I0546458

GENE GROSSMAN

...by REASON of SANITY

PETER SHARP LEGAL MYSTERY
NUMBER 2

1

...By Reason of Sanity

#2 in the Peter Sharp Legal Mystery Series

By Gene Grossman

From Magic Lamp Press
Venice, California

Magic Lamp Press ™

This is a work of fiction. Names, characters, places, and incidents are either the product of the author's imagination or are used fictitiously or with permission. Any resemblance to actual persons, living or dead, or any events is entirely coincidental.

...By Reason of Sanity
Peter Sharp Legal Mystery #2

Peter Sharp Legal Mystery Series
http://www.PeterSharpBooks.com

ISBN: 1-882629-13-2

Peter Sharp Legal Mysteries: the Complete Series

www.LegalMystery.com

Single Jeopardy

...by Reason of Sanity

A Class Action

Conspiracy of Innocence

...Until Proven Innocent

The Common Law

The Magician's Legacy

The Reluctant Jurist

The Final Case

An Element of Peril

A Good Alibi

Legally Dead

How to Rob a Bank

1

There's nothing worse than a reformed smoker. I know, because I'm one. I can smell something being smoked from a car pulling up next to me in traffic with its windows open. I can smell it from someone walking upwind of me a half block away. I'm insulted by the fact that some schmuck is polluting my air.

So here I am at thirty thousand feet above the Pacific Ocean, flying back from Maui, and the fat guy sitting next to me must have smoked two packs before boarding time. It's a good thing there's no smoke detector above us because his entire huge body and clothing reek of smoke. Every time he coughs, some smoke comes out of his liver-lipped mouth. He's been sleeping for the past two hours… probably tired from all that suction.

Sitting next to this guy reminds me of a long time ago, when I was going to Chicago's Roosevelt University days, and working nights playing piano downtown on Rush Street. After working from nine in the evening to three in the morning in a smoke-filled saloon, I would return to my parents' second floor north Kedzie Ave. apartment, where by my mother's orders, I'd get undressed in the hallway and leave my smoke-drenched suit hanging on the banister.

But other than the odors getting to me on this flight back, this vacation was a success.

With all of the book-time spent under Lahaina's Banyan tree, in my hotel room at the Pioneer Inn and on the flights both ways, I've been able to catch up on my reading with one by Robert K. Tannenbaum, one by John Lescroart, two by William Bernhardt and then John Grisham's *The Summons*, which I think he probably phoned in. Reading books by these burnt out lawyers gives me an idea: if reformed hackers can get hired by the government as computer specialists and reformed burglars can get jobs as security experts, why can't a reformed personal injury lawyer become a defense attorney? I've certainly got the credentials. In the past year alone I settled a huge asbestosis case with nothing more than a faith healer's report... and there was the two million life insurance settlement I got for that doctor who was accused of murdering his wife. I also successfully defended my friend Stuart when a lady using his weight-loss formula sued him claiming it turned her into a nymphomaniac.

Following up on that possibility, our office sent out some inquiry letters to a couple of insurance companies I bagged last year to see if there're any hard feelings. Knowing those corporate types, they don't have feelings. To them, all that counts is the bottom line. If Hitler came back as a winning defense lawyer, he'd be on their payroll.

When checking in from Maui, I was told that one of the insurance company's defense firms might have an assignment for me.

As promised, Stuart picks me up at the flight arrival area and I get in his car, only to be bawled out during the entire ride to the Marina. He doesn't let up, obviously having heard I was thinking of changing sides. "How can you do this? You're not one of those insurance defense guys who wanna cheat injured people out of a fair settlement. Those guys ruin the lives of people who're really hurt."

"You mean like you were with that faith healer's diagnosis of fatal mesothelioma? And if I remember correctly, you didn't complain when I acted as defense attorney for you with that crazy broad who sued you for negligent nymphomania, as a result of taking that weight-loss snake oil you sell. That saved your ass and made you even richer so what's the beef?" I had him there.

"Listen Stu, I know how you feel, but if you stop to think about it, a fair defense lawyer can do more good than a plaintiff's lawyer."

"Yeah, sure. You gonna just give away your client's money?"

"No, I wouldn't do that, but if a person really is entitled to a fair settlement I can advise my client to pay it, instead of helping them interpret their policy provisions into some perverted reason not to pay."

The discussion comes to a temporary conclusion as we pull up to the C-4200 dock, where the forty-two foot Californian motor yacht I live on is docked. This isn't exactly my dreamboat, but it'll have to do until the fifty-foot Grand Banks I covet becomes affordable. We're on the same dock as George Clooney's mega yacht and I still have some hope of bumping into him and starting a friendship.

Nothing's changed while I was gone. Being close to dusk, the electric cart driven by Suzi, an adorable little Chinese girl that I inherited, is parked in its spot near the boats. That means that she and her huge Saint Bernard are on the boat waiting for me, hopefully with a gourmet meal – and some word about new clients.

Suzi runs my life as well as the practice, but she hardly ever talks to me. I still haven't figured out why, but in the last year, about the only time she addressed me was to bawl me out for getting arrested. I didn't mind that conversation because it was just after she bailed me out. Fortunately, my doctor client and I beat that bad rap, ergo the boat we're now living on... it used to be his.

Suzi's a star at the Chinese restaurant around the corner where her late mother used to work, and where the food comes from many evenings. It gets delivered by the 'Asian boys,' a polite group of four young men who do everything from bus the restaurant tables at night, to cleaning and varnishing the boats on our dock during the day.

I still can't believe how smooth it's been going for the past few months. The kid's really been through a lot. Her mother died in a car crash when she was only three, leaving her to live with her stepfather, my old law school chum Melvin Braunstein. When she finally got used to that situation, Melvin perished in a plane crash while vacationing in Thailand - and now she's stuck on a boat in the Marina living with me, her legal guardian. Living on a boat some day used to be my dream when I was a kid, so maybe she'll learn to appreciate the lifestyle too. I certainly hope so, because until she's eighteen or goes away to school, this is it.

In addition to her office routine, she also volunteers at the local hospital. They have a children's ward there, so Suzi brings her Saint Bernard in once a week to visit the children.

Her computer skills are top-notch, she runs our law practice, and has two one hundred eighty pound animals to boss around... the Saint Bernard and me.

2

Big-time insurance defense attorney Charles Indovine calls the staff meeting together in his law firm's luxurious Century City conference room. "Gentlemen, we have a little competition now." He holds up a document. "It seems that our old friend Peter Sharp, the faith-healer case lawyer, wants to do some defense work. He's sent out some inquiry letters, and this one was received by one of our largest clients, Uniman Insurance." The junior partners see a smile on Indovine's face and sense that this amuses him, so they react in kind, with sarcastic smirks.

"So what, they'll never hire him. I hear he's a small-time jerk who practices off of a boat in the Marina," comments an associate.

Indovine disagrees. "I don't know. He beat us on that bullshit asbestosis case, and the Insurance

Industry's computer database shows that he's done a good job on some other matters of dubious merit. Perhaps there's an outside chance our client might take a flyer on him, just to keep us on our toes."

Another associate comes up with an idea. "Then let's beat everyone to it. We can farm out some stuff to him... like the losers."

Indovine takes the ball and runs with it. "Good idea. We can give him the crap to defend. That'll keep our batting average up and give him a bad track record from the get-go."

The associate responds. "I've got just the case: That slip and fall in the bank. The claimant landed on his side and broke two ribs. Plenty of witnesses to the spilled coke on the floor because it was there for almost twenty minutes before the claimant came in."

Indovine lays out the strategy. "OK, I'll advise the client that we have a chance to win this one because the claimant should have seen the dark colored spill on the floor. Then, we'll tell them that we're assigning it to attorney Sharp and let him take the blame for blowing it."

Nods of assent are given all around the table. All their heads are attached to the same string.

The Saint Bernard has just entered my stateroom with a message in his mouth. Around here we refer to this as 'dog-mail.' I remove the moist envelope, blot it dry and open it up to find a letter that came in while I was on vacation. It's from Indovine's defense firm:

Dear Mister Sharp:

It has come to our attention that you are desirous of doing some defense work, and we would like to welcome you to the true side of justice by offering to assign some cases to you.

If you would like to associate with us, our client has authorized us to send you the file on a claim that we feel can be handled successfully.

Please contact our office if you'd like to give it a try. Our current schedule allows for a rate of one hundred dollars per hour of pre-trial work, with a minimum advance of fifteen hundred dollars per file, once civil discovery commences.

Sincerely , Charles Indovine

This is encouraging. If I get some work of my own outside of Melvin's firm, I can keep the whole fee and only pay the office for secretarial services. My deal with Melvin was that as long as I get the firm's work done, my time is my own to try and build up an independent private practice. I send a message to Indovine's office that I'll give the first case a try and that he should send the file over.

To my surprise, a messenger shows up later that afternoon with a package containing a fifteen hundred dollar advance check and the case file.

I'll never understand why defense firms operate like this. The file indicates that a man named Mike Drago slipped and fell in the bank. Plenty of witnesses, wet floor, real damages, and now they want to spend more money screwing around fighting it than it would cost them to settle it outright. I guess it's to show people that they're not pushovers and if

11

you want to make a claim, you've got to be prepared for a fight.

Along with the file is a list of approved and authorized resources I'm allowed to use for private investigation, background checks, process serving, surveillance, and a lot of other services I'll probably never use. It looks like they want to use a one-ton fly swatter on this gnat of a case – but who am I to argue? It's their money and they obviously want to spend it.

The file indicates that the claimant already has an attorney named Richard Handelmann, with an office on Ventura Boulevard in Encino. I've never heard of him but with almost two hundred thousand lawyers in California, it's hard to keep track.

I get a notice of representation off to Handelmann's office, letting him know that I'm on the case and decide to see what the scene of the fall looks like. Taking Suzi's advice, I note my mileage before leaving and then head down Washington Boulevard to Culver City.

After introducing myself to the bank manager, I spend a little time with their seventy-five year old security guard, but he doesn't remember much about the incident. That's understandable. He doesn't remember much about anything.

Next, I check with the bank's security manager, to see if they caught the fall on one or more of their video cameras. I'm informed that yes, the fall is on tape, and the bank keeps copies of the videos for at least six months.

Wonderful. Not only do I have a losing case, it's even recorded on the bank's security cameras. Why the hell didn't this thing settle already? The claimant's medical bills are over four thousand, he doesn't claim any loss of earnings, and the file doesn't even contain one note about authorizing a settlement.

If I were handling this case on the other side, I'd make a demand of fifteen grand and wait for the defense to come back with a counter-offer. In this file, there isn't even a demand from the guy's lawyer. Something doesn't compute.

All this defense work has tired me out. Time to go back to the boat for a nap.

After only about an hour of dozing, the phone rings. The caller ID on my phone shows that it's my ex-wife Myra, the former deputy district attorney who had me indicted and arrested last year. Fortunately, I beat those charges. "Hello sweetheart, to what do I owe the pleasure of this call?"

"Don't sweetheart me, you idiot. My sources at the district attorney's office tell me that your picture turned up on some security tapes today."

"That's not surprising. Cameras are everywhere. I stopped for gas. They have cameras at that station. I stopped for a six-pack. They have cameras at the liquor store. Which one did you like best – maybe I can get you an enlargement for your bed stand... or perhaps some wallet-sized?"

"You're still the schmuck, aren't you? The cameras I'm talking about are the ones at the bank in Culver City."

"OK, honey, you caught me. I stopped off at the bank today. Is that against the law?"

"You were there at about two-fifteen this afternoon?"

"Yeah, some time around there. Why?"

"Because the bank was robbed minutes after you left."

3

Now that Myra's convinced I'm involved with some bank robbers, it's almost a relief to get a phone call from Stuart. I explain the day's events to him and let him know that it's just a coincidence, but he's a firm believer in the whacko world of hocus-pocus, so in his mind it's a big conspiracy that I'm now involved in. I tell him to go back to his faith healer for some therapy.

While he's got me on the phone, he tells me about his buddy Vinnie Norman, who was injured last week when a tree fell on him. Being a friend of Stuart's, he's looking for someone to sue. Why am I not surprised?

"Stuart, just because someone's injured doesn't mean that someone's at fault. There are accidents, acts of God, all sorts of reasons why someone can be hurt without having someone to sue."

"Yeah Pete, I know, but Vinnie was hurt because of a drunk driver."

"Stu, I thought you said that a tree fell on him."

"I did, but the tree fell because it was hit by a drunk driver."

"Well that's a different story. Do you know if the driver has any insurance?"

"Not likely. He was driving a Lexus that he had just stolen from a restaurant parking lot. He's in jail."

"What about Vinnie? Does he have any insurance, like uninsured motorist?"

"Naw, he's a poor guy. Doesn't even have a car. He works for me in my Van Nuys warehouse. Do you have any advice for him?"

"Yeah, tell him to take two aspirins and not call me in the morning."

"Come on Pete, there's gotta be some-thing you can do."

I tell Stuart that I'll look into the matter and that he should stop by the boat tomorrow with the police report of the accident. I really don't know where to start with this one, but I figure that the internet would be as good a place as any, so I do what any other normal professional person would do - I give the assignment to the little princess in the forward stateroom. She's the computer whiz. Besides, this'll be a case that the office will share in, so the office might as well do some work on it.

People who go to law school usually find out pretty early on how they'll wind up as professionals. There's an unwritten law that governs the careers of law students, and over the years it's been found to be quite accurate. Simply stated, the 'A' students become judges, the 'B' students become teachers, and the 'C' students make a really good living, working for the wealthy 'D' students.

I was a C-minus student, always hoping that someday my future might be as bright as that of a D student. It never hurts to aim low.

The reason the D students do so well is because instead of developing their knowledge of the law, they spend most of their time developing their knowledge of schmoozing. Law doesn't bring in clients. Schmoozing does.

If you go to a big accredited law school with ivy growing up the walls, you learn how to play golf. If you go to an un-accredited night law school with mold growing up the walls, you learn how to schmooze. I went to the latter, which was nicknamed the Betty Crocker College of Law, so I never learned how to ruin a perfectly good walk by stopping to try and hit a little ball with a club. All I ever learned how to do was get clients. You never have to worry about having too many clients, because former C-student lawyers looking for work are much easier to find than clients.

The next afternoon, Stuart shows up at the boat. He's looking as round as ever - obviously, he's not using the weight-reduction juice he sells all over the country. His buddy Vinnie is with him and I'm told that he's a former XXX film director, who used to turn out a new porno flick every week, until the vice squad put him out of business. Vinnie is a tall, gray man who looks more like a doctor than a pornographer. He looks surprisingly classy, but that image is destroyed as soon as he opens his mouth and I hear his 'New Joisy' dialect. Compared to him all the Sopranos sound like English professors. As we're talking, I can't help but notice the odor of grass coming from Vinnie's sweater... the smoking kind.

During the interview I hear his story. He was walking down the street late at night and stepped into the park for a moment to relieve himself, stopping behind the first tree he saw. While standing there watering the roots, the defendant came speeding down the street, lost control of the vehicle he was driving, and slammed into the tree. It splintered and fell on Vinnie. I can't recall ever seeing a Perry Mason television episode entitled "The case of the prolific, pot-smoking, peeing pornographer," but I'll bet that if it ever appeared in the TV guide, the ratings would have gone through the roof. This may not be a profitable one, but should definitely make it into some legal 'believe-it-or-not' book.

I tell them both that I'll look into the matter and suggest another meeting after I've read the police report. As much as I try to hint that the meeting is now over and they should get the hell off of my boat, Stuart can't resist the opportunity to tell me about the new business he's starting, with Vinnie's help.

"Pete, this one's a winner. You know the old saying 'you can't take it with you?' Well now, you can. I'm buying a used armored truck that Brink's wants to get rid of, and we're changing the name on the side of the truck from 'Brink's' to 'He's taking it with him.' Vinnie will be the uniformed driver and we'll rent it out for funeral processions. I figure that every disgruntled relative who gets shortchanged in somebody's will should be interested in paying three-fifty to have my truck in the parade to the cemetery. I told a whole bunch of funeral directors that I'd pay a hundred off the top for each job we get from them. Vinnie here'll get a hundred for the driving and I figure we can do two funerals a day. Whattaya think?"

There are very few times in my life can I remember being at a loss for words, and each time was the result of some outrageous business plan told to me by Stuart. I smile, nod in understanding, and wish him the best of luck in his new enterprise. I remind him to be sure to let me know when he gets his first job - and what the route will be, because it will be a genuine Kodak moment.

The local newscast doesn't mention Vinnie getting hurt while peeing, but there's plenty of coverage on the bank robbery story. As the razor-cut, blow-dried, empty-headed newsreader drones on, this is just another in a series of well-planned jobs that the authorities believe are being done by an organized gang.

After most bank heists, some frightened teller gets interviewed on camera, then the reporter asks the security guard about the incident, but he doesn't seem to remember too much about it. They usually attribute his memory loss to shock, but it's probably senility.

I start to go over the police report of the slip-and-fall case. I can't think of a defense for this case, so I might as well do the next best thing - build up my billable hours. Indovine's defense firm is probably billing the insurance company over two hundred an hour for the time that they're paying me one hundred for, so they'll no doubt be pleased by my wasted efforts.

I make a note to give Jack Bibberman an assignment on this case. He saved my rear end last year during my State Bar hearing, when he nailed the guy who framed me on an 'aiding the un-authorized practice of law' charge, by identifying another attorney as the one who was behind the whole plot.

Since then I've learned that he's a real stand-up guy, so I try to toss whatever business I can his way for investigation, process serving and whatever else comes up. I know I'm supposed to use one of Indovine's private eyes, but I convinced them to let me use Jack and Suzi... for the same billing rates.

Jack's assignment is to get copies of all the bank's security videos over the past couple of months, so I can watch them, look for patterns of customer behavior, see if anyone else slipped, see if the security guard remembered to close his fly, and build up my billable hours.

4

Suzi came up with some interesting stuff on the drunk driver case. She helps the local police agencies out with some of their computer work, and since she's like a goddess at the local Chinese restaurant where all the local cops feed at the trough, she usually can get information that normal earthlings aren't privy to.

The police report lists the vehicle that the drunk stole as an elephant-gray Lexus sport utility vehicle that was in the parking lot of a Mexican restaurant on Washington Boulevard. The keys were left in the ignition because the driver ran in for a minute to pick up a to-go order of vegetarian burritos. The drunken defendant was staggering out of the restaurant just as the Lexus pulled up. The rest is history.

The phone rings. It's my ex-wife Myra. "Hello my dear, what is it this time? Am I going to be arrested again?"

"No, I just got another phone call from an old friend at the district attorney's office."

"Myra, I think you should go back to work there. That's where all your friends are and with your old boss gone, there's a tremendous vacuum that needs filling... and you're just the person to take over as acting chief of the office."

"They've already got that position filled with another jerk, just like my last boss... but you're right about one thing and if you say anything to anyone about this, I'll have you killed."

"Don't tell me, let me guess. You're running for District Attorney in the next election?"

"You suck. How did you know that?"

"It figures. Listen, I hate to sound rude, but there's a gourmet dinner being delivered for me shortly, so let's cut to the commercial. I know you didn't call because you want to get laid, so what's up?"

"As a matter of fact, I *do* want to get laid, but not by you. The reason I called is to let you know that by some stroke of luck, you've won another case. You were working on the defense of that slip and fall matter at the bank, right?"

"Yeah. What about it?"

"The claimant just died in the hospital."

21

"Died? Did I hear you right? Did you say he's dead? How the hell could that happen, all he had were two broken ribs and a bruised kneecap. I don't believe that the fall could have caused his death. Damn! This went from a slam-dunk case to a quagmire. How did he die? Are there any details available?"

"Yeah, someone smothered him with a pillow."

Hoping this isn't the end of my career as an insurance defense attorney, I dash off a quick e-mail to the claimant's attorney, Richard Handelmann.

Mister Handelmann:
Please relay the condolences of this office to Mister Mike Drago's loved ones. Now that he has passed on, we will be closing our file.

I send an invoice for my hours to Indovine's office and decide to spend the rest of the afternoon reading *Center Street*, a new novel by Leonard Wise.

It never fails. Every time I get com-fortable to read a book, something hits the fan. I hear the pitter patter of huge paws and see that I'm being brought some dog mail. This time it's a message from Richard Handelmann's office – a copy of his e-mail:

Dear Mister Sharp:
This office is not closing its file on the Drago incident. It is our contention that the homicide was a foreseeable act and that liability for his death in the hospital should also be your client's responsibility.

As for the pain and suffering experienced by Mister Drago prior to his death, although precluded by California law, we will be filing our actions in the Federal Courts of Illinois, the state in which the federally licensed defendant bank was chartered.

Wow! This guy's got stones of steel. He actually wants to hold the bank's insurance company liable for his client's murder in the hospital - and wants to make a federal case out of it. This is not a good development, mainly because I know absolutely nothing about federal law... not even enough to advise Indovine about the client's possible losses in the federal court system.

I think it best to simply let Indovine know everything that's going on and let him communicate with the insurance company. For once, it's good to just be a hired hand. All you have to do is your specific job, with no responsibility for decisions.

I instruct the office to forward copies of our correspondence to Indovine's office and make copies of the police report. Then I call Jack Bibberman. Some investigation is in order because I want to know all there is to know about the late Mike Drago. I'm sure that Indovine will appreciate my help on this case, and I might even be assigned to second-chair at the federal trial. Jack tells me that when he went to the hospital to get a statement on the day that Drago was admitted, he noticed that there were security cameras all around the place. That's good to know because maybe the police can get some leads on his killer by watching them.

With the pressing matters taken care of, I can now devote some time to putting up my Lahaina Yacht Club burgee on the small decorative mast of our motor yacht. I remembered to pick up a replacement during my recent trip to the island because my other burgee went with the old boat when it was towed away by my ex-wife. There's a certain amount of pride in showing your yacht club's colors. If I didn't know better, I might even think I was rich. Yacht clubs here in the Marina charge entrance fees that can be quite costly. In one of them, you've got to come up with ten grand to get in.

Fortunately, the Lahaina Yacht Club isn't like that. It's for the cruising sailor and is quite reasonable. And because it requires you to personally post your picture on their bulletin board during your probationary period, anyone who's a member is recognized as actually having been in the Maui location. I try to get back there at least once or twice a year. It's about the only time I can get some serious reading done without interruption. And speaking of interruption, it must be mail time because the dog has just brought me another juicy item to read. Now that the red burgee is flying, I open the envelope and see that it's a copy of the police report on Vinnie's drunk driver case.

There isn't much in the report to hang my hat on. All it covers is the accident itself, with nothing mentioned about the vehicle theft. I guess that's in another report, which I also expect to be coming soon. The only item interesting in the report is the driver's blood alcohol level percentage, which was 0.19.

For many years the legal blood-alcohol percentage limit for driving was 0.10, but organizations like MADD (Mothers Against Drunk Driving) finally got it lowered to 0.08. Because of my experience with drunk driving defense cases, I know that depending on body mass and tolerance, the average person reacts differently to various alcohol blood levels. At the legal limit of 0.08, your reflexes are at least slightly impaired. This I know for a fact because not too long ago, after just two beers at the Chinese restaurant, I almost caused an accident while pulling out of the parking lot. That taught me a valuable lesson, so I don't drink anymore if I intend to drive within two hours.

In California, if you're brought to the police station as a drunk driving suspect, you're given three types of test to choose from to determine the percentage of alcohol in your system: blood, breath or urine. Bartenders usually advise their customers to opt for the urine test, because that requires an extra hour for the police to take you to a local hospital for the test. They're wrong... the extra hour doesn't help that much, because if you're drunk enough to be stopped and brought to the station for testing, an extra hour isn't nearly enough time to allow your percentage level to go down enough towards the legal limit.

At the old legal limit of 0.10, a guy who's not too bulky might be a little wobbly on his feet and probably fail the FST: that's the touch-your-nose, stand balanced one leg, and walk-a-straight-line Field Sobriety Test that cops make you take when you get stopped for being a suspected drunk driver.

Levels between 0.15 and 0.20 will usually make one's speech slur and the driver will obviously appear under the influence, even to an inexperienced observer.

Once you hit 0.20, the official designation is "shit-faced' and with that much booze in your system, an average person will most probably have slurred speech and difficulty pronouncing any word with more than two syllables.

Anything over 0.25 will usually result in wet pants and a terrible body odor. Readings over 0.30 can cause special conditions like unconsciousness or death.

In Vinnie's case, the guy 'blew' a 0.19 at the station. This may have been as much as an hour after the accident, so he probably was at the 0.20 level or higher at the time he interrupted Vinnie's pit stop, and that is definitely drunk, no matter how much body mass or alcohol tolerance you've got.

I call county jail to see if there's any chance of getting to interview him, but they tell me he never got there because Fradkin Bail Bonds took him out of the West Los Angeles Division jail and his sponsor picked him up. I call the bail bond place but they won't reveal the name of the sponsor, the person putting up the bail.

The County of Los Angeles owns all of the waterfront property in Marina del Rey and they lease out large parcels for people to build apartment buildings and boat slips. This evening there's a fireworks celebration in the Marina, being put on by the new buyer of a large leased anchorage and apartment parcel. He obviously can afford it because his family makes about a million every day, selling oil to the U.S.

At about nine PM, some surprising events take place. First, the fireworks start. They're on the other side of the Marina, so I can't see them from our boat, but the sounds are quite loud. Suddenly I'm being pinned to the couch by a heavy weight against my chest. At first I think I might be suffering a heart attack, but when I look down I see that the fireworks have obviously frightened the Saint Bernard, so he decided to jump up into the safety of my lap, where he promptly buries his head under my arm and whines for the next ten minutes until the noises stop.

After it's over, he looks up at me with a sorrowful face. I return his look with one that says "I've got your number now, pal. You're a big baby."

Embarrassed, he retreats to the little princess' forward stateroom, where he could have never gotten away with that stunt because he's not allowed up on the bunk. It's a good thing he tried it with me, because if he jumped up on Suzi like that we'd probably need a spatula to scrape her off of the bed.

I turn on the evening news and am surprised to hear that they made an arrest in the Mike Drago case. Evidently, the security cameras paid off, because Drago had been moved into a special intensive care unit where everything in the room is videotaped. To make matters even more interesting, the newsreader goes on:

"We have learned that the district attorney has decided to bring in a special prosecutor on this case... Ms. Myra Scot, a former employee of the district attorney's office."

27

The phone rings. Caller ID is a great invention because it gives me a few seconds to compose myself whenever Myra calls me. "Hello my dear, I see you made the evening news again. Good luck with this one. With the whole act on tape, you should have no problems getting a plea."

"Peter, I want you to watch me destroy the defense attorney on this one."

"No thanks sweetheart, I'm not that interested in watching a massacre."

"That's not fair. Up until now all you've seen me do is annihilate the former district attorney, who was incompetent. This is a capital case, so it'll probably be a really good lawyer on the other side who will be getting destroyed by my magnificent prosecution."

"So, what's that got to do with me?"

"You'll find out, Petey." I wish she wouldn't call me that.

As soon as I hang up with Myra, it rings again. I don't recognize the number on caller I.D., but pick up the phone anyway. It's a woman's voice. "Hello, Mister Sharp?"

"Speaking."

"This is Mary, Judge Axelrod's clerk. We just want you to know that on the recommendation of Myra Scot, the special prosecutor, you've been appointed as defense counsel on a capital murder case. We'll have the file delivered to your office. The arraignment has been scheduled for next Tuesday."

5

Losing is not fun, and I ought to know, because I've got plenty of experience in that area. When you practice criminal law, about ninety-nine percent of the people you represent actually did what they were charged with doing. The only reason I had a one percent acquittal rate had nothing to do with the defendants' innocence. It was only because of missing witnesses, evidence that confused the jury, technicalities like the Constitution's Bill of Rights, or some other reasons that drive prosecutors mad.

This case will not be going into the one percent success group because like all the others, it's a loser. I'll have to do my best, but this time there'll be no walking into court waving a document that clears the client and humiliates the prosecution. I'm afraid those days are over for everyone but Ben Matlock and Perry Mason.

About the only thing I can do on this one is try to break down the timeline of the video. I send a request over to Myra's office for copies of the tapes they've no doubt made for me. The only time that the prosecutors are happy to provide you with their evidence is when it nails your client to the wall beyond any reasonable doubt. I guess it's time to go downtown, pick up my appointment file and visit the new client.

After checking in the front desk of Twin Towers, Los Angeles' modern county jail, and presenting my State Bar card, a Deputy Sheriff leads me back to the attorney interview area, where I sit and wait about twenty minutes for my client to be brought in.

No client appears. Instead, a jailer comes in and tells me that my client would rather not see me.

This is a new one. After over twenty years of doing this, I've never been refused an interview before. And to make it even weirder, I wasn't forcing myself on this guy, because the court clerk said that he approved of my representing him when the court appointed me.

Just to make sure I'm not missing out on something, on the way out of the building I stop by the Captain's office to find out exactly what their policy is for inmates who don't want to see their lawyer. My client was right and I was wrong. The Captain tells me that an inmate does have a right to refuse a visit – even by his own attorney. Not only did he not want to see me – he also gave me an important indication of how difficult this case will be to handle...it's going to be uphill all the way. If he's smart enough to avoid meeting with me, I hope he's also smart enough to figure out some strategy to beat this case – because I sure can't.

Approaching the Marina, I see some-thing that's now familiar to me but almost caused me to wreck my car the first time I saw it – a huge Saint Bernard driving an electric cart. Actually, as I now know very well, the dog doesn't drive – it's Suzi. The dog sits up on the front seat next to her but if you see them from a certain angle, she's hidden behind the dog.

Her usual routine during the week includes stopping by the private mailbox place to pick up the firm's incoming stuff, making a deposit at the drive-up ATM window and stopping by the Chinese restaurant around the corner, where she and the dog disappear inside for an hour or so.

Because her late mother was a head waitress at the place, she's treated like royalty there. And since all the local cops eat lunch there every day, she's become their official mascot, so she can do no wrong in their jurisdictions.

On today's trip, when she sees me, I'm honored with a wave of her hand as she speeds down the alley towards the rear entrance to the Chinese restaurant.

Suzi's late stepfather Melvin explained to me that she's got the authorities convinced she's being home-schooled, so as long as she keeps passing their quarterly tests, she has her days free to run the law practice I work for and volunteer at the hospital with that huge animal of hers.

I still get a kick out of how she taught the dog to stand up on his hind legs, open the mailbox door with a paw and then deposit the mail from his mouth into the slot. During the rainy season, she has the dog trained to do the mail run all by himself. Of course none of this is amazing compared to how she's got me trained during the past six months. Each morning I make my bed, throw away yesterday's newspapers, wash my breakfast bowl (she can't reach the sink), and take out the garbage.

If it's early enough in the morning, I usually bump into Laverne, who lives on a small houseboat a few slips down on the dock. If I've had enough to drink in the evening, I've been known to allow myself to be abducted by Laverne, while walking past her houseboat. This happens at least once a month, but I never complain... it must be some form of the Stockholm syndrome, named after an event that occurred in 1973 when four Swedes were held captive for six days in a bank vault during a robbery. According to psychologists, the abused bonded to their abusers as a means to endure violence.

In my case, it's a situation of bonding to my abductor because even though she's got plenty of miles on her, she's still a smooth ride.

There's a knock on the hull. It's a messenger with two packages for me. The court file on my lawyer-shy murderer and a stack of videocassettes – copies of the surveillance tapes from the hospital. What a pain in the ass. I'll never have time to watch them all. Each one is eight hours long, recorded in stop-motion intervals of one second. Fortunately they're all labeled with a digital stopwatch appearing on the bottom of the screen that constantly displays the date, hour, minute and second of the taping. I've been told they call it time-code.

This is all the fault of a guy named Harry Lillis Crosby, who was a great old-time crooner nicknamed 'Bing.' You should remember him from a bunch of old 'road' movies he made with a comedian named Bob Hope. There's also an old song called *White Christmas* he recorded that sold quite well. Bing was a golf nut, but his game was interrupted quite often because he had to do his weekly television show twice during each broadcast day. The second show for local stations; the first one was show earlier, and broadcast from California to the East Coast, to allow for the time difference. Everything was shot 'live' in those days.

Bing came across a guy named Jack Mullin, who had an idea for a new invention called 'videotape.' With the help of Bing's fifty thousand dollar investment, a process was started in the 1950's that resulted in me now having an entire week's worth of crime-scene videotapes to watch. Good work, Bing.

I leave the videotapes on the boat's dinette table and start to read the file on Vinnie's drunk driver case. Maybe I'll have more luck with a broken tree than I had with my reluctant murderer.

I can read a book in one sitting if it's something that I'm really interested in. I usually can usually get through about fifty pages an hour if it's a 'page-turner,' so the average four-hundred-page paperback takes me a full day. There's no break necessary for eating because I've mastered the art of doing both of those enjoyable tasks at the same time.

Unfortunately the same doesn't apply to anything other than a suspense thriller or some mystery written by Arthur Conan Doyle or Rex Stout, so after about five minutes with the police report, my eyelids are starting to get heavy. It's such a beautiful day in Southern California, it seems like a good time to take a walk up and down the dock. Maybe I'll bump into George Clooney. I've been told he bought

33

the huge mega-yacht that's parked on our dock's large end-tie from the estate of Johnny Carson.

A friend of mine who's about my age, told me that after he turned forty, he started to feel old when the cops started looking like high-school kids to him. They look young to me too, but my introduction to the aging process happens now as I see a young mother carrying a baby in her arms and holding the hand of second youngster walking next to her. They're obviously coming to visit a boat-owning friend or relative on our dock.

As they pass by me, the eyes of the young one walking bulged out as he looks down the dock and sees that mega-yacht parked on our end tie. He looks up at his mother and asks her whose it is. She tells him that she doesn't know, but that he should ask the nice man standing there (me). The kid, shy at first, looks up at me. "Mister, do you know who lives on that big boat." Cute kid. He's got his eyes on Johnny Carson's former boat, now owned by George Clooney I look down at him and answer his question.

Not wanting to violate George's privacy, I tell the kid that huge yacht once belonged to none other than Johnny Carson." The kid looks at me with a blank stare on his face. I don't want to leave him completely confused, so I try to help him out. "Your mommy will tell you all about Johnny Carson."

That's when my age creeps up on me. As I smile and look into the young mother's face, I realize that she doesn't know who Johnny Carson is either! How can this be? The most famous talk show host in history – the greatest interviewer who ever lived – a guy who spent thirty years entertaining people – and she doesn't know who he is? She must be from a foreign country. And then it dawns on me: If this young mother is now in her twenties, which it looks like she is, then Johnny Carson retired when she was still in elementary school, when she had to be in bed before his show started. Boy, time sure flies.

I look at her and tried to explain in a way I'm sure she'll understand. "He's an old time television personality."

Realizing how fast time flies, I'd better get back to the boat and finish reading that police report before the cataracts kick in.

6

Long, long ago, places selling booze would dole it out in very small amounts called 'drams,' and if you want to really get technical, you should know that a dram is about one-eighth of an ounce. Those shops that sold booze by the dram were called 'dram shops.' That's about as clever as they got naming businesses back in those days.

Nowadays, with all the damages and deaths that drunk drivers cause, most states have enacted laws that trace liability for drunk driving injuries back to the last place where the drunk driver was served. Those laws are called 'Dramshop laws,' and they now exist in all but seven states, but California isn't one of them.

This means that if I can construct my case properly by using California's current Dramshop law, I might be able to bring an action on Vinnie's behalf against the bar where his defendant got drunk.

But even if I can put that together by showing he got drunk there and not somewhere else before going to that last watering hole, the restaurant will probably argue that his criminal act of stealing the Lexus was an 'unforeseeable' event, and therefore it cuts off their liability for his further actions. This is going to take some heavy-duty research. Jack Bibberman may have to spend time on some barstools for this case, but considering how well he holds his liquor, it will be a fun assignment for him.

Fortunately, Suzi was successful in getting us a copy of the police report on the auto theft portion of the case. It gives a lot of facts about the vehicle, the lack of any owner's permission to use it, yada yada. All that's missing is how long the defendant was in that place drinking. I'd like to avoid any surprise that could jump up and bite me if the guy did all his drinking somewhere else and just stopped in this place to say hello to someone. The defendant obviously didn't have his own car, so I tell Jack to check other saloons within walking distance. He's got the defendant's mug shot to show around.

I feel better now that there's a slim possibility to hang my hat on for Vinnie's case. Maybe now would be a good time to goof off for an hour or so and read a Sherlock Holmes story. Usually, getting comfortable to do some reading causes some interruption. This time it's different. Just the thought of doing some reading causes the phone to ring. It's Stuart.

"Hey Stu, what's up. Oh, by the way, I think I've got a way to go on your friend Vinnie's case, but we're going to have to do some investigating on it."

"That's great Pete, but I'm afraid I've got another case that's a little more important to me, right now."

"Stu, I'm really not looking for any new cases this month. I've got an arraignment on that murder case next week against Myra, Vinnie's case will be taking up a lot of my time, and I'm still trying to defend that case where the slip and fall guy got killed in the hospital."

"Pete, you don't understand. It's me this time. I'm getting sued again."

"For what?"

"You know that small claim court thing I'm doing for people who get junk faxes? Well one of the defendants we filed against had the case moved up into the Municipal Court and they're counter-suing me for some things like Barratry, Champerty and Maintenance."

I don't want to admit that I haven't the slightest idea what he's talking about. "Stuart, bring whatever they served you with over to the boat this evening. I can't give you any advice until I see the papers. We'll have some dinner and talk about it."

"Are we eating out?" I sense some apprehension on his part.

"No, Stuart. I'm cooking." He doesn't comment.

After we hang up, I reach for my copy of the thick Black's Law Dictionary that always occupies a prominent position on my desk. Let's see now, what were those things he's being sued for?

A message from Jack Bibberman comes in. He only had to make one stop on Vinnie's case. Two cocktail waitresses confirm that the defendant was definitely in the bar where he stole the car from for at least six hours. Good! Now they won't be able to point the finger at some other saloon. This case is going ahead right on track.

I'll be in court in a few days for that murder case arraignment, but something doesn't compute. If I'm defending the bank's insurance company against the claim of Mike Drago who slipped and fell there, how can the court appoint me to defend the guy who's charged with killing him? I call Myra's office. Maybe this is my chance to get off this losing case. I get put right through to her.

"What is it Pete? I've got a lot of work piled up on my desk."

"Well, I'm glad to see that you're so busy. Maybe I can get out of your way on the murder case."

"He wants to plead out?"

"No, I want to plead out. Out of this case. I think there might be a potential conflict here."

"No way, Josè. If you want off this case, I'll meet you in chambers. We can discuss it there and we'll let Judge Axelrod make the decision. As far as I'm concerned, you and your client are both going down in flames on this one."

Judge Axelrod's clerk shows us into his chambers. The judge cleared up his calendar early today, so he's got some time to meet with us. He's in a good mood. "What's up people?"

I start with my pitch. "Your Honor, first of all I'd like to thank you for appointing me to this case. It's an honor to get on the capital crimes appointment list, but I'm afraid I've got a conflict on this one."

The Judge and Myra exchange glances. I get the sinking feeling that they've already covered this ground and I've already lost.

"As I was saying, my client the Uniman Insurance Company has a vested interest in Mister Drago's death. If he can't appear and testify in his slip-and-fall case and the claim for pain and suffering doesn't survive his passing, then it's to the insurance company's benefit to have him dead."

They both question me, almost in unison. "So?"

"So, if I win the murder case, it might mean that Drago did not die at the hands of another, which would mean that his death may have been a result of the slip-and-fall case. That's against my insurance client's interest. In other words, the better I do on the criminal case, the worse I do on the civil case." The judge looks at me over his bifocals.

"Mister Sharp, you've appeared in my court on many occasions and I obviously approve of your talents as an attorney, or I wouldn't have appointed you on this capital case. The county jail informed my clerk that you were refused an interview with your client, which tells me that he isn't interested in assisting with his own defense. According to Miss Scot's interview on the evening news, the prosecution has a videotape of your client committing the act with which he's charged. In view of these two facts, I would say that the chances of your winning this case are slim and none... and Slim's out of town."

"Yes, your Honor, I agree it doesn't look too good for the defense, but..." He cuts me off mid-sentence.

"There are no buts, counsel. No jury trial was requested on this case. It's going to be heard by just me. And to tell the truth, I don't think Siegfried and Roy could create an illusion of innocence in this matter. Now this doesn't mean that my mind is already made up, because I haven't seen any evidence yet, but if for some reason it doesn't get admitted properly then you might have a chance.

"I'm willing to risk that you're not creating any conflict here and I'm also going to have my clerk type up a memo to that effect on my official letterhead for you to present to your civil client and to the State Bar, if you feel that might be necessary in the future. Thank you for coming in today – I'll see you both in court next week at the arraignment."

Okay, I'm still on the case. I'll just drop this whole thing in Indovine's lap. If they still want me on the civil case, then I'll stay on, but I have to let him know that I'm going to do my best on the criminal case.

The email is sent to Indovine. He calls me back personally. "Peter, I've received your message and we're all quite pleased at your honest attempt to avoid a conflict here, but not to worry."

"Oh, thanks, I see you think I'm going to lose the criminal case too."

"Peter, it doesn't matter. Even if by some miracle you get your criminal defendant off, it still doesn't mean that our claimant wasn't murdered... it just means that your guy didn't do it. The videotape clearly shows that the claimant was murdered... and that should cut off our liability. It's a criminal act and no court will hold that it was foreseeable. That shyster Handelmann doesn't stand a chance – now go and do the best you can for your criminal client."

As I hang up the phone I see that the Saint Bernard is sitting here looking at me. He must be psychic. Suzi is busy studying this evening for her quarterly home-schooling test, so I'm left on my own to make dinner. The dog is rarely more than two feet away from her, unless he knows that I'll be trying to prepare food. Not being the neatest guy in the world, he knows I can be counted on for some food droppings, so when I start cooking, he goes on 'crumb patrol.'

Tonight's gourmet feast will be pasta a la Marina. Poured on top of the cooked, large elbow macaroni will be a can of Campbell's low-fat cream of mushroom soup, a small can of sweet peas, three slices of non-fat mozzarella cheese, some chopped garlic, and whatever else I can find in the refrigerator.

This is a win-win situation. Stuart will be here this evening with his lawsuit and whatever's left over after the dog and my cooking mistakes, we will both have for dinner.

Stuart shows up promptly at six-thirty and the three of us sit down to eat. Suzi is spending the evening at her computer, but will probably be listening in to every word Stuart and I say. Stuart hands me the papers he was served with. It seems that one of his defendants decided to fight back. Our federal government passed the Telephone Consumer Protection Act, which gives any person who receives an unsolicited fax, the right to sue in small claims court and get five hundred dollars in damages from the fax sender.

Stuart solicits people in Santa Monica to assign their TCPA actions over to him. He finds out who the California fax broadcasters and their clients are and then files suits against them in small claims court. When he wins, he gets his court costs back and then splits the rest with whatever client assigned the claim to him.

In this particular case, one of the fax spammers wants to make an example out of Stuart, so that he can stay in business by clogging up the fax machines of millions of Californians with notices of free cellular phones, travel bargains, stock tips, health plans, new mortgages, etc., etc.

He states three ways that Stuart is violating the law and asks for the small claims suits Stuart filed to be dismissed, and that Stuart be stopped from filing further ones. His contentions are that Stuart is guilty of *Barratry*, which is the stirring up of litigation for profit; *Champerty*, the participation in someone else's action for some percentage share; and *Maintenance* - the financing of a lawsuit he shares in.

"Pete, these things sound like they're from the middle-ages. Are they still on the books?"

"I'm afraid so, pal. In California, we've got two sections of our Penal Code, numbers 158 and 159 that make barratry a misdemeanor."

"Exactly how serious is that?"

"In California, the seriousness of a crime is determined by the severity of the punishment. A misdemeanor is punishable by up to a maximum of one year in the county jail, or a fine, or both. A felony is more open-ended, with the punishment starting out at a minimum of one year in a state penitentiary, and going all the way up to life in prison and in some instances, a lethal injection."

"So if this is only a misdemeanor, I'll get fined, huh... I mean, they won't send me to jail will they?"

"Nah, jail time probably wouldn't be a risk for you Stu, not for a first-time offense, but the fine can be a thousand dollars for each violation and you've filed quite a few of these things."

"Jeez, that could really cost me a lot. Is there any way we can fight this? I'm making several grand a month off of these cases and junk faxes to Santa Monica have dropped off since I started. That's good, isn't it? I mean, like I'm providing a service to the public."

"Yeah, Stu, you're my hero, but we'll need more than that to beat this guy down. Let's just finish our dinner. I'll work on the case a little more and have Jack B. do some snooping for us. Don't worry - we'll beat it. I've got a good feeling about this one."

Stuart calms down and the three of us finish our dinner. The dropped salad croutons and cake crumbs have a floor-life of about ten seconds and the table almost tips over every time the huge beast below goes after another morsel that hits the floor.

Now that Stuart has been temporarily taken care of, it's time to get to the real serious stuff. I've got stacks of videotapes to go through. Where are they? I thought I left them out on the dinette table. I don't remember seeing them earlier today. No problem. Any time something strange happens on this boat, there's a simple answer. The little princess is doing something that I know nothing of. I scribble a note quickly and drop another crouton on the floor. As soon as the dog comes to retrieve the dropping, I slip the note in his collar. This is his signal to make a delivery to the foreward stateroom.

The next morning, there's a message waiting for me. The videotapes were sent to some lab to be digitized. I don't know what that means, but as long as Suzi's behind it, it must be a good thing, so I'll just wait to find out.

A couple of days have passed and I now see a videocassette on the dinette table. I don't know what happened to the other twenty or thirty of them, but I hope to find out. I pop this one into the VCR and hit the play button. This is amazing, because this one tape contains all the action from all the other tapes. The parts where nobody moves have been eliminated and the action has been speeded up to eliminate the one-shot-per-second jittering that was on all the other tapes. What we're left with is a smooth-action video of exactly what happened in Drago's hospital room.

As pleased as I am to find out that thirty or forty hours of my time have been saved, I'm not too happy with what I see on the screen. It's my reluctant client. He's moving around in the room, stops at the closet for a minute, then picks up a pillow off of the unoccupied bed next to Drago's and proceeds to smother Drago to death. He then returns the pillow to the empty bed and walks out of the room. For some strange reason, he even looks up towards one of the security cameras. His face appears plain as day, with no effort at all to avoid the cameras or escape guilt. They must have found him by showing his picture around the neighborhood. There are a few quirky spots on the tape but that's probably a result of the digitizing process, which I now know is what they call it when you load video footage into a computer.

45

About two minutes of this stuff is all that Myra will need to deliver my client to the guy with the needle. She might be willing to offer me a plea bargain of some sort if I have something to give her in return, but since my client won't even talk to me, I rule out a deal. Maybe he'll talk to me at the arraignment.

7

My client has been brought in from the holding cell area and he's already sitting behind the counsel table when I get there. I look at him as the bailiff calls the court to order. He doesn't return the look. He looks terrible, but that's understandable. The County Jail is not a vacation spot. Only the really rich defendants have enough resources to get brand new suits delivered to the holding cell, so they can walk into court looking like they just came from a Brooks Brothers store. My client is not rich, so he's wearing one of the fashionable orange jump suits they give out to prisoners. As far a juries are concerned, on the back of the jump suits they should have the word 'guilty' silk-screened on. It's now 'show time,' so the bailiff makes his announcement.

"Remain seated and come to order. The Superior Court of the State of California is now in session, the Honorable Ronald Axelrod, presiding."

The bailiff's announcement having been made, the judge sits down behind the bench and calls the case. "People versus Harold Blitzstien." He looks down toward the counsel tables. "Appearances?"

Right on cue, Myra stands up. "Myra Scot for the People, Your Honor."

My turn. "Peter Sharp for the defendant, Your Honor. We waive reading of the charges and statement of rights."

The judge looks down at my client. "Well Mister Blitzstien, it's your turn. In the charge of Murder in the First Degree, a violation of California Penal Code Section 187, how do you plead?"

My client just stands there and glares at the judge. Silence. After about ten seconds of pin-drop quiet, the judge takes over. "Okay, tell you what I'm going to do. Mister Sharp, I have a feeling that you really haven't had a chance to properly interview your client, so I'm going to put this matter over for another ten days, during which time maybe the both of you can get to know each other a little better. Then, next time we all get together, perhaps a plea might be forthcoming." He looks over to Myra, and then to me. "Any objections?"

We both answer almost in unison, "No, Your Honor."

The judge then looks over towards the calendar hanging on the wall over his clerk's desk. "I see that we've got an opening on either the 13th or 14th, so if either of you would like to make a reservation, please go right ahead."

Both Myra and I check with our calendars and agree that the 14th would be a good day to come back.

She checks to see if she had anything else going on that day. When I check my calendar, I see that I'm free for the rest of my life. The judge bangs his gavel on the desk. "Done. See you then." He stands up and heads back to his chambers.

Just before the bailiffs lead him away, I take the opportunity to try a conversation with my client. "Listen Mister Blitzstien, you don't have to like me, but at least give me the courtesy of acknowledging my presence here. I'm going to do whatever I can for you so please, if I come to the jail to visit you, at least come to the interview room. If you don't want to talk okay, you can just sit there silently. That's your decision and I'll respect it."

No response. The bailiffs are on the way to escort him back to the holding cells. I try one more time. "If I come to the jail tomorrow will you see me?"

As he's led away, he looks back at me and utters the first words I've heard from him. "Knock yourself out."

I don't know if that's an acceptance or not, but I'll go to the jail tomorrow to find out. If he refuses to see me again, I'll notify the judge and then do whatever I can for his defense. About the only chance we have is to block Myra's having the videotape evidence admitted – and if they document the chain of custody and bring all the right witnesses in, then I have no chance at all.

For some reason, this matter has attracted the press' attention – probably because of Myra's recently gained notoriety in beating her former boss a few months ago and forcing him out of office. There are several reporters in the long hallway outside the courtroom. When Myra sees them, I'm once again reminded of her love affair with any camera. They crowd around her, asking those inane questions that they get overpaid to ask. After stalling the exact right amount of time to build the suspense, she breaks it by making a statement. "As you've already seen by that footage leaked from the district attorney's office before I was appointed to this case, not only did the defendant do the act with which he's charged, but even my predecessor, former District Attorney Bill Miller, could win this case."

A reporter asks her a leading question. "Does that mean you're you willing to stake your reputation on a conviction here?"

Myra's a smart cookie. She sidesteps that one. "I don't have any reputation to stake. I'm not the district attorney, I've just been appointed as a special prosecutor for this one case. When it's over, I'm back to my private practice."

The reporter won't let up. "In other words, can we assume that if you lose this case, you won't run for district attorney in the next election?"

Myra wasn't ready for that one, but she tries to answer as tactfully as possible. "Let's put it this way, anyone who loses a dead-banger like this one doesn't even deserve to carry the district attorney's briefcase."

The press acts like it's in a feeding frenzy and I can see that Myra's getting uncomfortable with it. I try to help her out by grabbing her arm and pulling her into the elevator, which is going up to the second floor. She appreciates the extraction. "I'm just going up to the second floor cafeteria for a cup of coffee... come on, join me."

"You buying?" She's still as stingy as ever.

"Yeah, why not. I'll write it off as a celebration for our working on another case together."

The coffee break is a cordial one. After the usual small talk, she apologizes to me.

"Pete, I can't give you anything on this case."

I guess she's talking about a plea bargain, which I'm really not interested in here. "That's okay, I don't think I'll need one."

I catch her by surprise with that one. "What do you mean, you won't need one? You think he'll plead straight up, to the 187?"

At this point, I figure it's time to rattle her cage a little. As I've said many times before, knowledge of the law isn't as important as knowledge of the prosecutor. "No, I mean that maybe he's insane. I've always thought that anyone who can take another life in cold blood like that can't be sane... even if it's a cat or dog they kill. No reason it shouldn't apply here. I looked in those gray, cold eyes of his today and it creeped me out. I think the guy's nuts."

Wow, that sure presses a button. She starts to come unglued. "No you don't – you're not doing that to me. You know damned well that my run for district attorney may depend on a straight conviction in this case, so don't you go pulling any of your crap on me." When she sees me embarrassingly looking around the room, she realizes we're still in a public place, so she immediately stops yelling at me and leans across the table. In almost a whisper, she gives me an ultimatum. "You try that on me, and I'll cut you right off at the knees in open court. I'll fillet you like a fish. I promised the public a conviction and that's what they're going to get." With that, she gets up and storms out of the room. There's never a reporter around when you need one.

Driving Myra crazy was always a specialty of mine and now that I don't have to be worried about her threatening to throw me out of the house, it's even more fun. It seems that we're having much better fights now that we're divorced.

While I'm at the courthouse I might as well get some use out of their law library, so I start some research. I've got several areas I need to know more law about and if I don't doze off reading this stuff, maybe I'll learn something that might help with my cases.

I pull out a bunch of books and start reading up on Barratry for Stuart, Dramshop for Vinnie, and client refusal to cooperate, for my own edification. And while I'm at it, I make a note to research how far the bank's liability could extend to deceased claimant Mike Drago.

While scanning through one case after another, I notice one that mentions one of the most celebrated cases in criminal law... one I should know more about for possible use in Blitzstien's defense.

In 1843, a paranoid young woodworker from Edinburgh named Daniel McNaughton was convinced that Sir Robert Peel, the Prime Minister of England, was conspiring against him. Daniel got a gun and tried to assassinate Peel. Unfortunately, Daniel shot the wrong guy in the back by mistake –

he killed Mister Edward Drummond, Peel's private secretary.

Of course McNaughton was caught and arrested. The cops in those days couldn't catch Jack the Ripper, but that failure was understandable because all he ever carved were prostitutes - and Sherlock Holmes was probably on vacation that month. It might have been a different story if Jack tried to whack the Prime Minister. What a terrible thought... then he might forever be known as Jack the Whacker. My mind drifts in and out of reality when I read about the law.

When McNaughton was brought to trial, he must have had what was the 'dream team' in those days because they came up with a new argument for his defense. They said that because he believed his life was in danger, he acted in self-defense when trying to kill the Prime Minister. Not quite as creative as 'if the glove doesn't fit, you must acquit,' but it seemed to get the job done anyway. The court accepted the dream team's argument, and found McNaughton not guilty by reason of insanity.

That case gave rise to quite an uproar in the legal community, and it hasn't stopped yet. Modernly, the casebooks contain many celebrated trials where the insanity defense was put forth. Some of the most memorable cases include the one involving Wade McClave who thought his parents were vampires, so he butchered them. It worked for him. Andrea Yates drowned her five children but it didn't work for her. Probably because her trial was in Texas and they really like to execute people there.

The insanity defense was never more hotly debated then when John Hinckley shot President

Ronald Reagan, outside a hotel in 1981. The very next year, Hinckley was declared not guilty by reason of insanity.

I've never asserted that defense for a criminal client, but maybe that's because I haven't had that many capital cases. You don't waste your energy on a defense like that for a shoplifting charge... although it has been done. I think an attorney tried to convince a Beverly Hills Municipal Court that his movie-star client was not responsible for stealing thousands of dollars from Saks Fifth Avenue's store because she was mentally impaired and under the influence of prescription drugs. She lost.

One of the big downsides of an insanity defense is that you have to admit your client actually did the act with which he or she is charged, before you can claim that they didn't know what they were doing. That removes all the fun of trying to destroy the eyewitnesses. Another bad thing about it is that it turns the trial into a battle of the shrinks, who'll say anything for the right amount of money. In order to be successful I'll have to show by a preponderance of the evidence that my weird defendant, because of a mental illness, either didn't understand what he was doing when the crime was committed or that he didn't know that his actions were wrong. A tough sell, especially when you can't back it up with a nice history of prior craziness.

Partly in jest, I threatened Myra with the not guilty by reason of loonyness defense. Now it's starting to look like a better idea. Everything will depend on whether or not I actually get a chance to meet with my client tomorrow at the jail. It's bad enough when I can't get my legal ward to talk to me. I don't want to fail with a fifty-year-old killer too.

There's still time left this afternoon to get a message of representation off on Vinnie's case, so I use Jack Bibberman's information and send an email to the restaurant where the drunk got drunk.

The kid is doing her volunteer dog act at the hospital today, so I'm going to turn off the phone, get comfortable, and do some reading. I copied over fifty pages from the courthouse library books, which should take me at least three hours to get through. By that time, the Saint Bernard will be hungry, so maybe Suzi will be generous and feed me too. She usually stops by the Chinese restaurant on her way back from the hospital, or calls the Asian Boys to deliver something for us.

8

A surprising message comes in from Ms. Patty Vogel, counsel for the restaurant where Vinnie's drunk driver got loaded. She informs me that they are denying all liability, which is pretty standard practice for defense attorneys. They want you to get the feeling that it's going to be an uphill fight all the way if you threaten their client. Just for the record, I email her that we have several affidavits from independent witnesses who have placed the defendant driver in her client's place of business for a minimum of six consecutive hours prior to his driving into the tree and injuring my client.

Ms. Vogel responds by letting me know that they are aware of our affidavits and that they still deny all liability. She goes on to state that her office will accept Service of Process in this matter. Suzi likes this because it means that we won't have to spend the money to have the Summons & Complaint for Vinnie's case served on them by Jack B., or the Marshall's office.

Come to think of it, she's really got some nerve. Not only is she denying the claim, she's daring me to sue and even offering to let me mail the papers to her office. This is the first time I've come across this much boldness, which probably means that they know something that I don't know - and that worries me.

My cell phone rings and I recognize Myra's number on the caller ID display. "Hey, what's up?"

"Pete, I'm calling to apologize."

"For what?"

"For the way I acted yesterday in the courthouse cafeteria. I totally lost it when you brought up that insanity defense and I shouldn't have. You're representing a client in a capital murder case and you certainly have the right to assert any defense on his behalf that you think is warranted."

"Gee, that's nice of you Myra. I really appreciate your consideration like that."

"Yeah, well, listen, I know you're going to try and visit with your client again today, so after you're through, why not call my office and maybe we can get together for another cup of coffee... one that I promise to finish without going ballistic."

This looks encouraging, but I'm still worried. That's twice in the same week that a female lawyer has been agreeable with me. First it's Patty Vogel agreeing to accept service by mail for her restaurant client and now it's Myra, apologizing for being the ball-buster that she is. If things keep going this well for me, maybe my own client will grant me the honor of his presence. I should know soon, because I'm now pulling into the jail's parking lot.

After going through the usual check-in procedure, I'm led back to the attorney interview room, where I sit down with a magazine to wait for my client to either show up or send a jailer back with his refusal to see me.

To my pleasant surprise, the steel door opens and in walks my esteemed murder client, Harold Blitzstien. He looks like shit – even worse than he did in court yesterday. He sits down on the other side of the table and gives me a blank stare. I ask him how he is but as usual, he doesn't answer. Okay, the silent treatment. I can take that. It's a step in the right direction – at least he came to the meeting. I figure that at least one of us should talk, so I start in.

"Mister Blitzstien, do you mind if I call you Harold?" No response. "Okay, I'll take that as a yes. Harold, we've got a serious problem here. You're charged with murder in the first degree and the prosecution has a videotape of you committing the crime. Just in case you weren't aware of it, the hospital has security cameras all over the place. Now that doesn't give us too many ways to go. We can deny that it was you on the tape, which would be tough since you looked right into one of the cameras in the hospital corridor, and they've got a beautiful shot of your face. Self-defense is probably out of the picture because the guy in bed looked like he was unconscious when you held the pillow over his face... he didn't even put up a fight.

"With self-defense and it-was-someone-else gone, the only things left for us are NGRI or GBMI, which mean Not Guilty by Reason of Insanity, or Guilty But Mentally Ill." Still no response. I know he's listening but he won't give me even an inch of acknowledgement.

"Can you at least nod to let me know that you're hearing everything I'm saying?"

Success. He gives me a slight up-and-down 'affirmative' nod. Now that communication between us has actually begun, I continue. "I don't want to fight with you about the defense we use. If I stand up in court and tell the judge that we're pleading insanity, I don't want to be surprised by your vanity kicking in and making you jump up to deny that you're insane. I'm trying to save your life here... will you work with me?" Another slight shrug. That's okay, I'm not expecting a well thought-out legal discourse from him. At least he's letting me know that I can try something in court without any surprise reaction. Now I'm going to try to push it one step further. "Harold, can you at least tell me why you did it?"

He gets up and walks towards the door. The jailer and I both know what this means... he has decided that today's interview is over. So much for the fine art of client control. Just as he starts to leave the room, he turns around and says the exact four words I didn't want to hear. "I needed the money."

Damn. That makes it a murder for hire – a special circumstance case that qualifies for the death penalty – and I know about it. Now I'm in deep doo-doo. Putting him on the stand has just become an impossible option. If he tells the court he's a paid killer, both of our careers are over. And now that I know he's admitted to doing it as a murder for hire, I can't put him on the stand as a witness, because I can't allow him to perjure himself by denying the crime.

Criminal defense attorneys walk a tightrope whenever they interview a client. You want to find out all you can about the case but you really don't want to hear the client confess to the crime by admitting that he did it. If he does, then as the defense lawyer, you're between a rock and a hard place. The only reason to ever put your client on the stand in a criminal trial is to tell his or her side of the story, deny guilt, establish an alibi, or try to point the finger of accusation at another person. If you're the one doing the questioning and know that the client actually committed the crime, then every question you ask to help his defense is soliciting an answer that will be perjurious... and as a sworn officer of the court, you just can't do that. It's never worth it to put your entire career on the line like that.

Of course there's always the possibility that even if your client confesses guilt to you, he might insist on testifying on his own behalf. That's an even stickier situation. Some criminals are such sociopaths that they think they can convince a jury of their innocence. In cases like that, a criminal defense attorney should advise the court that the defendant insists on testifying against the advice of counsel. This way, the attorney is at least on the record as having been against the defendant testifying, so he may be off the hook if the client gets nailed for perjury. The only danger there is to watch out that you don't ask your client if he did it or not. Let him tell the story in his own words, but leave that question for the prosecutor to ask... and get lied to.

There's nothing I can do to help Harold keep his career of crime going, but I'd at least like to continue with mine. And if the court orders the prosecution's shrink to examine him, I'll be shot down that way too. If he readily admits things to me, he'll admit them to the shrink too. I'm afraid it's all over for Harold.

It's time to call Myra's office and make arrangements to meet her for lunch. I now know that I can't assert any kind of defense for him, but she doesn't know that yet. Maybe there's still hope I can get some kind of deal out of her. If she at least takes death off the table, maybe I can talk him into a plea.

Driving over to the restaurant, I mentally go over all the 'designer defenses' that have been tried by various dream teams over the years, seeing if anything might be worth a shot. One after another, they all get ruled out in order. Starting with the Twinkie Defense, PMS, Sleepwalking, Black Rage, Post Traumatic Stress Disorder, Battered Woman Syndrome, Postpartum Psychosis, Adopted Child Syndrome and Brief Reactive Psychosis. Not only will none of them work - I don't even understand what half of them mean, but every defense lawyer worth his salt can usually rattle them off for conversational purposes, to show how smart he thinks he is.

What really bothers me isn't just that I can't figure out a defense for this guy, it's that I can't figure out why the hell he did it. He says it was for the money, but why should anyone want to have a slip-and-fall claimant killed? I know that the insurance companies can be pretty evil at times but I can't believe they'd have a nuisance claimant whacked. There's got to be something here that I'm missing, and if I don't figure it out soon, Harold Blitzstien will be looking at a visit from doctor death.

Wait a minute. If I can think this thing through, so can Myra. She's got me up against the wall, so why the hell is she being so nice to me and wanting to get together? I smell a rat. Looks like it's time for a change of plans. I call Myra's cell phone and tell her voicemail that something urgent just came up and I'll have to take a rain check on our lunch – maybe we can reschedule it for next week. I've got to get back to the boat to think all of this out and come up with some defense for Harold. Maybe I can find something in all that video footage that might help.

Back at the boat I draft a complaint against the Mexican restaurant, mail it to the court for filing and send a copy to their attorney Patty Vogel's office with a note that I'll email her the court case number once I get my conformed copy back. Just to cover all the bases, I also send a short set of written Interrogatories over too.

I tell our office manager to use whatever connections we have with the local cops to run background checks on both Mike Drago, the deceased slip-and-fall claimant, as well as the defendant drunk driver in Vinnie's case. There's got to be something somewhere that will give me a clue as to what's happening with these cases.

I was told that all those videotapes were digitized into some computer. The courthouse newspaper rack has a selection of magazines, one of which specializes in digital video, so I bought a copy on my way out of the building, the last time I was there. While reading through it, I learned quite a bit about non-linear video editing, which is all done on a computer after the footage is loaded in. From what I understand, you can isolate any frame you want out of the video and there are plenty to choose from because, as my magazine education revealed, videotape runs at a speed of about thirty frames a second.

Once a frame is chosen, a hard-copy print of it can be made. I think they call if 'frame-grabbing.' With this knowledge, I once again go back to that single videotape and take a look at it. Although it's only a compilation of the other tapes, there is a time-code marker running at the bottom of the screen, which tells what reel it's from, as well as the day, minute, hour and second of the action that took place. I start to make a list of the frames I want pictures of.

And while I'm in this scientific detective mood, it might also be a good idea to do the same with the security camera footage from the bank. I'd like to see how Mister Drago fell and hurt himself, so I send a message requesting that those tapes get digitized too. I may not be learning much, but at least I feel busy.

I save the most interesting stuff for Jack Bibberman, who gets the assignment of trying to find out from under what rock the mass fax spammer who counter-sued Stuart crawled out.

Now that we know the fax-spammer wants to play hardball, we might as well make the game interesting. I draft a set of Interrogs for them to answer.

The standard rule for trial lawyers is to never ask a question that you don't already know the answer to. When non-lawyers hear that rule, they always ask the same thing. "If you already know the answer, why ask the question?" The reason is really quite simple. When you're in court, you want to tell your client's story to the trier of fact, whether it be a judge or jury. It's not good enough to have your client or his mother take the witness stand and lay things out. You're much better off having it come out of the mouths of some independent witnesses – people who have no apparent agenda or desire to help either side.

In order to do this you should have a list of the things you can't use to build your side of the case up. Along with the list, you should also know which witness will testify to each item on the list. Then like a puppeteer, you call witness after witness, ask the questions in any order you want, and elicit the answers you need. There's no need to worry about the proper order, because you can straighten all that out in your closing argument, when you 'sum up' all the answers you received and put them in the proper order for the jury.

Of course if you're going to have the answers to all the questions, you must have some way of getting them in advance of the trial, so the courts allow for what's called 'civil discovery,' which takes the form of written 'interrogatories' (Interrogs), or the taking of oral testimony under oath at a 'deposition.' There are also some other tools in our kit, like the right to subpoena documents, demands for admissions, statutory offers, and some other tricks that are better left to qualified paralegals. All the trial lawyer wants are the answers.

On Stuart's case, I plan to use the Interrogs not only as a means of getting answers to some questions I'd like to ask, but also as a 'spear,' to give them some indication of how deep I want to probe the other side's affairs.

Accordingly, my questions to them include information as to how they get the fax numbers they send their junk out to, as well as what those numbers are, what their procedures are for removing people who complain, how many faxes they've sent out over the past year, and on and on. They've obviously retained an attorney to help them, so there's no reason not to make him work for his fee.

I've always had the suspicion that when you get one of those unsolicited junk faxes containing a number you can contact to be 'removed' from their list, it's a number that doesn't really work to remove you. Instead, it lets them know for sure that yours is a valid fax number – one that they should continue

63

sending their junk to and sell to other junk fax broadcasters. With that in mind, I send Jack Bibberman to the nearby Santa Monica courthouse to do a naughty errand for me.

The written Interrogs are completed and sent along to the defense firm's office, along with a formal Answer to their complaint – a general denial of everything. The real trick to sending Interrogs is to disguise the question you really want the answer to along with all the others, and hope that they don't figure out which one you're most interested in. My big question is in there and if Bibberman does a special task for me, that answer might make our case.

9

Vinnie is calling. He wants to know if anything's happening on his lawsuit. I try to be tactful. "Vinnie, you don't have any property damage, you don't have any lost wages and you have no medical bills to speak of, so let's not get greedy on this one. It's not going to be your retirement nest egg."

"Yeah Mister Sharp, I know that, but they should still have to pay something... even a little maybe, for my inconvenience."

"You're right Vinnie, but if you're looking for big numbers, I don't want to see you disappointed. Just to give you an idea, I filed the case in Municipal Court, so if we get a settlement offer above five hundred dollars, I'd recommend that you accept it."

"Okay, Mister Sharp. Stuart says to trust you completely, so I'll leave it in your hands."

It took a few days, but now I'm starting to get results on some background checks that I requested – and there aren't any surprises. Mike Drago, the slip-and-fall claimant has no record. He's a single guy who lives alone with no family to be found, and not even a parking ticket. Same results came back for Harold Blitzstien, with the exception of the fact that Harold has an ex-wife and a couple of kids somewhere. They both appear to be honest, hard working blue-collar types who never got into trouble with the law. The only real difference between them is that one is dead and the other is headed for death row, and both show the same amount of concern for their respective conditions.

The other one isn't as clean, because as expected, Vinnie's drunken stolen-car driver Harry Michaels has several 'deuces' on his record over the past couple of years. The section of California's Vehicle Code pertaining to drunk driving was number had formerly been 502. When the code was re-written, the code section became number 23102. Because both sections ended in the number '2,' that particular violation took on the nickname of a 'deuce,' which is a term instantly recognizable by anyone remotely connected with the criminal justice system in California.

Being a repeat offender, it's no wonder that he didn't drive his own car any more. Some judge probably lifted his license for at least a year. I don't see any need to waste our assets going deeper into his record, because there's no doubt he did what we think he did. Our case will depend on whether or not I can get the facts within the purview of the Dramshop laws and how bad of a guy the driver is or what his past record shows isn't really relevant to our case. He could be either a mass murderer or a choirboy and the law should still be applied the same. Maybe a slightly different sentencing, but no change in the law on the way there.

The same goes for Mike Drago, the murdered slip-and-fall claimant, and Harold Blitzstien, the murder-on-video client. Add Stuart's spammer into the mix and you have four cases where background, criminal history and character don't come into play. All that counts is their actions.

If I have to go to trial with these cases on matters where all that counts is the evidence, and there's no problem interpreting that evidence, then I'm going to have to come up with some strategies that test the law itself, and not the character or credibility of any witness.

Almost two weeks have gone by. Answers to both sets of Interrogs have just come back on Vinnie and Stuart's cases. I'd like to spend some time going over them but I've got an appearance to make on Harold Blitzstien's case. His arraignment was continued ten days last time and it's set for this afternoon. I still don't know what I'm going to do for his defense.

Once the bailiff's announcement is made and Myra and I both state our representation for the record, it's my turn to offer a plea on my client's behalf. I think I've got a win-win way for us all to handle this – if it works. The Judge looks down at me. "Well, Counselor, you've had some time now. How would Mister Blitzstien like to plead? I'm sure you're familiar with the menu. Today's specials are Guilty, Not Guilty, Not Guilty by Reason of Insanity, or Nolo Contendere. Would you like to make a selection?"

I spend a few seconds telling Harold that Nolo Contendere means 'no contest,' and that they can do whatever they want, because you just don't care. He's not very talkative today. The judge is getting impatient.

"Mister Sharp, can we please move this along? Not Guilty has traditionally been our best seller, would your client like to try it out?"

I can't keep the judge waiting any longer. "Your Honor, if the court pleases, at this point we're down to two choices you offered that look attractive today." I look over to the prosecution table. Myra is glaring at me, nervously tapping her pencil on the counsel table with one of those 'what the hell is this schmuck up to now?' looks on her face. I haven't seen that look since we were married. I continue. "We seem to be on the fence between Not Guilty and Not Guilty by Reason of Insanity, so to save everyone a lot of trouble down the road, we would ask that the court order a psychological examination of Mister Blitzstien, to determine, among other things, his ability to understand the charges against him, his ability to cooperate with the defense, and whether or not he's fit to stand trial." The courtroom is silent. I can hear the gears grinding in Myra's head. Not hearing any immediate objection, I go on. "In this way Your Honor, once the court has had an opportunity to examine the Defendant, we will go along with whatever the result is. In fact, we'll stipulate to an agreement right now, that the plea will depend entirely on the results of the court's psychiatric examination."

The judge wants to make sure. "Mister Sharp, are you telling this court that if the examination I order shows the defendant to be fit to stand trial, that you will not consider an insanity plea and go with a straight Not Guilty?"

"That's correct, Your Honor." The judge looks over to Myra."

She stands up. "No objection, Your Honor."

The judge bangs his gavel down. "So be it. You'll both be notified when the report comes in."

I look at Harold, just before they lead him away. "Harold, just be yourself." At this point, I have no idea what he really is, so I'm as curious to see what the shrink will say as Myra and the judge are. I can only say one thing about him – he looks really terrible. I hope he's physically okay.

Back at the boat, I start to go over the responses to Interrogs returned to us. I scan through both sets, looking for answers to certain questions. On Stuart's spamming case I see the answer I'm looking for. On Vinnie's case I don't.

The questions asked of the Mexican restaurant were about employees and customers. I specifically mentioned the night that the drunk driver was there, but their answers completely deny that he was either a customer or an employee. This is not good for us. If he wasn't working as a bartender or waiter and he wasn't an employee, then how the hell did he get enough booze in his system to blow a 0.19? The restaurant didn't report him to the police for stealing alcohol, so he must have been drinking it over the six hours he was there. Was it free? I don't think so.

The property report from his arrest didn't indicate any credit cards, so if he paid for the drinks, it must have been by cash. This calls for more investigation. I call Jack Bibberman and tell him to re-interview the witnesses. No wonder Patty Vogel was so smug when I talked to her. I was right; she knows something that I don't know and it bothers me.

I call the public defender's office and try to locate whatever deputy has been assigned to the drunk's Grand Theft Auto charge. After what seems like an hour on hold, I finally reach a deputy PD who is handling the matter for arraignment. "Hi, this is Peter Sharp. I filed a civil matter against your client Harry Michaels. He's the one charged with driving that Lexus into a tree after leaving a Mexican restaurant on Washington Boulevard, out here in the Marina, and I understand you're representing him.

"That's right, Mister Sharp, I caught that case. What can I do for you?"

"Well, as you probably know, he wound up wrapping that car around a tree."

"And you represent the tree?"

"Not quite. It so happens that my client was standing next to that tree, taking a leak, at the exact same time that Mister Michaels decided to attack it."

I hear laughter on the other end of the line. "Is your client claiming some invasion of privacy, or maybe peeus interruptus?"

"Not exactly, but the tree did fall on him. We filed a Municipal Court action to recover for some new clothes and minor pain and suffering. This is a small matter but the client is an employee of one of my bigger clients, so I'm trying to keep him happy."

"Okay. It's time for the commercial. You want to interview him, right?"

"Right." The Interrogs I got back from the restaurant that served him last don't dispute the fact that he was there for six hours, but I can't establish him as either a customer or an employee. I'm trying to figure out what the hell he was doing there."

"Sharp, I appreciate your situation but I can't arrange for an interview. I'll tell you what - I'm pleading him out later this week. If you want, you can be there in the courtroom. Maybe you'll get a chance to ask him a quick question while he's standing next to me at the counsel table."

"Do you think he'll do some time?"

"Yeah, but it won't be hard time. I've talked to the City Attorney and they're willing to let him do six months at County Jail. They're pretty overcrowded there, so he'll probably be out in a month or so. If you really want some cooperation, I'd like to be able to tell him that you've authorized me to deposit some cash to his prisoner account, so while he's in there, he can buy some grooming stuff. Nothing big, maybe ten or fifteen bucks."

"It's a deal. I'll give it to you in court before I talk to him. If anyone sees me handing you the money, you can just tell them it's a drug deal."

Just as I hang up the phone, there's a knock on the hull. It's a messenger with the still pictures I ordered off the security videos from the bank and hospital, so it looks like I've got some work to do now.

The dog is sitting and watching me. This means that he knows something before I know it – that I'm cooking tonight. Suzi must be busy doing something, so she told the dog that I'd feed him. He obviously doesn't want to be late for dinner.

Tonight's pasta dish will be a special combination that includes the usual small can of sweet peas, eight ounces of large elbow macaroni, a can of almost fat-free vegetarian chili, plus a few dashes of Paul Newman's Spaghetti sauce. Added to the mix will be three slices of veggie imitation cheddar cheese and some garlic salt. I call this combination my chili-mac special. The dog smells the open can of chili, but because it's up on the sink and he can't see the label, he doesn't know it's the vegetarian kind.

As I'm walking around the galley, I notice that the door to the little princess' stateroom is ajar. She's peeking out at me.

"I'm preparing one of my pasta dishes tonight. Would you like a bowl of it?"

For the first time since I've met her, I see a slight smile on her face as she nods 'yes' and then immediately hides behind her door. I must have done something right, because this is the first time she's agreed to voluntarily eat my cooking.

The phone rings. "Myra, my dear. Your number is always a pleasant sight when it appears on my caller ID display. What can I do for your tonight?"

"You stood me up last time. I had to sit there and eat lunch all alone."

"I called."

"Yeah, but I was already waiting in the restaurant, so I stayed to eat."

"I'm sorry, but you know how it is when you've got a busy private practice."

"Sure Pete. How many cases do you have now, three?"

"It's four, but who's counting? To what do I owe the pleasure of this call?"

"I thought I'd give you a heads-up on that murderer you're defending. We did a thorough search of the hospital and found a discarded latex 'mission-impossible' type of facemask that looks exactly like your client. That means someone else may have done the crime and then looked up at the security camera with the mask on, to make it look like your client was the guilty one.

"It's probably something the CIA is involved in, so we'll be dismissing the case and releasing your client with a letter of apology signed by everyone in the District Attorney's office. I hope that helps you out a little."

She must really enjoy torturing me. "Oh gee, Myra, thanks a lot. That's exactly what I've been hoping for to clear this innocent man. I'd better get down to the county jail to pick him up... or will you be sending your driver to take him home? There! You feel better now? I know it doesn't look too good for us but there's no need to rub it in. You'll get your conviction and you'll get elected as District Attorney."

"Yeah, I know. But it's still going to be fun beating your pants off in court. In all the years I've known you, I've never seen you at such a loss for words or strategy. Your client is going down and there's nothing you can do about it."

"The shrink's report isn't in yet, you know. There's always a possibility he can be found unfit to stand trial."

"No way Petey, and you know it. He's just as sane as you and me. I'm glad we've got him on tape because the only weak link in our whole case was the motive. After this is all over, maybe you'll tell me why he did it."

"Sorry beautiful. I'd like to assert the Attorney-client privilege, but all I've gotten from his so far is silence. And I do mean silence. The guy hasn't said one complete sentence to me since I was appointed to defend him. Oh by the way, I'm preparing one of my special pasta dishes tonight – want some?"

"No thank you, I'm off of gruel this month. But I'll make it easy for you. If you win this case, I'll buy you dinner anywhere you want."

"Anywhere?"

"You got it, pal."

"Myra, if I win this case by proving that my client didn't do the crime, I'd like to have dinner at the club."

"What club would that be, Peter? Have you joined the 'Y'?"

"Not exactly, my dear. I mean our club – the Lahaina Yacht Club. I'll pay for the plane – you pay for the food."

There's a brief lull while she's thinks it over. This will be the real test to see how much she believes in her case. My macaroni timer is approaching eight minutes, so I try to move the conversation along. "Myra, I don't want to sound rude but my pasta is almost done cooking."

"Okay Petey, you get an acquittal on this case and I'll buy you dinner at the club on Maui."

She can call me Petey as much as she wants, as long as it's accompanied by an offer to go to Maui with me. The last time we were in Maui together was during our first few years of marriage, and it was really great. Maybe because that's before she started law school.

Now I've got some extra incentive to win this case. Even if the court only awards me fifty bucks an hour, by the time the trial is over I'll have about two hundred hours invested. Ten grand will help to make it like a second honeymoon - and we'll go first class. Now, all I have to do is figure out some way to win an impossible losing case. No problemo. I'm sure that with the dog's help, it's in the bag.

During dinner I browse through the still pictures that were 'frame-grabbed' from the hospital security tapes. There are several that I requested and they clearly show Harold walking into the hospital room, standing by the closet door, walking over to the vacant bed next to Drago's, picking up the pillow from the vacant bed, lowering the pillow onto Drago's face, pressing and holding the pillow down on Drago's face, and then putting the pillow back onto the other bed.

There were another few minutes or two of photos I didn't ask for, during which time the nurses ran into the room and tried to revive Drago. Evidently, his flat line showed up on the nurses' station computer, letting them know that they'd lost another customer, so they rushed into the room. When they ran in, Harold hid behind the vacant bed's curtain and then walked out while they were trying to revive Drago. That's when he looked up at the hallway security camera outside Drago's room.

According to the added time-code on the bottom of the photos, the whole act took no more than two minutes. The hospital staff used those electric paddles and spent several minutes trying to bring Drago back to life, but it was to no avail.

I spread the ink-jet printed pictures out on the coffee table in chronological order and scan back and forth over them, looking – I don't know for what – just looking.

The Saint Bernard is coming out of the forward stateroom with his leash in his mouth. This is the signal for me to do the trick he taught me. When he brings his leash over to me like that, I'm supposed to attach it to his collar and take him for a walk. As I'm fastening the leash, he drools on one of the pictures, completely obscuring the upper portion of the one that shows my client lowering the pillow onto Drago's face. No problem. That's a picture I'm not particularly fond of.

On the way back from our walk, I can't help but notice Laverne smiling in our direction from her window. I hope it's me she's smiling at. I let the dog go back to our boat by himself, and smile back at Laverne. Aw, what the hell. I've worked hard today – I might as well take a break from normality. If I perform the tricks that she taught me, I'll get rewarded with French toast for breakfast.

10

I've received the bank's security tapes and just like the hospital cassettes, they were digitized into a computer somewhere. I now have a single tape that contains all the action in the bank concerning Drago's fall. Because there's constant traffic in the bank, there aren't any dead spots with no motion, so all I'm concentrating on is the thirty minutes before and after the fall.

This one-hour cassette is not a compilation of footage – it's the actual real-time account of what happened in the bank the hour of the accident. I see a kid spilling his coke on the floor near the counter where the deposit and withdrawal slips are. I see Drago come in and walk over to the counter. Boom! He goes down on his ass. Once down, he just lays there with a grimace on his face. People come over to help him up but he waves them off, obviously in pain and afraid to be moved by anyone but professionals. The old security guard must have finally noticed the accident because he walks over to where Drago is lying. In less than ten minutes, the paramedics arrive, get him onto a gurney, and remove him from the bank.

I watch the part where Drago falls, over and over again. It looks strange that a fall like that would injure his ribs. This doesn't compute, so I ask the office to prepare a subpoena for his hospital records and X-rays. I want to get an independent medical opinion on this because if his ribs were damaged before the fall, then our client may only be responsible for aggravating a pre-existing injury. I also want to know if he hurt anything else when he landed on his ass.

This is where working for an insurance defense firm really comes in handy. Getting medical records out of hospitals and finding doctors to testify is their bread and butter, so everything gets done at warp speed.

I also want to know if there's any connection between Blitzstien and Drago, so I instruct the authorized investigation service to run credit reports and extensive civil background checks on both of them to see if there's any way they might have known each other before the murder. No wonder it's so tough to beat an insurance company. I now appreciate the benefits of having unlimited assets to avail myself of the services of the big investigative firms, but nothing beats the personal service of a guy like Jack B. and his dedication to the case, and not the fee.

Harold's shrink exam results probably won't be back for at least another month, and the special investigations I requested won't be completed for at least a week or two, so now's a good time to concentrate on Stuart's defense to those barratry and champerty counter-claims.

At this point I'm a little confused. According to the common law definitions of Champerty and Maintenance, anyone who finances another person's lawsuit and then shares in the proceeds is guilty of the offense, but that's what lawyers do every day. It's the main basis of an attorney's Contingency Agreement. The client pays nothing unless the lawyer wins the case. In the typical contingency case, a lawyer advances all costs of litigation and if there's a victory, the lawyer gets reimbursed for his expenses and also takes a percentage of the recovery.

Several years ago the legislature saw fit to prohibit private investigators from also working on a contingency basis, because they're usually called to testify. It was felt that no witness' credibility should be tempted by monetary reward. That's the reason why people who've already sold their story to a magazine are looked upon as less than credible witnesses. If they change their testimony in court in any way that differs with the exaggerations contained in their previously sold story, they run the risk of being asked to return their fee from the magazine.

I guess that because most of the legislature is composed of attorneys, they rationalized exempting contingency lawyers' fees because the lawyer can't be called to testify in a case he's working on. Also, contingency fees give people access to legal representation that they'd probably never be able to afford.

But this reasoning doesn't help Stuart. He can't claim he was working on a contingency, because he's not a lawyer. And if he were a lawyer, he wouldn't be allowed to bring all those actions, because they don't allow lawyers to represent people in Small Claims Court.

It's true that Stuart advertises for clients who have received un-solicited faxes but he doesn't create unfounded claims. Unlike a recent situation where some Beverly Hills law firm filed actions against hundreds of small businesses claiming that the risk of consumer fraud might exist, Stuart has actual fax receivers who have valid claims. All that Stuart does is organize them and process their claims. He's one step above those typing services that help people fill out divorce and bankruptcy forms, because he goes the extra mile and appears as their assignee in the courtroom.

It's quite obvious what's going on. The business of sending out huge numbers of un-solicited faxes is big business and those fax broadcasters are all probably organized into an association of telemarketers with some political clout. If they allow someone like Stuart to get away with what he's doing, it might get publicized and set a precedent, so that they'd be facing someone like Stuart in every jurisdiction in the country. They can't afford to have that happen, so they've ganged up on Stuart with this outrageous counter-claim, to stem a possible tide of costly litigation. They're fighting for their lives here and I've got to come up with some good defense to stop them in their tracks. I really can't blame them for trying to defend themselves, but a lawyer can only be on one side at a time, and in this battle, Stuart is my client.

If I try to fight the law, I don't have much to work with, so I'll have to completely destroy the witness in this case. That's why I'm glad Jack Bibberman did that secret, naughty task for me at the Santa Monica courthouse. I've now got the answers to their Interrogs, so I'm going to push for a trial on this case as soon as possible. It's only a municipal court action, so we should be able to get a trial date pretty soon. They're not as backed up as the higher courts are.

The only snag so far is that Jack B. has failed to come up with anything derogatory about the fax spammers. They report their income, pay their taxes and have no criminal records. They're also young, attractive guys who work very hard and will probably make excellent witnesses on their own behalf. That would ordinarily be tough to combat, but I've got an ace up my sleeve. I'm having our office fax a very small set of supplemental Interrogs to the other side's lawyer. It's about time their side received an unsolicited fax.

The Mike Drago medical reports and evaluation have come in. Other than the damage to his ribs, the only other injury the x-rays showed was a bruised coccyx, or tailbone. That's understandable, because the bank's security video shows him falling on his ass. Protection of the coccyx is why people wear padding on their rear ends when they go skating. Other than wrist and head injuries, the coccyx is a target part of the body for anyone who falls over backwards like Mike Drago did.

Unfortunately, the medical experts all agree that his broken ribs were not pre-existing injuries. Knowing how anxious insurance doctors are to find pre-existing conditions, when *they* say something wasn't there before, you can take it to the bank. The only other possible conclusion is that the slip-and-fall in our insured's bank caused his broken ribs and bruised coccyx.

But the doctors are as confused as I am as to how landing on his back like that could damage his ribs. This is just another in a series of unanswered questions I'm faced with on this case. I send a statement to Indovine's office and to my surprise, he sends a note to me, expressing his satisfaction with the work I'm doing.

What the hell is he satisfied with? All I've done so far is show that the claimant's injuries actually were the cause of his fall at the bank. That's not good for us. What's good for Indovine is the fact that I'm putting in plenty of time on this case – all billable hours that he and his firm will make money on. Someday someone will make a scale of justice that shows the balance between the lawyer's bank account and the client's welfare. I wonder which side will outweigh the other. And I'm part of it now because shortly after sending in each of my weekly hourly statements, a check from Indovine's firm comes in the mail – and neither me nor the teller at my bank refuse to accept each one.

Harry Michael's court date is today and I intend to be there, with a twenty-dollar bill in hand for his jail inmate account. If the Public Defender is true to his word I should have about fifteen seconds to talk to Michaels before he's taken away to start serving his sentence.

The courtroom looks like something out of a movie, completely packed with attorneys and relatives of the defendants, who are brought out from the holding cells in groups of twelve and seated in the jury box. After each dozen cases concludes, the court takes a short recess and another group of prisoners is brought out from lock-up and seated.

The bailiff points out the Public Defender I'm looking for. He looks harried, with a bunch of files under his arm and another batch on the counsel table in front of him. I introduce myself and hand him the twenty-dollar bill. He holds it up in the air so that his client can see it. I look over at the jury box and see one of the defendants nodding in recognition. The P.D. tells me that because I'm an attorney, it will probably be okay for me to go over to the jury box and talk to the defendant. Other lawyers are over there talking to their clients, so I won't look out of place.

I go over and introduce myself. "Hello, Mister Michaels, my name is Peter Sharp, and I represent....'

Harry cuts me off mid-sentence. "I don't care who you represent. All I care about is that you're the guy who's putting some money in my account at the jail. Whattaya wanna know?"

There's nothing like cutting out the small talk. "Mister Michaels, I wonder if you'd please tell me what you were doing in the restaurant that night you had the accident. Were you a customer there, or an employee?"

"I wasn't none of those."

"Well you were there for six hours that night, and you had quite a bit to drink, so if you weren't a customer or employee, what were you doing there?"

"I was working a private party upstairs in the banquet room."

"Doing what?"

"I was the bartender."

"Whose party was it?"

"It was for some rich old guy who lives in the neighborhood, but didn't want to dirty up his penthouse, so he had the party in his restaurant. They paid me fifty bucks and I worked until the party broke up."

83

So that's it. That's the reason why his name didn't show up as an employee, and he couldn't be picked out as a customer. He was upstairs working a private party and getting drunk. This is nice to know, but presents another set of problems with respect to the dram shop laws, because one of the requirements is that the liquor-providing establishment must have had notice of the drunk's intoxication or that his outward appearance should have given someone notice that he deserved to be cut off, or 'eighty-sixed' for the evening. But if he's the one who's doing the serving, who is supposed to cut him off from drinking? I can tell that it's back to the law library for this one. No wonder Patty Vogel was so quick to deny the claim. She must have known all of this from the beginning.

The only good thing about all this is that she doesn't know that I know. It's not a big advantage, but any time you have even a little bit of knowledge the other side doesn't know you have, you're ahead of the game.

This is another case that's going to turn on the law itself. No tricks on this one.

11

As expected, Stuart's case moved quickly through the court's scheduling process. I tell the court that as far as our side is concerned, the trial should take no more than one day - but the other side gives the court notice that they might need a full week to adequately present their case. The big guns are in town for this one, representing all the country's fax broadcasters. They obviously want to let all the other Stuarts out there know you can't stop them from sending out their unsolicited junk faxes.

From the looks of the briefcases that are being wheeled into court, they're probably going to present a history of the common law of England, to show how people who stirred up litigation were put into 'stocks' in the public square – those nifty wooden devices that only let someone's head and hands hang through, on display for all the townspeople to ridicule.

My entire case hangs on whether or not my ace in the hole came through for me. Stuart is as white as a ghost. In a desperate effort to be judgment-proof, he's already transferred all of his assets over to his accountant, just in case a nasty verdict comes down against him. In some ways, I don't blame him. Every time you walk into court it's a crapshoot. You never can tell what will happen.

The other side's attorneys introduce themselves to me in a polite professional way. There is no jury, but the box is full of people. The bailiff tells me that it's a small courtroom, so they're letting the press sit there. I recognize a representative of the ACLU. I guess they're against us too – maybe they feel the fax broadcasters' right of free speech is being infringed on.

The bailiff makes his announcement calling the court to order and the judge waltzes in through his private entrance, looks at the full house, steps up, and takes the bench.

The judge sees that we're all in place at the counsel tables, so he starts the ball rolling. "Civil case number C001838, Stuart Schwarzman versus Fax Broadcasters of Santa Monica, having been transferred to this court from the Small Claims Court Division, Defendant Fax Company being the moving party."

As usual, all of us stand, stating our name and representation for the record. The judge signals their head counsel to start his case.

"Thank you, Your Honor. Appellant in this matter intends to establish to the court's satisfaction that Mister Stuart Schwarzman's actions are a textbook example of what the courts of Europe and the United States have held for centuries as unsatisfactory conduct. He has made numerous attempts to exploit the people's courts for profit, by stirring up litigation among citizens who would not ordinarily be prone to institute these actions, fitting perfectly into the common law and statutory definitions of Barratry, which is not only actionable in a civil court, but is criminally prosecutable under the California Penal Code section 158, which we would ask the court to take judicial notice of.

"Furthermore, his conduct also falls within the purview of that same code's section 159 because he has, as stated in the code, executed suits or proceedings at law in at least three instances.

"At the end of this trial, we will be asking the court to have a transcript of this matter sent to the proper prosecutorial departments for criminal action against Mister Schwarzman."

I feel a tug at my arm. Stuart whispers nervously into my ear "can they do that?" I try to wave him off. Their attorney continues.

"And in addition to the offense of Barratry, we intend to show by a preponderance of the evidence, that Mister Schwarzman has made agreements with his assignors, so that he will share in the proceeds of each Small Claims Court action he has filed, thereby constituting the civil offense of Champerty.

"Our witnesses will testify to the fact that at no time was any claim assignor asked to expend any costs for the prosecution of these matters, all said expenses being borne entirely by Mister Schwarzman. This conduct has been termed Maintenance, and is also frowned upon by nearly all of the enlightened jurisdictions, one of which we feel is this venue.

"Therefore we will be asking the court to have all current actions being brought by Mister Schwarzman against our client, and against all other similar organizations, dismissed with prejudice, and he be ordered to pay statutory damages, our clients' legal fees and also cease and desist the bringing of any further actions of this nature in this court or any other court in this State."

The attorney holds up a list of all the small claims court actions that Stuart filed during the past months and hands it to the bailiff, to be given to the judge.

Once the judge starts looking over the list, the attorney continues. "Your Honor we would ask the court to take judicial notice of these fifty-nine Small Claims Court Actions filed by Mister Schwarzman, each one constituting another count in our Complaint. They were all filed down the hallway in this very building, in room 102.

"We also contend that it is Mister Schwarzman's intent to violate our client's Freedom of Speech rights under the First Amendment to the Constitution of the United States.

"Thank you, Your Honor." He finally sits down. His client looks at him warmly, as if they've just won the first battle of this war. And maybe they have.

The press is feverishly taking notes. The judge looks down at me. "Mister Sharp, would you care to say anything?"

"Not at this time Your Honor. We reserve the right to make our opening statement at the time of presenting our defense."

Once again I feel Stuart desperately tugging at my sleeve and whisper-shouting. "What? You're not going to say anything? How can you let that guy get away with all that? You should say something."

I lean over and whisper in his ear "Stuart, the reason I didn't say anything, is because so far, he's correct in everything he's said. I don't want to get into a pissing contest with him now, because it's not the proper time yet... just relax, I've got something planned that might end this whole thing."

Stuart sits back in his chair but I know he's not relaxed and I don't blame him. The only chance we have of winning this case is if people behave as I assume they will. I look to the back of the courtroom and see Jack Bibberman sitting there. He gives me the 'thumbs up' sign. I wish I felt as confident as he does.

The other side starts calling their witnesses, which are no surprise, because in accordance with the rules, we were provided a copy of their list. As each one is called to testify, I check his or her name off on the list. Included are several well-known scholars of Constitutional Law, the president of some national telemarketing organization, several clients who have built up successful businesses as a result of mass fax campaigns they conducted, some idiot lady who claims she likes to receive all those faxes – makes her feel like she's got friends, a mailman who testifies that without fax broadcasting cutting down on the mail being sent, he wouldn't be able to carry his mail bag every day, and on and on.

Notwithstanding Stuart's wrinkling my goin'-to-church suit sleeve with his incessant tugging, I pass on my turn at cross-examination of every witness – until they call their own client to the stand – Marvin Bennett, the nice young hard-working man who owns the company that sends out all of the faxes.

His attorney does a nice job of establishing him as a pillar of society, family man and one who donates to charities. The lawyer sits down. The judge is no doubt wondering if I intend to cross-examine any witnesses in this trial, so he politely addresses me. "Mister Sharp, do you have any questions for this witness? Any at all?"

It's now or never, so before Stuart goes into cardiac arrest, I stand up. "Yes, Your Honor, we do have just a few questions for this witness." The judge looks relieved, probably glad to see that I finally came out of what he must have perceived as some trance during the first portion of the trial.

I start out very politely, asking some softball questions about where he gets the telephone numbers that he broadcasts to. As expected, he explains how they are all on lists sold to him by companies that gather the numbers from people and businesses that have no objections to receiving the faxes.

Next, I let out a little more rope. "Mister Bennett, do you ever add to your list the numbers of people who have asked you to never send them a fax?"

He denies this very strenuously. I produce a list of names from my briefcase and one by one, start to read off the names. "Mister Bennett, do you recognize any of the eleven names I've just read off of my list?"

"Not a one, counselor." The judge looks at me with a puzzled expression on his face... and I know why.

I address the court. "Your Honor, with the court's permission, I would like to use a display, which is an enlargement of the affidavit which all eleven of the names just recited have executed.

The other lawyers all jump up to object on grounds of relevancy, surprise, failure to give them notice and some other grounds I never heard of before. I try to stop their objections and get permission to proceed with my display. "Your Honor, this display is not being offered into evidence, it's only being used to refresh the witness' memory." The judge overrules their objections and lets me continue.

Pointing to the display, which is a two-foot by three-foot enlargement of one of the affidavits that simply states "Please refrain from sending any unsolicited faxes to this telephone number," followed by the phone number. It is signed, dated and notarized.

"Mister Bennett, this is an enlargement of one of the eleven letters all sent to your office by certified mail, with a signature receipt requested. We are also prepared to offer into evidence the original signed receipts for the mailings. Does this refresh your memory?"

"Mister Sharp, our office receives quite a bit of mail each day… I don't see and read every piece."

The judge looks extremely interested now. I go over to the easel and remove the first affidavit, revealing a large poster, containing a collage of twelve faxes.

"Mister Bennett, do you admit to the fact that your company has sent out faxes like every one of these during the past sixty days? And isn't it a fact that you do in fact represent every one of these businesses, as their fax broadcaster?"

He looks at the faxes on my easel and then looks at his attorneys. He's getting a little uncomfortable now. "We may have sent out some faxes like that... they look vaguely familiar."

Now I tighten the rope a little. "Mister Bennett, if I were to tell you that every one of the eleven people on my affidavit list are willing to testify that not only have they received these dozen faxes but they checked with their employers, the people whose fax machines these were sent to, and that the employers all strongly denied ever subscribing to or opting in on any list which would allow you to send them faxes – what would your response be?"

He has a smug smile on his face. "I'd say that their employers were all a little weak in the memory department. They must have done business with some company or opted in on some list that gave us the legal right to send faxes to them."

"Mister Bennett, are you claiming here in open court, that you are right and that the superiors of every one of those eleven people are wrong?"

"That's right counselor, their bosses must all be mistaken and I don't think you can prove otherwise."

I look up at the judge. "That's all for this witness, Your Honor, and if the Appellant rests its case at this time, so do we." I sit down and Stuart almost rips off my sleeve.

"Pete, are you nuts? They'll kill us. You haven't done anything but show some posters. We're dead!"

The faxer's lawyer stands up to make a motion, but I cut him off by speaking first. "Your Honor, at this time we would ask the court for a fifteen minute recess, so that we might confer with the appellant to discuss a settlement of this matter."

As I look over to the other table, they are all jubilant. They think the war is over. The judge looks down at us with a slight smile on his face. "Mister Sharp, I think that's an excellent idea. I'll look forward to seeing you all back here in a while with a settlement for me to approve."

The judge steps off the bench and I signal to the other attorneys that we should use the empty jury room. Stuart looks like he's going berserk. He thinks I just gave the case away to the other side. His mouth is moving like a fish out of water, but no sound is coming out. I lean over and whisper in his ear that everything is going to be okay and that he should trust me. He sits down. Over at the other counsel table the lawyers are shaking hands with each other and with their client, Bennett. They all don't know it yet, but they're now experiencing a severe case of premature congratulation. We all walk into the jury room and after they're seated, I begin my presentation.

"Gentlemen, this case is over. In the next ten minutes, a settlement will be reached and we will all be out of here." They look at each other and exchange smiles of success.

"First of all, let me fill you in on a few things. Number one, the eleven people on my affidavit list are all clerks – for judges in this building. That means the employers your client was demeaning out there are all Municipal and Superior Court judges, all friends and associates of the judge in this case.

"Second, every one of the eleven received at least twenty unsolicited faxes from your client after they expressly informed him by certified mail that they did not want to receive any faxes from him."

"Third, each fax number on the list was a personal fax number assigned to the machine in each one of the judges' chambers – machines that were installed less than ninety days ago and assigned brand new numbers by the telephone company at the time of their installations.

"This means that your client is full of crap. He's a liar. These are all new fax machines and new telephone numbers. The judges never subscribed to any service nor did business with any company and never gave the fax numbers out to anyone but the presiding judge, who wanted the fax machines solely for the purpose of sending official court memos.

"Your client obtained their new numbers by using an unlawful 'war dialer, that automatically dials every telephone number in numerical order, hoping to randomly discover fax lines, or through some other unlawful means from an accomplice, who illegally provided him with newly assigned fax numbers on a regular basis, constituting a criminal conspiracy and therefore subject to forfeiture and seizure of assets through the federal RICO laws.

"Your client also received the notices to not send these judges any more faxes, and instead of complying with their requests, continued to bombard them with unsolicited faxes and then sold their numbers to other mass fax broadcasters who continued the same unlawful process.

"Your client lied in open court under oath, and you gentlemen have already asked that the court send a copy of the transcript of this trial to the prosecutors. You wanted to see my client nailed for a misdemeanor Barratry charge but instead your client may go to the penitentiary for felony perjury."

I look down at their faces and wish I had a camera with me to capture the scene. If it was printed up and distributed, I'll bet it would sell more copies than the ones of those dogs playing poker.

"Now here's what I suggest. You go out there and tell that lying client of yours that he is dismissing his counter-claim and agreeing to pay the minimum five hundred dollars damages on each of the first faxes sent to the judges' chambers. Due to the fact that he continued his practice after receiving notice to cease and desist, the damages on each of the other 19 faxes sent to each of the eleven judges' chambers qualifies under the federal law for a treble penalty of fifteen hundred dollars each. This portion of the settlement check will be made out directly to whatever charities the judges select.

"As for the remaining cases out of the fifty-nine actions you so generously told the court about, your client will pay the minimum of five-hundred dollars plus court costs, for each – said payment to be made to my client, the assignee, Stuart Schwarzman.

"And lastly, your client will agree to immediately remove those thirteen numbers from his list, along with any other numbers of people who ask to be removed in the future – and make no mistake about it. Every once in a while he may be tested by another request for removal and he'll never know if it was from us or not."

After a prolonged silence, I get up and walk out of the room. Shortly thereafter, all the big guns come slinking out of the jury room, tails between their legs. A note is given to the clerk, telling the judge that the action has been withdrawn and a settlement has been reached. Before we have a chance to leave, the clerk tells me that the judge wants to see me in chambers. This a request that no attorney ever refuses, so I follow the bailiff back into the private hallway.

"Mister Sharp, that was a nifty job you did out there today, but you realize that if they didn't 'cave,' I would have had to recuse myself from hearing the case."

"Yes Your Honor, I knew that. You can't be on any case where there's even the remote possibility that you or one of your staff might be called as a witness."

"You took a big chance there, Peter – you're lucky it worked."

"It's the old rule, Your Honor, you can't shake down an honest man. Bennett's a liar. He doesn't care who he spams with that junk as long as he gets his fee. Anyway, thanks for the courtesy Your Honor. As soon as your clerk sends me the list of the charities your associates want the donations sent to, we'll see to it that the checks are sent out."

As I step out of his chambers door he calls out to me. "Oh, by the way, I got a great deal on a vacation from one of those faxes."

12

The problem with performing magic is that you never want to repeat the same trick more than once to the same crowd, because if they get wise to your slight-of-hand, you'll never get away with anything again.

Once again I got lucky and won a case without using any knowledge of the law, which has always been my weak suit. I explain to Stuart that he really owes his thanks to the guy driving our car, Jack Bibberman, for getting all the judges' clerks to go along with our plan.

With this case out of the way, I'll have some time to concentrate on designing new illusions to use for my other clients. On Harold Blitzstien's murder case, I'd like to be able to create a cloud of smoke and disappear from the courtroom just before the guilty verdict comes in.

I'm also definitely going to need some magic for the other two cases on my plate. Mike Drago's ribs were definitely broken by his fall in the bank, which may increase the insurance company's liability. Not only did the claimant die, but he probably took my insurance defense career with him.

Vinnie's defendant wasn't a customer at the restaurant – Harry Michaels 'self-medicated' himself into a state of drunkenness, so I probably won't be able to use the Dramshop laws against Patty Vogel's restaurant client. Things are definitely not looking too good for me. If it weren't for the steady paychecks from Melvin's old practice, I'd be in deep doo-doo, because all of my fees from previous cases are tied up in CDs.

Every time I see a magician he seems to have a beautiful long-legged female assistant who wears a Playboy Bunny-type of costume and sensuously parades around the stage handing him things.

My assistant is Jack Bibberman, who isn't particularly long-legged and if he ever shows up at my boat wearing one of those Bunny suits, he'll immediately be fired. The one thing he does have going for him is his ability to get the assignments done.

Today his assignment is to find out anything he can about the party that Harry Michael worked. Who hired him, what the party was for and anything else we might be able to use, because once I wrap up Vinnie's case I intend to spend full time on the Bank matters – both the slip-and-fall and the murdered claimant.

Somewhere in the back of my mind I have the strange feeling that these two cases are tied together. It's just too coincidental that I happen to be representing the insurance company for the bank where a guy fell and also the guy who is charged with killing him. There must be some fate at work here.

With Jack concentrating his efforts on finding the facts, I think I'll try to hold up my end of the work by concentrating on the law – and the law is kind of strange when it comes to liability of land owners to people who injure themselves on that land. If this were going to be a California case, we wouldn't have much of a problem because claims for pain and suffering don't survive the death of a claimant. But the lawyer representing Drago's family will be filing this case in the Federal courts of Illinois, and that puts me back at square one.

Under the old laws of England and the United States, the liability of a land owner to people who were injured on his property depended on the classification of the injured person – whether they were a business customer – referred to as 'invitee,' social guest, or trespasser. Each category of visitor was owed a greater degree of care.

In a landmark 1968 decision, the California Supreme Court said "...A man's life or limb does not become less worthy of protection by the law nor a loss less worthy of compensation under the law because he has come upon the land of another without permission or with permission but without a business purpose..." With one stroke, they eliminated the distinction between the categories – but in my mind they still exist.

Although it may sound rather pompous for an attorney to disagree with his own state's Supreme Court, I don't think I should be blamed for feeling that a burglar who breaks into your house shouldn't be able to sue you because he tripped over your kid's toy fire engine and fell down the stairs. Maybe the court would be happier if the burglar didn't trip and instead made it into the upstairs bedroom, where he might have gotten shot – with no chance of recovery at all in a court of law.

This may not make much of a difference as far as the black letter of the law is concerned, but it sure will count in the minds of the jury. In a case like that they might get an instruction from the judge that the burglar is entitled to an award for damages, but I'd be surprised if the jury gives him much more than the minimum of one dollar.

With respect to the Drago case, we're still waiting for the bank to come back with some info on whether or not he had an account there, or with any other branch of that same chain of banks. If our search shows that he did have an account, then he was a business invitee while present in the bank and that category of visitor gets the highest treatment, outside of California.

If Drago didn't have an account at the bank, then he would only be a business invitee if he was there to open an account, apply for a loan or other service offered, or to transact some business with a teller.

His personal property stored in the police evidence locker didn't contain any check to be cashed, money to be deposited, or any other documentation that would make him a customer of the bank, so the question still remains as to what he was doing in the bank on that day. He is lucky about one other thing though... he was taken out of there before the bank robbers arrived.

If I can get his status lowered below that of a business invitee, it might save the insurance company some money. Even better would be if I could get him lowered to 'trespasser' status, but that's a magic trick I haven't learned yet. Jack Bibberman is out working on the case, so anything's possible. I see Jack's cell phone number on my caller ID display as the phone rings.

Jack checked criminal court records over the past two years and we've had subpoenas issued to the bail bondsman who bailed Harry Michaels out each time he was arrested for drunk driving. Big surprise – the sponsor on his bail bond each time was a Mister Robert Palmer, who I crossed swords with once before on a sexual harassment suit. He owns two restaurants on Washington Boulevard in the Marina, a seafood place next door to our favorite Chinese restaurant, and the Mexican place across the street, where Harry Michaels did his bartending the night of Vinnie's tree injury.

I tell Jack to concentrate on the party Michaels tended bar for, and to find out the names of some guests who attended. We certainly could use some witness statements on this case if we're to have any hope of hanging liability on the restaurant under the state's Dramshop laws.

Until Jack comes up with anything interesting, all I have to work with are the videotapes. There are only two five-minute portions crucial to the cases. On the bank tape, it's the one where Drago slips and falls, and on the hospital tape, it's when Harry Blitzstien 'visits' Drago and smothers him with the pillow.

There are several UHF and cable channels that keep re-running the old *Matlock* and *Diagnosis Murder* shows. Andy Griffith and Dick Van Dyke both share the uncanny ability to look at the same photos or videos that the police and everyone else have seen, and miraculously spot some previously missed clue that completely destroys someone's alibi and reveals who the killer is. Van Dyke will usually create an ingenious plot to trap the bad guy. Andy

101

Griffith's Matlock character does it by cross-examination, getting the killer to break down on the witness stand and confess. I'll never be that good. No lawyer will. Things just don't happen like that in real life.

I've looked at these videos and the still photos of some frames over and over again. Nothing. I'm getting the feeling that there's nothing that I'm missing... there's just nothing to find. I've shown this stuff to Stuart, Jack Bibberman, the dog, and I'm sure that the kid has seen it all too. No comments from anyone. I can't believe that both Myra and Drago's estate lawyer are going to be able to walk all over me. It's not fair.

The only thing I can see that might help out a little is that in the bank, the kid who spilled his coke on the floor did it completely un-noticed by anyone. For the next ten minutes or so there was a steady stream of people over to the deposit-slip island in the middle of the bank lobby and with that morning's heavy bank traffic, it's no wonder that nobody saw the small spill to report it. That part of the bank isn't too well lit and the coke was almost the same color as the dark marble floor.

Maybe I'll be able to argue that it wasn't negligence on the part of the bank to not have discovered the spill and that because the tape shows numerous customers walking around it, that it wasn't hard to see, thereby making Drago partly to blame for not watching where he was walking.

I receive a brief email from the court clerk that lets me know the psychological examination results have come in on Harold Blitzstien. She was nice enough to give me an advanced tip that he was found fit to stand trial.

Last time we were in court on his case, I made a deal to abide with whatever the court-appointed shrinks decide, so now it's time for me to pay my dues. I'll appear with Harold at his arraignment and offer a plea of not guilty on his behalf, because he probably won't want to say that many words. He's the strong silent type.

The court is paying me to represent him to the best of my ability but with all the evidence that they have against him there's not much I can do, so I figure he's at least entitled to a visit from me. Traffic between the Marina and downtown isn't too bad this time of the late morning, so I head down to the county's central jail.

After the usual identification procedure, I go through the sallyport and into the attorney interview room. I finally get some respect. Harold comes down to see me.

As usual, there isn't much of a conversation between us. I tell him that the shrinks have declared him fit to stand trial and that his arraignment will be in a couple of days, at which time I'll be entering a plea of not guilty on his behalf. He finally says a word to me. "Why?"

I'm not surprised until the question sinks in. He wants to know why he should plead not guilty. "Harold, what's your question? Do you want to know why that's the plea we'll offer, or do you want to know why you're pleading not guilty at all?"

He answers me. "Why should I plead not guilty? I did it. Let's get it over with. There's no need for you to try and get me off."

"That's not the way it works, Harold. In our judicial system, it's the prosecution's job to prove your guilt beyond a reasonable doubt. What happens if they make a mistake and you're found not guilty? Would you turn that down and stay here anyway? I think not.

"Listen Harold, I know that things don't look too good for you with that videotape evidence, but let's do it by the book. I'll make sure that if they want to convict you that they do it fair and square."As usual, there's no response from him. He just sits there and glares at me. He finally breaks the silence. "You're my lawyer, right."

"Right. I'm your lawyer."

"Then could you do me a favor?"

"I'll try, Harold. What is it?"

"Could you deposit a few bucks into my prisoner account? I'd like to buy some candy and stuff."

I nod yes. He gets up and walks out of the room.

The last time I came up with some money for a prisoner's account it was given to the Public Defender in court. This time, it's up to me to make the deposit. I ask one of the jailers how to go about it and I'm told that as I re-enter the lobby from the jail hallway, immediately around the corner to my right is a cashier's window where I can make a cash or credit card deposit for an inmate.

Following his instructions, I go down the hallway and stop just before making the right turn. I want to open my wallet here in the hallway instead of out in the lobby. I've got a bunch of hundred dollar bills in there and I'd rather not let the general visiting population see them. I pull out a twenty, and just as I'm about to step around the corner, I hear a woman saying "thank you" to someone. When I stick my head around the corner, I see a short woman walking away from what must be the cashier's window. I hear the cashier calling out from the cage, "You're welcome Miss Vogel."

Hearing the name Vogel causes a reaction. For some reason, I step back into the hallway. That's one heck of a coincidence. Vogel is the last name of the attorney who's handling the Mexican restaurant's case against Vinnie's dram shop action. Could it possibly be her who just left the cashier's cage? I stand there for a minute trying to compose my thoughts. I'll only get one crack at this, so it has to be done right. I wait another minute or so and then step in front of the cage, hold up my ID and speak to the cashier.

"Hi, I'm attorney Peter Sharp and I was supposed to meet an associate of mine here to deposit some money to a couple of clients' prisoner accounts. I don't know if I missed her and I certainly don't want to make any of your customers rich by making a double deposit. Can you tell me if she's been here yet?

He looks at me with that typical cop-face. No emotion. "What's her name?"

"Patty Vogel – she's a short woman, about…" He cuts me off mid-sentence.

"Yeah, you just missed her. She already made a deposit."

"Great, now I'd like to make one too, but not if she already made it. Did she deposit anything for Harold Blitzstien?"

"Naw, she put the maximum of fifty in for Harry Michaels. Do you want to put some in for Blitzstien? If so, I'll need his booking number again."

I thank him for the information and give him the twenty, and Harold's booking number. After he gives me the receipt, I thank him and walk away in a daze.

Harry Michaels gets money from Patty Vogel. Why? What's the connection between them? I call Jack and ask him if he ordered copies of the court docket sheet on Harry Michaels' previous drunk driving cases. He tells me that he did and verifies the fact that Patty Vogel was the attorney on both cases.

I don't know why I should be so surprised. Here I am depositing money to my client's account, so why shouldn't she feel the same way and deposit money to her client's account? This will require some more looking into. I sense something here that may be more than the casual attorney-client relationship. Harry Michaels copped a plea and took a deal that the public defender made for him. With the jail over-crowding situation that's going on now, he'll probably be out in a month or so. So why come and deposit fifty dollars to his account?

On the way back to the Marina I call Jack Bibberman. The California State Bar has a website that lists all the licensed attorneys in the state. It provides information as to what Law School the attorney graduated from and what year they were sworn in to practice. I tell Jack to check out Patty Vogel. I then call Myra's office. She knows most of the lawyers in this town who practice criminal law and probably every one of the female ones.

No special information there. Myra knows Patty from some Women's Bar Association meetings but to the best of her knowledge, Patty doesn't do any criminal work. While we're on the phone, Myra informs me that the court called her office and wants us both to appear tomorrow at two in the afternoon for Harold Blitzstien's arraignment.

Back at the boat I have a chance to sit down in silence and think over what I've learned today. It's always nice to have someone to bounce your ideas off of, so I invite the huge Saint Bernard into my area of the boat – he's an excellent listener. After we kick the idea around for a while, the logical answer we come up with is that after Harry Michaels wrecked the Lexus he stole from the restaurant's parking lot – the one he drove into Vinnie's favorite tree – the owner of the car put a claim in to his own insurance company.

Insurance companies try to recover their losses by going after the people who cause them. In this case, after the insurance company paid off the Lexus owner, it would be logical to assume that they then went after both Harry Michaels and the restaurant, in an effort to recoup some of the claim money they paid out. Harry Michaels obviously doesn't have any money, so the insurance company is concentrating on the restaurant, using the same dram shop strategy that I'll be trying. The restaurant is

Patty Vogel's client, so she's probably defending Harry Michaels too, hoping that by keeping him happy with a fifty-dollar deposit to his inmate account, he won't say anything nasty about the restaurant that might help the insurance company's action.

We both agree that this scenario is the right one and celebrate our logical victory by sharing a biscuit.

Confidence is a good thing to have, but what if the dog is wrong about this one? Now that I'm a member of the insurance defense clique, I decide to see how far the benefits go. I send off a message to Charles Indovine's office, asking if he can do me a little favor. I tell him I'm working on another case and would like to know the name of the insurance company that insured the Lexus and how much they paid to their insured for the damages. I provide him with the date of loss and the license number of the Lexus.

To my surprise, a day later there's an answer from Indovine's office. It gives me the name of the insurance company that insures the car and also says that no claim was put in for damages to that vehicle during the past twelve months.

I've watched countless programs on television where some insurance-funded safety institute buys new cars and crashes them to see how safe they are, and how much it costs to have them repaired. On one of those shows they had a Lexus similar to the one that Harry Michaels wrapped around Vinnie's tree. In a low speed collision that didn't cause much visible damage, the repair bill was several thousand dollars. Judging by that, I'd estimate that after knocking over the tree, it would cost about ten thousand to put humpty dumpty back together again. I've heard of people who refrain from making claims to their insurance company because they fear cancellation or future rate increases but when the damages exceed five figures, it just doesn't make sense to hold back and bite the bullet.

Whenever I come across things that don't compute it bothers me. It's time for another meeting. I call the dog back into the room again.

The only thing we can figure out this time is that the restaurant has decided to cover the Lexus owner's losses – not out of good will, but because they don't want a dram shop precedent against them – and because they'll write it off anyway.

Okay, that answers one question. We now think we know why there was no claim made against the insurance company for damages to the Lexus. But it opens up another problem. If there's no dram shop suit against the restaurant, then the dog must have been wrong. Why would Patty Vogel be making that deposit to Harry Michael's account? There's no need to keep him quiet or stop him from cooperating with the insurance company.

Indovine's office will be sending me a printout of the insurance company's under-writing report on that vehicle. When it comes, I'll send Jack Bibberman over to interview the owners of the Lexus, to find out exactly what their story is and why they never put in a claim for property damage.

The bailiff makes his usual announcement and the court is now in session. When Judge Axelrod calls the case, Myra and I both stand and make our statements of representation. Harold looks absolutely terrible. It seems that every time I see him he looks worse.

The arraignment goes quickly. today. Reports from the shrinks are put into evidence and in accordance with my previous stipulation, a plea of not guilty is entered on Harold's behalf.

Because Harold wants to get this matter over with as quickly as possible, we refuse to waive time and ask for the soonest possible preliminary hearing date.

Real life is a lot different than those criminal legal dramas on television, where after you see a person arrested and plead not guilty to murder, the next scene takes place in a trial court. That's because they leave out what the California judicial system considers a very important element: a Preliminary Hearing, affectionately called 'prelim' by the legal community.

On misdemeanors that only carry a maximum one-year sentence in the county jail, cases will go directly to trial after a municipal court arraignment, but felonies are much more serious. When a person is charged with a felony but not indicted by a grand jury, they are entitled to a preliminary hearing, at which time the prosecution doesn't have to prove guilt - but does have to establish beyond a reasonable doubt that the crime charged actually took place and that there is enough probable cause to hold the defendant over for arraignment and trial in the superior court.

In this case, a grand jury was never convened. The district attorney's office obviously felt that it wasn't necessary because of the hospital's videotape evidence of the crime. I've also learned that Harold has a distant cousin who at one time worked for the district attorney's office, so that's why they brought an outsider like Myra in to act as an independent prosecutor.

All this means to me is that I'll have two chances to get trounced by Myra – at both the prelim and the trial. It also means that she has two chances to screw up, but the possibility of that happening is so remote that I'm not even hoping for it.

Myra doesn't object to our insistence on speed. She doesn't need any more time to prepare her case – Harold did it for her, with his hospital appearance on prosecution-TV, the new network designed to bring the viewing audience timely convictions. I tell Harold to try and get some rest. He thanks me for the deposit I made to his account. The way he doles out words to me is second to only one other person I know.

On the way back to the Marina, I can't help but feel that Harold doesn't seem like a bad guy. I'll never know why people do things.

About twenty years ago, when I first started practicing law, I was retained to represent a man who was an executive at a defense contracting company. Here was a guy with a wife and family, a security clearance, and high-paying job. He got arrested in a public park restroom for sodomy. He was the stickee.

I handled the case and arranged for him to plead to second-degree burglary. This kept a sex-related offense off of his record, so he was able to keep his security clearance. Several other attorneys and I were having dinner that evening and they all seemed curious about why a guy like my client would risk his family and his job to do something like that? I took out some of my business cards and passed them around the table, saying "okay guys, take a look at my card. You see what it says under my name? It says Attorney at Law, not mind reader, or psychic. All I do is the same thing that you guys do – I represent them, I don't get into their heads. That's not included in the fee... and it's not a place I want to be."

Maybe with a sex-related offense, a lot of prior psychological baggage comes into play. But with a cold-blooded murder for hire, there's just no way I can start to figure out why Harold did what he did. I don't want to know the deep dark thoughts that can go through someone's mind. There was an old radio show called *The Shadow*, in which the main character would say: "Who knows what evil lurks in the hearts of men...?"

Back at the boat there's a moist envelope waiting for me on the couch – obviously a dog-mail delivery. It's from Indovine's office and contains two items: a check for my past week's efforts on the Drago case, and a one-page computer printout on the Lexus policy. I see that there's a damage estimate in there for over fourteen thousand dollars, a requirement in any theft report but as Indovine told me, there was no claim put in by the owners, who are listed as Walter E. and Patricia F. Vogel.

13

I don't know where to start. I'd like to give Jack Bibberman some instructions, but I can't figure out what he should check out first.

The State Bar's website confirms that Patty's real name is the same as the one on the Lexus' ownership, so unless Patricia F. Vogel is a really common name in this town, that Lexus is her car. Maybe that's where Jack should start. I tell him to check out Patty Vogel the attorney, just to make sure she's the owner of the car – and while he's at it, to try and get a photo of her from one of the many lawyer publications, her law school yearbook, her drivers license portrait, or from wherever he can.

I don't think it would be a good idea to talk to her about this yet. I like to know the answers to the questions before I ask them, and in this case there are plenty questions and no answers.

A knock on the hull jars me out of my deep thought. It's a delivery guy with a big gift basket that contains wine, cheese, cakes and other goodies that must have set someone back at least fifty bucks. I hand the guy a two-dollar tip and bring the basket into the dining area to see which cop is sending a gift to the little princess. To my surprise, I see that the gift is for me. It's from Stuart. The note says, *Peter, thank you very much for your successful handling of my barratry case. As a result of the publicity, my business has doubled. Please let me know when you'd like to be my guest for dinner at the Chart House.*

That's very nice of him. He's become another hustler making money by working our judicial system like a slot machine. That's not a nice thought, but I still can't get it out of my mind, even though he's a friend of mine and I'm glad to see that he's doing well. On second thought, maybe I shouldn't condemn him like that. I've had an opportunity to see one of his defendants close up in person and if that's the type of industry that Stuart's shaking down, then more power to him.

At least he has a really good choice in restaurants. The ChartHouse is a really close- by restaurant that's a walking distance from our dock, and serves a good meal. I wish I could get myself to spend the money to eat there – it's one of the higher-priced places on the water. I guess you can take a guy out of a Chicago tenement neighborhood, but you can't take the neighborhood out of the guy. I can't see spending fifty bucks for a dinner there that I can get around the corner for twelve. I guess the tourists are willing to pay twice the price for a view of the water. If I want that view, all I have to do is look out my window. Nevertheless, I call Stuart and thank him for the basket... and arrange to meet him at the ChartHouse tomorrow evening at seven PM.

I can't wait any longer. My curiosity is killing me. Jack Bibberman has confirmed the fact that the Lexus does in fact belong to Patty Vogel and her husband. I have his work number, so I call him, under the guise of working with the insurance company. That's not too far from the truth because after all, I am an insurance defense lawyer.

Walter Vogel owns a women's clothing business in Van Nuys. His secretary puts me through to him.

"Hello Mister Vogel, we're following up on your Lexus damages and just want to know how the repairs are going."

"Oh yeah, the Lexus. Well it took long enough, but the body shop finally got it back to us. I guess it's okay."

"That's good, Mister Vogel. By the way, there are a few unanswered questions on your claim form. Would it be okay if one of our people came by to talk to you?"

"I really don't handle that stuff. My wife Patty is a lawyer – she takes care of the forms, but she must have done it correctly because otherwise you guys wouldn't have paid the claim so quickly. Why don't you call her office? I'll give you the number."

"No, that's okay Mister Vogel, we have it in our files. We just want to make sure that everything was done to take care of your claim."

Hmmmn. He says that the insurance company paid the claim. The insurance company says that no claim was made. I'm going to have to stop bringing the dog in on these meetings – he's batting zero for two on this case.

If I have to choose which one of them is telling the truth, I'll go with the insurance company. But I don't think that Vogel was intentionally lying to me. He probably believes that his wife put in a claim and that the insurance company paid to have the car repaired. If that scenario is correct, then the answer must be with his wife, the mysterious Patty Vogel, attorney at law.

I call Jack Bibberman and learn that he was successful in getting a recent picture of her, so I give him a new assignment.

The clock is ticking on this case, because a hearing date is approaching. Instead of going to court with this lawsuit, I opted to choose arbitration instead. There's a non-profit organization called the JAMS Foundation, which is an acronym for Judicial Arbitration and Mediation Services. They're the premiere nation-wide provider of alternative dispute resolution and they do it with a distinguished panel of retired judges and other judicial-types of people that they call 'neutrals,' who hear the cases.

One of the reasons I want to take this to a JAMS hearing is because I'll have the opportunity to select from a group of hearing officials who actually may know something about the law involved in this case.

Sometimes when you take a case to trial, you discover that the judge hasn't the slightest idea of what you're talking about. If it's a subject or concept of law that he or she has never heard of before, then instead of presenting your case in an orderly fashion, you're forced to waste time and energy trying to educate a judge whose learning ability has decreased a few percentage points for each year served on the bench.

I've spent years teaching law to students; I don't think I should have to teach judges too. If they don't know the law, they shouldn't be sitting up there on the bench. In arbitration, both sides first agree on the exact area of law that's involved and are presented with a list of arbitrators who are familiar with that law. It's then up to both sides to agree on which arbitrator to choose. They don't have any axe to grind for either side, so you can get a fair hearing by a knowledgeable person.

Patty Vogel agreed to sidestep the courts and take our case to arbitration. All I had to do was tell her that I didn't want to embarrass my client by having the fact of his peeing on a tree discussed in open court. Over the years, I've found it a useful tool to always give the other side a way to go without their losing any face.

In this case I have a strong feeling that it's Mrs. Vogel who has something to hide, so I made it easy for her to agree to arbitrate by letting Vinnie take the rap for being ashamed. Actually, I think Vinnie wouldn't hesitate to pee in the middle of Hollywood and Vine if he had the immediate urge, but that's beside the point. We're going to arbitration, and that's what counts.

Over the past few days I've had time to do some research, and it looks like both Drago's case and Vinnie's action will both hinge on the court's interpretation of one word: FORESEEABILITY, and I'm sitting right on the fence – arguing for it on one case and against it on the other. The thing that makes both of these cases so much alike is the fact that a crime took place before the plaintiff's injuries – and an intervening act like that sometimes acts to cut off liability.

In Drago's case, his estate's lawyer is contending that since the hospital had security cameras installed all over the place and because Drago's room was on the same floor as the psychiatric ward, that intentional harm might come to a patient there, so that his getting murdered was a foreseeable event. That makes the bank's liability extend past the slip-and-fall, all the way to the death in the hospital.

Naturally I'll be going to argue *against* foreseeability there, because I don't want to see the bank stuck on a wrongful death action.

In Vinnie's case, I'm on the opposite side. I'm contending that it *was* foreseeable that a drunken customer would leave the restaurant and drive, so that when he crashed into that tree Vinnie was watering, the restaurant's liability extends all the way to Vinnie's injuries.

Attorney Patty Vogel argues that the unforeseeable intervening crime of car theft breaks the chain of liability and that the restaurant is not responsible for Vinnie's injuries. She contends that the restaurant's liability was cut off by the intervening car theft.

Personally, I'm torn. In both cases there was an intervening crime and there are only a few special types of cases where the courts have decided that a crime was foreseeable. The most common ones are assaults in unlit parking areas of commercial establishments located in high-crime areas. The courts will usually look to past events. If the plaintiff can show that there were several recent similar incidents in the business' parking lot – and that the business was aware of these incidents, then the court would be more likely to find that the business had a duty to protect its customers with proper lighting and security.

On the other hand, when there is no record of past crimes and the one complained of appears to be an anomaly, it's a different story.

In Vinnie's case, I'm arguing that it doesn't make any difference whether Harry Michaels stole a vehicle or not. He was driving, and that is something that the restaurant should have foreseen. That's why they have a parking lot... so that their drunken customers can drive home. The very same customers who the restaurant causes to be drunk by taking their money and providing them with liquor.

In Drago's case, I've got statistics to show that there's never been a murder in the hospital, so that this one is a freak incident and one that shouldn't be labeled as foreseeable.

I'm glad I'm not a judge. This is what they get paid to decide, and on cases like this, they really work for their money.

Wait a minute. Something just hit me. When I was in the courtroom talking to Harry Michaels, I happened to see his file on the Public Defender's table. He was charged with felony drunk driving. What happened to the auto theft charge?

I call the Public Defender's office and ask for the Chief Deputy. It so happens that he was part of our of night student study-group back at Betty Crocker college of law on Sepulveda, so he does me the favor of pulling out the file. I only have one question for him and it's about the Grand Theft Auto charge. To my surprise, he tells me that the GTA was never filed. It had been on the prosecutor's list, but apparently the alleged victim refused to press charges, so all the defendant made a plea to was the felony drunk driving charge.

That's odd. Not only did Patty Vogel lead her husband to believe that the insurance company paid for fixing the car when it really didn't, she also refused to press charges when it was stolen. Why would she do that? I call Jack Bibberman and tell him to get Patty Vogel's picture out for some canvassing.

The mail just came in with a copy of the lawsuit filed by Drago's attorney and I see that he followed through on his threat - it's been filed in the Illinois Federal Court. I call Charles Indovine at the insurance defense firm to give him the news.

For some strange reason, no matter what happens on the Drago case, he's pleased to hear it and tells me that I'm doing a fine job. As for the Illinois filing, he inquires about my status in the Federal Courts. I tell him that because I've been sworn in to the Supreme Court of the United States, that I'm allowed to practice in any federal court in the country. To my surprise, he says that he'd like me to stay with the case and to send him receipts for my travel expenses.

Is he serious? It would cost only a fraction of that to hire a local Chicago attorney to appear on this case. No specialist is required – it's only a slip-and-fall case and any personal injury defense lawyer should be able to argue against the foreseeability of Blitzstien's intervening act of murder. I know he doesn't have any particular fondness for me, so what's his reason for spending all that money just to keep me on the case? Another unanswered question I'll have to deal with.

14

Patty Vogel and I both agree on an arbitration date and also upon one of JAMS' 'neutrals,' to act as the hearing officer. The date for the hearing has been set for next week at their downtown location in the Los Angeles World Trade Center, so I'm now in the process of getting my argument ready... not the argument I'll give to the arbitrator – the one I'll be giving to Patty Vogel, to get her to settle the case before the hearing begins.

If Jack Bibberman comes through for me, I should have the information I need to do my usual pre-hearing rant.

Patty Vogel introduces herself to me in a polite professional manner, while at the same time maintaining an attitude that lets me know that she means business. I can't help but feel that she has a subtle smirk on her face – like she knows something that I don't know. I've seen that before and one of my great pleasures in life is being lucky enough on some occasions to remove the smirks from smug lawyers like that.

At the last minute, Jack Bibberman came through and provided me with some smirk-removal ammunition, so my only decision now is how to go about using it; the soft way, or the hard way. Normally, I prefer doing it as politely as possible, but people who smirk usually make it impossible for me to do it that way – and I have a feeling that Patty Vogel will be doing just that.

Patty Vogel tells the arbitrator that she'd like a few moments to discuss a settlement with me before the hearing starts. The arbitrator doesn't care because he gets paid his minimum whether we have a hearing or not. She motions to a small conference room and invites me to join her in there. I tell Vinnie and Stuart that this will only take a few minutes and that they should wait for me in the lobby. Vinnie is surprised, but Stuart knows me well enough to have confidence in me, so he assures Vinnie that everything's okay.

I've already discussed this case at length with Vinnie and he knows my feelings about it. If he gets anything out of it at all, it'll be some low nuisance amount, probably less than a thousand dollars – and he agreed.

As I go into the conference room with Patty, I notice that something is turned around here. Usually it's me who does the inviting into a conference room to talk about a settlement. Now it's someone else inviting me into the little room. Does she think she's going to do me the favor of allowing me to settle before the hearing? Boy, she's got stones.

I've always had the reputation of being a good sport, so I politely accept her invitation and we both step into the conference room. She motions for me to sit down. This is going to be good. I'll bet she's practiced her speech all the way down here today. Now it starts.

"Mister Sharp, I want to give you a chance to save yourself some time and avoid embarrassment in front of your client. If we settle this matter before the hearing, I'll lie about it and tell him that you did a great job."

She must want me to think she's a warm, considerate person. Actually, she's a little out of touch with reality, but I'll try to correct that in a while. I smile at her with my most sincere look of appreciation for how wonderful she must think she is. She goes on in a quiet tone of voice. If you watch the bad guys in the movies, you may note that the most menacing ones are those who can make a deadly threat in a quiet voice with a slight smile on their face ala Christopher Walken or Clint Eastwood. It doesn't take any particular talent to shout and swear like Tony Soprano when you're making a threat, but to keep your cool and be soft-spoken takes a quality that Patty Vogel must think she possesses. She continues, like a gangster in some 'B' movie.

"You are going to settle this case here and now, in this room, because if you don't, you will receive nothing.

"I've had it up to here with cheap personal injury ambulance chasers and I know what you want. All you care about is stealing a few dollars from the insurance company, so I'm going to give you a little, just enough to make bottom-feeders like you and your peeing client go away."

Hmmmn. Not exactly as eloquent as I'd expected, but she does manage to convey her feelings. As I've said before, one of the first rule of holes that a person learns is, when you're in one, stop digging. Evidently, Patty doesn't know that rule, so she continues burrowing down further and is now about to ask for an even bigger shovel.

"Sharp, you've got no case here. First of all, the defendant was not an employee of the restaurant. Second, he wasn't even a customer... he was a bartender for a private party that had nothing to do with my client's restaurant.

"Third, nobody in the restaurant knew whether he walked to his bartending job or drove and no one paid any attention to whether or not he drank. They had no duty to and no responsibility to.

"When he left work, he was on his own. Liability for his decision to take that vehicle from the restaurant parking lot can in no way be traced back and neither can any event that took place subsequent to the taking.

"To sum it up, you have no case. Your client is the scum of the earth, a pornographer, who was relieving himself in public. If anything, it should be your client who should be arrested for lewd conduct.

"Do yourself a favor and settle now. I've been authorized to offer you a five hundred dollar nuisance amount and because I feel that both you and your client are nuisances, if you have a brain, you'll take the five hundred and advise your client to accept it. If it was up to me it would only be fifty cents, so why not do yourself a favor, take your money and get the hell out of here with your tail between your legs?"

This is what I get for trying to give her some respect. My decision now is how to let her know that we aren't going to settle for the five hundred, and instead would like five thousand. I think it best to remain calm and be as polite as possible. To be any other way would mean that I'm no better than she is, and that's no good. I start out by asking her a question. "Are you through now?"

She still can't let it go. Her answer shows it. "Yes Mister Sharp, I'm through now and so are you, and I hope you finally realize it."

It's really hard to be nice to someone who is so obnoxious, but I'm going to try. "Please sit down, Patty my dear, I've got a few things to tell you. They may have nothing at all to do with the law, but I'm sure you'll be interested in hearing them, because it might help you to re-adjust your attitude about this case."

She looks up at me astonished. Her eyes are bulging out at me and the expression on her face is rapidly turning to one of anger. As she starts to turn red, I continue.

"First of all, we are not accepting your offer of five hundred dollars, and if for any reason there actually is a hearing today and we are not successful, we intend to file a municipal court action against you and your husband."

She gasps for breath in disbelief. That's a good sign. If I really do my job, maybe she'll start to hyperventilate. I go on. "Secondly, the reason that the restaurant's liability is not cut off by Harry's intervening act of taking the car is because there was no grand theft. In fact, there was no theft at all because not only did you refuse to make a charge of theft, you never filed a police report, never made a claim to your insurance company, lied to your husband about the claim and who paid for the damages and also because Harry Michaels had permission to use that vehicle as he had in the past, because you were having an affair with him."

It worked. She's starting to hyper-ventilate. I must be on a roll. Usually, all they do in situations like this is glare at me angrily. I only hope she stays conscious long enough for me to finish up, because I'm not through with her yet. If she only had the control and professionalism to show me some respect and apologize for the fact that all her client authorized was five hundred, I would have probably tried to talk her up to seven-fifty and the matter would be a done deal. But nooo, she had to try and stick it to me in the rudest way I've ever seen, so whatever she gets now she really deserves. I have an emergency paper bag in my briefcase, so if she starts to black out, I'll come to the rescue.

"Mizz Vogel, here is the affidavit signed by my private investigator, in which he states that your picture was identified by several of Harry Michaels' neighbors, who fingered you as being a constant visitor to his apartment. We also have discovered by subpoena that you were instrumental in getting him bailed out on two occasions after he was arrested for drunk driving. You had your employer act as his sponsor on those bail bonds and Mister Robert Palmer, owner of the restaurant, was also the person who hired him as bartender at the party. That means that both you and Palmer were aware of Harry's drinking problem – but you still hired him to tend bar and dole out booze all evening, much of which he proceeded to ingest, as both of you should be charged with knowing.

"When he finally stumbled out of the restaurant, your husband had just pulled up and walked inside. Harry didn't know your husband was going to be there, because you arranged for him to come and pick you up after you were sure that Harry would already have finished for the evening and gone home. Harry never saw your husband before and didn't recognize him if he did. All Harry saw was the car that you had let him use on numerous occasions, so he probably figured you wouldn't mind him using it one more time to drive himself home.

"I don't know what story you told your husband, but I do know that you lied to the police when you told them that your husband had stopped in just for a moment to pick up some vegetarian burritos – and making a false statement to the police is a violation that can get your license to practice law pulled for a while.

"Now that we've established that there was no car theft here, and because Harry was really driving that vehicle with your implied permission, you and your husband liable for negligent entrustment of an automobile and that's not too good for you either.

"So, I have to agree with you. This case will be settled right here and now. You were certainly right about that, but it won't be to save me any embarrassment, it will be to save your sorry rear end from being sued, suspended, and probably divorced. Now, as for the amount, I'd like to be able to tell my client that he'll be getting five thousand dollars for his troubles, so while I'm out there getting congratulated, I'll expect you to compose yourself, make out that five thousand dollar check directly to my client, go tell the arbitrator that we've settled and that you'll be paying his fee and then come out and tell my client what a great job I've done."

15

Now that Vinnie's case is history I intend to devote my efforts full time to the two remaining really important matters – the Drago case and poor Harold Blitzstien's defense. I still have no idea what I'm going to do on either one of them, and can't get rid of the feeling that somehow they're both connected in some way.

Harold's prelim is coming up in another week or two and I've convinced Drago's lawyer to give me an extension of time to answer his lawsuit until the murder case is over. If my feelings are right, maybe I can kill two birds with one stone. I certainly hope so, because there's nothing I'd rather avoid more than flying to Chicago in the winter for federal court appearances.

If I'm going to find anything to work with on Harold's case, it's got to be in the pictures of him committing the crime. Where's Dick Van Dyke's Doctor Mark Sloan character when you need him?

The time flew by faster than I had expected and it's now time for Harold's prelim. It always amazes me how rapidly something you're not looking forward to comes around. If you're waiting for something like the results of a medical test, every minute until the doctor calls can seem like a week.

Tomorrow morning I'm going into court with nothing to say. No fax-spammer to roast, no Patty Vogel to knock off her high horse, no law, no facts, no nothing. I feel like a condemned man being walked out to the firing squad. Of course what I feel is probably nothing compared to how Harold must be taking it, but I'm not a cold-blooded killer, so I deserve a little more consideration.

Preliminary hearings are nothing like trials because the defense doesn't put on a case – it doesn't have to. The burden of establishing a case rests solely on the prosecution and can be a good chance for the defense to see a preview of almost every card the prosecution will play at the trial.

During the previous century, O.J. Simpson's case was on every television station and the people were glued to their sets during the entire preliminary hearing. That's when O.J.'s dream team had a crack at the county's medical examiner and forensic experts.

I don't think they considered for a moment that the case wouldn't be bound over for trial, but the ammo they got during the prelim was extremely useful in showing them exactly where the prosecution's weak points were - and they used that ammo in every gun they could find when the case was brought to trial.

Many legal experts fault the district attorney in that case for what they consider to be a whole slew of mistakes, including not getting a grand jury indictment, which would have eliminated the need for a preliminary hearing altogether. If they went the indictment route, the case would have gone from arraignment in the superior court, right to trial, thereby not giving the defense all their ammo on a silver platter. The defense team would never have had a crack at the prosecution's witnesses in that sideshow they called a preliminary hearing.

Unfortunately, Myra is a lot more experienced than the clown upstairs who tried to micro-manage the Simpson case, so the only opportunity I'm going to get out of this prelim is a chance to see how badly I'm going to lose at the trial. Too bad this isn't taking place back in the year 1278, when a guy named Hugh de Misyn hanged his daughter in a fit of madness. He was found not guilty by reason of insanity and released to the custody of twelve men, who pledged to keep him under control.

What a great idea. Instead of sending people to jail, each convicted person would be sent to a 'foster jail,' where volunteers would keep an eye on him. I'll have to suggest that to the governor – maybe that way I can get committed to a mental institution and miss this whole prelim and trial.

The court is called to order by the bailiff, Myra and I stand and state our representation for the record, and the prelim begins.

Myra starts out right at the top, establishing that the deceased is actually dead. That probably sounds silly to a non-lawyer, but it's really the first step in any murder case. She does this by calling in the doctor who was in a group that ran into the hospital room to try and revive Mike Drago. The doctor testifies as to the time that he made his life-saving attempts and states that he's the one who officially pronounced Drago dead.

To support his testimony, Myra introduces the death certificate her doctor signed. When Myra finishes with the doctor, the judge gives me the wonderful opportunity to cross-examine. I have nothing to ask, but always look forward to a chance to practice my cross-examination skills, so I take a couple of shots at him.

"Doctor, how long after the patient died did you sign the death certificate?"

He's a pro. Probably been on the stand many times. "About two hours later, in my office. When I pronounced him dead, I had two nurses make note of the exact time and that's what I put on the death certificate."

"Doctor, during the two hours that transpired between your pronouncing him dead and your signing the death certificate, did you see the footage from any of the hospital's security cameras?"

He thinks about this one for a minute, but has a plausible answer, which I believe is true. "Yes sir. We were told that a person was seen leaving the room, so we checked the cameras, to see what might have happened."

I guess he didn't perform an autopsy. Maybe a question or two about the cause of death might be in order here.

"Doctor, would you please tell the court what you listed as cause of death?"

"Yes, we have it down here as asphyxiation."

I think I'll quit now. I was waiting for him to say something in addition to his testimony so far but he didn't, so I might as well not push him any further. It looks like he determined the cause of death by videotape instead of by autopsy. This is a medical breakthrough and certainly a great time-saving device.

Myra is offered the chance to ask him more questions on 're-direct,' but she passes. The witness is excused.

Her next witnesses are several people who work for the hospital's audio-visual department. They testify to the security camera set-up, how the time codes are synchronized so that all the cameras work off of the same clock, the chain of custody of the security videocassettes and everything else that Myra needs to lock up her case – and my client.

I have very few questions for these witnesses, other than to inquire what clock all the cameras work off of and who tests the accuracy of that clock. My questions are answered. They don't give me anything I can use, but I was curious to know those answers. It's interesting to know that the hospital uses the same clock that I do. On the boat's navigation station, I have a small twenty-dollar clock ordered from a catalog that receives radio signals from the national observatory in Colorado. The signals keep the clock's digital display accurate to something like a millionth of a second. With accuracy measured in nano-seconds, I wonder why it still takes so long for a nurse to show up after a patient calls for one.

I was given information about Myra's next witness in the stuff that the prosecution must provide the defense with, including witness lists, statements obtained, evidence to be introduced, etc., etc., but I didn't know exactly what this guy was going to testify to. He's a security expert on retainer to most of the casinos in Las Vegas, Nevada. His field of expertise is the operation of a facial recognition software program he designed. He sells this software to the casinos and trains their personnel how to use it, to spot professional crooks, card cheats, and the faces of other unsavory sorts who have been previously scanned into the computers.

In this case, the expert brought his software to the Culver City Police Department's headquarters, and installed it on their computer, where he used it to compare the face on the videotape with all the photos of men in our Department of Motor Vehicle's database of drivers' license photos.

Harold Blitzstien's face was a match, so he was picked up, arrested, and charged with Drago's murder. That's interesting. I was under the impression that they took Harold's photo off of the videotape and showed it around. I must really be out of touch with the new technology. It's a good thing the kid backs me up.

Myra goes on to show the two minutes of videotape footage of Harold using the pillow to smother Drago. I try to object, but since she did such a good job of verifying the tape's chain of custody, I don't have a chance. The video is admitted into evidence and the judge sees it. For one time in my life, I definitely am not happy to be associated with a video celebrity.

Myra rests her case and I don't offer any defense. This isn't only because the prelim is not the place to put one on, but in this instance because there is really no defense I can think of. Harold doesn't have an alibi for the time of the murder and at this point, the only weakness in the prosecution's case is the motive. That ordinarily would be a good opening for a defense lawyer, but not with a televised celebrity murderer like Harold. Any decent prosecutor could successfully argue, "we don't know why he did it, but the evidence shows that he did it, so what's the difference what his reason was?"

As expected, the judge binds Harold over for arraignment and trial in the Superior court. Myra and I check our calendars and agree upon a date less than a month away.

Harold shows no emotion at the judge's holding, but that's not surprising – he hasn't showed any emotion since the first day I saw him. He seems to look worse every day.

On the way out of court, Myra hands me a stack of statements that the D.A.'s investigator got from the nurses, doctors, technicians, and everyone connected to the case – including people not called at the prelim. Suzi mentioned that she has a program that can scan text documents into the computer, so I toss the paperwork into my briefcase.

All the way back to the Marina, the only thought on my mind isn't about the witnesses who testified for the prosecution - it was about a particular one who didn't testify - the county's medical examiner. Whenever there's an allegation of murder, the prosecution will usually order an autopsy. Then, the coroner will come into court and testify as to cause of death. In this case it looks like Myra has decided to go with the new 'autopsy by video.'

I don't know if all this is important but it sure raises a question. If I really pushed I could probably have the court order the coroner to autopsy Drago's body, but what's the use? All it would probably do is be further verification of what was already testified to and would nail Myra's case even more towards conviction.

Back at the boat, I take all the statements that Myra gave me and leave them in a big folder for Suzi to scan into her computer. Later that day, I see the folder on my desk with a note that because this is not one of the firm's cases, she doesn't have time to do the scanning.

I send a message to her by dog-mail that the court has approved the use of minimal office staff and since she's the most minimal person I know, she'll receive a stipend of thirty-five bucks an hour for going through the statements and scanning them into her computer program. I then walk over to the Marina del Rey Liquor Store to get the new Playboy. When I return to the boat, I see that the big folder of witness statements is no longer on my desk.

Miraculously, her schedule must have had an opening. For a pre-teen kid, she has the business instincts of a twenty-nine-year-old gold-digger. Not only is she a multi-millionaire because of the lawsuit settlements from two separate accidents that caused the deaths of her mother and stepfather, she's now working for more money than most adults in this country earn. Her hourly rate is equivalent to a yearly salary of more than seventy thousand dollars – and that doesn't take into consideration the money she gets as managing partner of her late stepfather's law firm which she runs, with Jack Bibberman and me as employees... and the interest her trust accounts is probably more than all this other stuff combined. Maybe I should ask for a raise. I'll talk it over with the dog tonight. Naah. It wouldn't do any good...he's on her side.

The subject of a raise doesn't come up this evening because instead, there's a roundtable discussion of Harold's murder case. The Asian boys delivered a feast that's now being shared by all six of us including me, Suzi, Jack B. Stuart and Vinnie. The sixth member of the dinner group is at his usual station, waiting for some morsel to be dropped to the floor. Four of us cover the case from all angles but nobody has any suggestions for me. As usual, Suzi just sits and listens to every word.

Stuart complains about a filling that came loose. His dentist is out of town on vacation, so he tells us that he's going to call the number that's advertised in all those TV commercials – 1(800) DENTIST. If you're looking for a dentist, I guess that's as good a way as any to find one. Their advertising mentions that they carefully screen and select all applicants before putting them onto their listings. I'll bet that the main qualification is an ability to sign a check, and that their 'rejection' list is slim, if at all.

During dinner I mention my concerns about no autopsy having been done on Drago. We hear some electronic beeps and notice that Suzi, who hasn't said a word yet during the entire dinner, is dialing a number on her cell phone and has the small speakerphone turned on. When the phone number answers, to everyone's surprise, a recorded announcement plays. "Hello, this is one eight hundred autopsy, we offer private and forensic autopsies to families, mortuaries, and the legal profession..."

I don't believe it. There' actually is a real 1(800)AUTOPSY. It's understandable that you could call a 1(800) DENTIST, or 1(800) LAWYER, or even 1(800)PLUMBER, or other service provider, but in a million years I'd never think you could get an autopsy like that too. As serious a subject as it is, we all have a good laugh about it.

While everyone is here, I decide to play a little parlor game. We've spent a good deal of time talking about the murder case, so I take a sheet of paper and tear it up into small sections about two inches square. I then pass one section around to each person at the table, asking them to write down what they think is the real verdict on Harold's case. There is silence in the room. After everyone's had a chance to write down their verdict, I collect the pieces of paper and tell them that I'll read each anonymous verdict out loud. No surprises here... two 'guilty' verdicts, probably from Vinnie and Stuart. There's one 'not guilty by reason of insanity,' probably from Jack B. It's the last one that gets to me. I can tell by the almost calligraphic penmanship that it's from the kid and for someone her age she really knows how to turn a phrase. It only has four words 'guilty... by reason of sanity.'

Last night's dinner was very informative. Not only did I discover a criminal plea I've never heard of before but I learned about a business that's so out of the ordinary, I don't know why Stuart has never thought of it. When checking it out, I discover that they actually do perform private autopsies. They're located near Pasadena and have a mobile lab that's fully equipped to do autopsies on the road. A guy named Victor Gutierrez, who used to work for the Los Angeles Coroner's office, runs the whole operation, and he's a really nice guy to talk to on the phone. I politely declined his invitation for a tour of his business facility.

I didn't realize that the general public might have much use for a business like this, but due to hospital downsizing, many post-mortems are 'outsourced.' He seems busy enough and is planning on franchising his services to all of the states and then to sixteen foreign countries. I guess that both he and the I.R.S. are the only two establishments with true job security, both guaranteed by inevitability.

I convince the office that the court will probably reimburse us for the expenditure, so the next move is to decide whether or not to go ahead with it. There are too many unanswered questions in this case, so I push to have the private autopsy done. First step is to call Myra. "Hi, it's me. I need to ask you a favor."

"Peter, you know I can't make a plea bargain on this case... it's a murder, possibly a special circumstance case..."

I interrupt her. "No, no, I don't want any deal, it's something else." Nothing but silence on the other end. She's waiting to hear what her moronic ex-husband has come up with this time. "You know, I also represent the insurance company against the murder victim's estate."

"So?"

"Well, they feel that with all the unanswered questions, they'd like an autopsy on Drago."

"No way. The district attorney's office is quite satisfied with the hospital doctor's death certificate, and we're not going to re-open the cause of death issue to satisfy some fat cats at an insurance company."

"Hey relax, I'm not asking you to do anything. I've made arrangements with a private autopsy company. They'll pick up the body, do their business and return it to your morgue. I'll even toss in a free copy of their report... and the insurance company will pay for the whole thing."

"... I dunno."

"What's the problem? All I'll be doing is making your case better for you. Are you worried that my lab will come back with the Flu as cause of death? I'll tell you what... you can have your own medical examiner observe the whole thing and I'll even get the insurance company to pay his overtime. How about it?"

The five seconds it takes her to make her mind up seems like five minutes. She finally agrees.

"Yeah, what the hell. Will they do it on a Saturday? I don't want to see one of our M.E.s lose hours of valuable time from an already overloaded workweek."

"Not to worry. A Saturday it is. I'll have my office make all the arrangements and we'll have the autopsy place make an appointment to pick up the merchandise."

"Okay Peter, but no funny stuff. I'll have one of our guys looking over their shoulders. And say hello to Suzi for me."

Good, it's a done deal. She went for it. I don't know why I'm so happy. Maybe because it's probably the only small victory I'll ever get in this crazy loser of a case. Nevertheless, the wheels have now been set in motion.

The private autopsy place coordinates their schedule with the county morgue and an off-duty medical examiner and the examination is set for the Saturday after next. They invite me to attend. I explain that the true definition of a lawyer is 'a college student who can't stand the sight of blood,' and I respectfully decline. That adds 'autopsy' to my list of 'do not go to,' events, along with bullfights, opera, hockey games and ballet.

When we were married, Myra was always bugging me to take her to the opera and to see a ballet. It was always me who was backing out for one reason or another. This time, it's her turn. When I asked her if she was going to the autopsy, she told me she couldn't make it – she was having her hair done that day. Me too.

The thought of having over a week with nothing to do is too tempting. Usually, when I try to take only an hour or two off to do some reading, some emergency pops up. I'm afraid to think of what could happen if I actually plan on taking a whole week off. Maybe an earthquake or some other natural disaster.

While I'm sitting up on the boat's flybridge trying to imagine what situation will destroy my week off, good friend Stuart calls and provides the answer to my question. He desperately wants me to meet him at the Pacific Division of the Los Angeles Police Department. Vinnie's been arrested.

16

I meet Stuart, who has already had Fradkin Bail Bonds post the five thousand dollars to get Vinnie released. When Vinnie comes walking out to the lobby he's dressed in a two-tone gray police costume, complete with one of those over-the-shoulder leather straps that attaches to his belt, like a school crossing guard. He's also wearing a badge and a holster and there's a stain on the front of his trousers.

Something tells me that I don't want to hear this story, but it seems unavoidable. Stuart starts. "Remember that great idea I had to convert an old Brinks truck into a funeral armored thing?"

I think back a ways. Yes, he did mention that crazy idea. "You mean the 'He's taking it with him' armored truck for stingy dead guys?"

"Yeah Pete, that's the one. Well, I promised Vinnie a hundred for each funeral he did and today was our first job."

"Okay, no problem with that, but where did the uniform come from?"

"Oh, you like it huh? I thought it would be nice touch, so I went to a military supply house and bought the whole thing for Vinnie. He's supposed to be the ultimate armored car guard."

"What about the empty holster on Vinnie's belt?"

"That's one of the problems."

At this point the story looks good enough for me to make an offer to buy the screenplay rights. Little do I know that it gets even better. Vinnie tells the next part.

"Well Mister Sharp, we get this nice funeral job. All I gotta do is be at the funeral home at one in the afternoon, put the truck in the procession and go with them to the cemetery, about five miles away."

"That sounds straight enough Vinnie. So how did you wind up in jail?"

"Well, Stuart told me that the air conditioning in the truck wasn't rebuilt yet, so I brought along a cooler full of colas. When we got to the cemetery, the guy directing traffic had us pull up so close together, that I wasn't able to get the truck out of there and had to wait until the whole funeral was over.

"Anyway, I had about five cokes and really had to take a leak, but there was no toilet in sight."

I have a weird feeling what's coming next. Vinnie proves me right.

"So, I walked a couple a hunnert feet away from where all the people were and saw a real big tree behind a bush."

"Don't tell me Vinnie, I've already seen this movie. You were peeing against the tree, weren't you?"

"Well yeah, but that wasn't the problem. All of a sudden there were about ten cops surrounding me with their guns out. They shouted that I should put my hands up, so I did. That's when I soiled these pants. I was right in the middle of peeing. I'm sorry, Stu, I'll pay for the cleaning."

"Vinnie, where did all the cops come from?"

Stuart has the answer to that one. "The dead guy was an older cop who was the watch commander at one of the local precincts. He died of a stroke, so there were plenty of cops at the funeral. His ex-wife was cut out of the will and she was mad at the deceased. She's the one who hired us."

Vinnie has the rest of the answers. "Yeah, there were a lot of cops there. I guess one of the cemetery's groundskeepers saw me peeing and didn't know I was the armored car driver, so he told the cops that there was a guy with a gun behind a tree. He fingered me."

As usual, whenever Stuart and Vinnie are involved, there's a fantastic story. I don't think that Jimmy Breslin or Dave Barry could create anything better than this. Maybe Donald Westlake, but he's the only one.

"Vinnie, do you have anything against regular bathrooms? You know, if a person gets arrested for petty theft, the first time it's usually just a misdemeanor. If they get arrested for it a second time, it can be charged as a felony and it's called 'petty with a prior.' In your case, we've already had one case with you peeing on a tree. This time, they might be justified classifying it as peeing with a prior."

143

They are not amused. Vinnie is charged with one count of carrying a weapon, and one count of lewd conduct. In mitigation, Stuart tells me that the gun isn't real. It's one of those replicas they sell that look and weigh like the real thing. I remind him that in most of the catalogs I've seen, they don't ship those things into the state of California. Stuart tells me that he had a friend out of state get it for him.

I don't know what to tell him on this case. At first I think that maybe I can get the gun charge dropped because it isn't a real one, but it's also a violation to expose a replica. California Penal Code section 417 covers the drawing and exhibiting of any deadly weapon, whether it's a loaded or unloaded gun, or any other deadly weapon. They call it 'brandishing.'

In Vinnie's case, the only weapon he was exhibiting wasn't his gun, but he was still wearing one.

There's even a law covering security guards that specifically prohibits the carrying of an "...inoperable, replica, or simulated firearm."

The bottom line is that police are really down on people who have replica guns. The only thing that Vinnie has going for him in this case is that the replica was holstered and not being used in any attempted crime, unless 'peeing while armed' is now against the law. I'll have to check the Internet for that one. The only break we've gotten so far is that the Sierra Club hasn't been bringing any actions against Vinnie for his treatment of trees.

If a criminal attorney can get to the City Attorney before charges are filed, he can sometimes explain away what's been interpreted as criminal behavior. I don't know if it'll work in this case, but the facts are so outrageous that I have to give it a try. I call an old classmate who works at the City Attorney's office and make an appointment to come in and meet with the head deputy in charge of filing complaints. The police were nice enough to provide me with a copy of the 'incident' report, so I've got more than just my word to offer as to exactly what went down.

I also get Stuart to sign an affidavit to the effect that he bought the costume and replica weapon and hired Vinnie to wear them both – and supplied him with the cooler full of cokes. Next, we take some pictures of Vinnie in uniform standing next to the armored truck and I get Stuart to have a port-a-potty installed in the truck. A copy of the receipt for its purchase and installation is included in my presentation package. All of this, along with the argument that because the truck can be mistaken for a real armored vehicle, Vinnie should be allowed to wear the holstered replica as a crime deterrent, should get me either a laugh, a dismissal, or both. Vinnie suggests adding a picture of the tree to my presentation package… I pass on that one.

Walking through the City Attorney's office, package under my arm, at each desk I pass, someone is smiling at me. Is my fly open? Would that deserve a smile? When I get to the Chief Deputy's office, I see that they've got six people in there. They invite me to sit down at the conference table. I think I'll keep my mouth shut for a minute or two and let them start the meeting for me.

The chief starts. "Peter, this is an interesting case that the Pacific Division detectives brought to us. Do you think we should file on it? And if so, what charges would be best here?"

I know what they're all in there for – to have a good laugh at Vinnie's expense. And because I'm there on his behalf, the laugh will be on me too. I didn't practice law for over twenty years to be humiliated like this, but it's difficult to see how to avoid it today.

"Gentlemen, I appreciate your giving me the opportunity to come in here and make a fool out of myself and I'm sure you're all waiting for a good laugh at the expense of my client and me, but all I have for you is some statistics on deaths of armored car guards. If you want to laugh about that, then please be my guest.

"As for my client, he was just working for a living. I noticed on the way in here that there were several restrooms out in the hall. My client didn't have one, so that's another reason for you to laugh. If you can stop laughing long enough to give an honest, hard working guy a break for taking a leak when he had to, then I'd be grateful. If not, then I'll just have to go to court and face a jury with twelve hard working stiffs, just like my client, who found himself in an embarrassing position while at work and took care of it the only way he could.

"As for the brandishing, the weapon wasn't real and it was holstered – not waved or exhibited in a menacing way. The only time he exited the vehicle was when he felt that nobody was watching him, so I don't think any fair-minded person would consider that to be a rude and threatening exhibition.

"I'll leave all my data here for you guys to go over and if you decide to file on this case, I'll be very disappointed. In my past twenty years of doing business with this City Attorney's office, I've found it to be a responsible, professional group of lawyers who don't look forward to wasting the taxpayers' money with frivolous prosecutions. I hope you'll continue to uphold that reputation.

"If you don't have any questions, then you'll have to excuse me, I've got a capital case coming to trial next week and there's a lot of preparation work to finish."

I stand up and wait for a few seconds. The chief speaks. "Thanks for coming in Pete, we'll see what we can do on this one."

I thank them all again and make my escape, feeling that my integrity is still intact. I don't hear any laughter coming from the room as I exit their department. No smiles from the people at the desks either – it wouldn't surprise me if they had the meeting piped through the public address system, as a form of office entertainment. I hope they were disappointed.

Because the Drago and Blitzstien cases still are connected in my mind, I've got to figure out why. The sequence of events is simple to see. First, Mike Drago slips and falls in the bank. Second, he's brought to the hospital. Third, the bank gets robbed. Fourth, Mike Drago gets killed by Harold. What's wrong with this picture? Let's see – we have a slip-

and-fall, a hospital admittance, a bank robbery and a murder. If this were a puzzle of some sort, I would separate out two pairs of happenings: the slip-and-fall and the hospital... then the bank robbery and the murder.

I already know about three of the four items in our chain of events. The only thing I don't know anything about is the bank robbery. The fact that it took place in the same bank where Mike Drago slipped and fell, and on the same afternoon, is just too coincidental to be random. I send a dog-mail message to the kid, telling her to pull some strings and get a copy of the police report on the bank job. The local cops handled it for the first day until the Feds stepped in, but I should still be able to get copies of reports, security videotape, interviews, or anything else that our locals have.

It takes a few days, but the kid comes through and I'm given a bunch of pages from the police files that smell like chow mein. Hmmmn... I wonder what restaurant could have been the 'drop zone' for this stuff.

From the police reports, witness statements and notes taken from viewing security cameras outside the bank, it looks like this gang is composed of two or three guys who make no getaway. That's interesting. If you're going to pull a bank robbery, I would think it's nice to have a getaway strategy – some way to take the fruits of your crime away from the scene of the crime. But not here. No getaway, no getaway car, no getaway driver, no nothing. The bank robbers and their loot simply disappear into thin air.

I start to compare the police notes on the other three robberies that this gang pulled off since starting their career a month or so ago. None of the banks were in freestanding buildings of their own. Each bank was on the first floor of a large office building.

Okay, that can answer one question. They didn't have to drive away – they just melted into the scenery of the building. Maybe they used the elevator and went up to an office. Wrong. The witnesses had them carrying sacks of money out of the bank, but lobby cameras in each building show nobody getting into any elevator carrying anything like that.

We're still at square one. No wonder so many crooks get away with things. It's tough for us armchair detectives to sit here and figure how they did it.

Rex Stout created Nero Wolfe, the original armchair detective. He rarely left his brownstone and instead sent his legman Archie Goodwin out to do the fact gathering. Wolfe would then summon all the usual suspects to his home, and at the end of the story in true black-and-white-movie style, he would conduct the 'show down,' during which time an antagonistic police inspector would stand there and watch while Nero Wolfe explained his solution to the mystery and named the culprit.

Unfortunately I don't have an Archie Goodwin. I do have a Jack Bibberman, but he doesn't even come close to Archie's talent level. Jack has to write things down. Archie had a photographic memory. Archie carried a gun; Jack carries a cell-phone and a small pepper-spray, to protect him from dogs when he serves papers on people. The comparison could go on and on, but suffice it to say that I'm no Nero Wolfe and Jack B. is no Archie Goodwin.

Therefore, without the pairing of such talented detectives, it's unlikely that I'm going to solve these bank robbery cases. The phone rings. It's Stuart, in another panic. Vinnie's been arrested again, but not for peeing on a tree. The Feds have him and they think he pulled off the bank robberies!

17

The FBI has a nice suite of offices in the West Los Angeles Federal Building on Wilshire Boulevard and Sepulveda, just off the San Diego Freeway and Stuart is waiting for me in the lobby as I get off the elevator on the tenth floor.

"Pete, this is terrible. They think Vinnie did the bank robberies and they've seized my armored truck. I think they're going to arrest me too. I don't know what to do."

There's no calming him down, so I just let him babble on for a minute or so and then walk away, go over to the receptionist, show my State Bar card and ask to speak to the senior agent in charge of the bank robbery detail.

After a few minutes, Special Agent Bob Snell comes out to greet me. If you look up 'FBI Agent' in the dictionary, you should see a picture of him. He's about six-foot-three, full head of straight silver hair, conservatively dressed in a dark suit with a white button-down shirt, shoes with laces, and he's got a square jaw with a dimple right in the middle of it. If you saw him on the street you would immediately place him as either an FBI agent, politician, or an airline pilot. He asks me to follow him back to his office. Stuart starts to follow us, but when he gets cold stares from both Agent Snell and me, he retreats to a chair in the lobby.

Once in his office, Snell tells me that the only information he's at liberty to disclose is that Mister Vincent Norman was arrested outside of a supermarket with a bag of stolen currency in his hand. He was putting it into the rear of his own armored truck. Snell was surprised at the level of sophistication that Vinnie achieved. He said that he's never encountered a bank robbery gang with their own armored truck.

There are only two kinds of people in this world - those who think that Vinnie is sophisticated and those who have already met him.

I'm shocked, but not like Claude Rains was shocked when he found out that there was gambling in Humphrey Bogart's club in Casablanca. What really surprised me was his thinking that Vinnie was sophisticated. I mean, I like him a lot, but of all the words in the English language, the one that just doesn't apply to Vinnie is 'sophisticated.'

I tell him that there just has to be some mistake here and let him know about Vinnie's 'peeing with a prior' incident. It doesn't work. He assures me that their case is solid and if I'm representing Vinnie, he'll send me copies of the report. I ask to see my client and Agent Snell tells me that he's still being processed, but I can visit with him tomorrow at the Federal Detention facility on Terminal Island. That's a nice little facility the feds have near San Pedro, a few miles from the Port of Los Angeles.

Out in the hall, I firmly grip Stuart by the arm and walk him into the elevator. "Stuart, I know that Vinnie didn't rob any banks, but he did have the stolen bags of currency in his hands and he was putting them into the back of your armored truck. I think you've got some explaining to do because I haven't got the time to get involved in a federal criminal case this month."

It's late in the afternoon now and the feds always tire me out, so I tell Stuart to be at the boat tomorrow morning – and to have his explanation all ready. I expect a full report of how Vinnie got into this situation – and it better be good.

Stuart followed my instructions and he's here at the boat. His explanation is just one more reason why I'd like to own screen rights to 'The Vinnie Story.' He tells me what the unbelievable chain of events were.

After a long day at the cemetery and completing two funerals with the armored truck, Vinnie stopped by a Ralph's Market at about nine in the evening, to get some milk and food for his apartment. The armored truck was too wide to fit in the normal parking spaces, so he pulled up right in front of the main entrance and left the truck's blinking emergency lights on while he was inside shopping. He also left the back door to the truck slightly ajar, so that with arms full he could manage to get the doors open to put his grocery bags in.

After his shopping was done, he put his bags into the rear of the truck, slammed the door shut and drove home. When he got to his apartment, he had two things to do. First, he wanted to get his groceries inside so that the milk and ice cream wouldn't go bad. Next, he wanted to drive over to a sewer, where he could pump out the porta-potty that Stuart had installed for him to use on those long hot days. When he went inside to hook up the drain hoses, he noticed two bags of money in the back of the truck. At first he didn't know they were full of money, but upon opening up one of them, he realized what they were. One main clue is that stenciled quite clearly on each bag were the words "property of Brinks Armored Transit," and an ID tag from Ralph's Market.

Vinnie called Stuart and told him what happened. Stuart reasoned that when the truck was parked in front of the market, they must have thought it was Brinks coming to make the evening's regular pick-up, so a helpful market employee, seeing the truck's back door open, walked out and tossed the money bags in.

Stuart's advice was that Vinnie should immediately go back to the Ralph's Market and return those moneybags to the store's manager.

A little while later, but before Vinnie returned, the real Brinks truck pulled up and found out that the cupboard was bare. An all-points bulletin was immediately put out to the local police to be on the lookout for anything that looked like a Brinks truck, but really wasn't one. The Feds were also notified that a search was being done for a possible suspect.

Following Stuart's advice, which is always risky, Vinnie drove the truck back to the market and was in the process of taking the bags out of the rear of the truck when he was nabbed by a local police squad car who had heard the bulletin on their radio and were staking out the market just in case another robbery attempt might be tried.

If what Stuart tells me is true, Vinnie wasn't trying to steal the money... he was trying to return it.

Okay, that sounds amazing enough to be a true 'Vinnie' story. No one but Vinnie could get into a situation like this.

I don't think that going to the feds with this story will do any good, so I figure the next best thing will be to try a manipulation of the press – those ignorant, blow-dried anchor people who bring us the local news each evening, which is actually a neighborhood crime report with pictures, and an occasional car chase.

Stuart has a police scanner in his car, so he can alert Vinnie to where police activity might be blocking traffic that a funeral procession might be going into. I know that most news crews monitor those scanners, so we decide to plant some info.

I call the L.A.P.D. metro division and let them know that I'll be giving a press conference tomorrow morning on the steps of the Federal Building and that there should be some crowd control there. The police dispatcher notifies a few squad cars to remind them of my conference. The press hears the police broadcast and the game is afoot.

This is all helped along by the pompous federal authorities rushing to make an announcement on the evening news that they've made an arrest in the bank robbery cases and have recovered 'one hundred percent' of the loot from a related robbery. When it comes to blowing your own horn, nobody does it better than our gendarmes.

Next morning the reporters are waiting for me as I walk up the dock gangway to my car. I've already made a phone call to Special Agent Snell, asking him to meet me at the Federal Building, but he has other business and declines my invitation.

As usual, the press is pushing their microphones in my face and asking the most inane questions I've heard since the last time this happened to me on a high profile case I was handling.

It never ceases to amaze me how these reporters actually expect to get answers to the questions they shout out at you. I can't remember how many times I've seen these goofs on television, at the scene of some arrest or appearance of a well-known lawyer or client near the courthouse. They shout out things like "did your client really commit those crimes?" or "do you think your client is innocent?" Are they kidding? Are they actually getting paid to ask those questions? Do they really expect an attorney to ever answer with a "yes, my client is guilty?" – That's not going to ever happen, but they keep trying. It reminds me of the Saint Bernard watching me eat a steak. He sits there waiting for me to offer it to him. He's got a better chance of getting that steak than those reporters have of getting a scoop-making answer like some lawyer or criminal defendant shouting out an admission of guilt. I politely smile and tell them that my statement will be made at the Federal Building and they're welcome to meet me there.

Jack B. knows the routine. We pull up in front of the courthouse in the Yellow Hummer rented yesterday from Budget on Lincoln Avenue. It always pays to make a nice impression – you never can tell how many prospective clients are watching. After I step out of the Hummer and walk up the courthouse steps, Jack turns on his portable TV set, so he can monitor my speech and know when to circle back around the block to pick me up. I walk up the steps and give the press a chance to focus their cameras and get some still shots. I then pull a stack of papers out of my briefcase, all copies of Stuart's extensive statement. It's been slightly refined to depict Vinnie as the victim.

It's Showtime. I've got my Sunday suit on and I'm ready to start. "Ladies and gentlemen, I want to thank you all for coming today. The purpose of this conference is two-fold. First, I want to state that my client, Mister Vincent Norman, is not the culprit here, he's the victim. And we want to state here and now, that we are hereby putting in a claim for any reward that may have been offered for the return of misplaced currency to Ralph's Market.

"I called Special Agent Robert Snell and invited him to join me here, but he declined, stating that he had more important matters to take care of today. Well, if Special Agent Snell can tell us what's more important then letting an innocent person out of custody, then I'd like to hear it.

"Here in my hand is a notarized affidavit from Mister Norman's employer. It explains quite clearly how Vincent was in fact attempting to return funds to their rightful owner. He found the moneybags, and being the honest hardworking citizen that he is, made an effort to return them. It was at this point that the authorities, not coordinating the proper timeline, arrested him.

"I only hope that the federal authorities take note of the injustice of his confinement before they go too far. He should be released immediately, and because I have such great respect for the press, I'll be looking forward to your respective organizations doing the investigation that the authorities neglected to do. Thank you." I hand out copies of Stuart's statement, complete with pictures of the armored car and Vinnie. Also included is Jack's affidavit of the off-the-record conversation he had with the clerk who actually made the mistake of putting those moneybags into Vinnie's truck.

Jack knows when I'm done and when to pull up with the Hummer so that I can make my clean exit. Once back in the car, Jack asks me how it feels making a statement up there, in front of all those people and cameras.

"Jack, my good man, the toughest part about it all is trying to keep a straight face while telling the press about the great respect I have for them."

This evening's local news shows all carry my press conference and also show the reporters descending upon the Ralph's Market, not stopping until they ferret out the employee who tossed the bags into the back of Vinnie's armored truck.

Apparently, the FBI can't handle the real truth because shortly thereafter, Vinnie is released. I guess that after talking to Vinnie for a while, they compared his level of sophistication with what they considered to be the minimum required for grand theft, and decided he wasn't their man.

Now it's back to trying to figure out how those truly sophisticated people knocked over a couple of banks during afternoon business hours. Like a cop friend of mine once said, 'crime doesn't pay, but the hours are good.'

There were three banks robbed within a one-month period of time. They started one month before Drago's slip-and-fall and continued until the afternoon of his accident. That's interesting. There's always a bank getting robbed somewhere in Southern California, but the authorities have only linked three to this particular gang. I assume that's because the methods of the three were unique and therefore separated out from all others. All three first-floor banks in office buildings, always two or three robbers in the bank, no getaway car and the perps disappearing into the office building with no trace of the stolen money.

The cops cross-indexed the tenant lists in all three of the bank office buildings: there was no overlap of tenants. No one lessee had places rented in all three of the buildings. This means that if they were hiding in the building of each bank robbery, they'd have to find new places to hide after each job.

Security tapes show that the robbers wore business suits. They didn't flash guns, but discreetly showed that they were being carried in shoulder holsters or shoved into belts. They didn't wear masks. Instead, they merely put on large sunglasses and made their threats by passing one note to a teller and another to the bank manager, both at the same time. The note to the teller would be a demand to quietly fill up some bags with large bills – and if he or she didn't, the bank manager would be killed. The note to the bank manager was to let him know that his bank was being robbed and that if he did anything to stop it, his family would immediately be killed. To make themselves appear more threatening than usual, they signed the notes as representatives of a mid-east terrorist organization, which was a threat discounted by the authorities as bogus and only done for shock effect.

The only thing surprising is that the Department of Homeland Security wasn't brought into the mix. They should have been very interested in the fact that a mid-east terrorist organization was at least mentioned.

All the robbery notes were examined by the best federal CSI investigators in the business and were found to be ink-jet printed on cheap copy paper, with no fingerprints or other identifying marks.

Not one dollar of the stolen money has been recovered, and because a trace was put on the serial numbers, not one dollar has been spent yet.

This doesn't sound too tough to figure out. All I have to do is plan a bank robbery and try to think like a robber. Where would I go, where would I stash the loot and how would I get away?

I don't have an Archie Goodwin - I run a one-man and one-kid shop, so I make a personal visit to all three of the banks. One of them I'm already familiar with because that's where Drago fell. The other two look quite similar, but that's no surprise because most banks look the same to me. They all have counters with tellers, desks with people to open new accounts, and senile uniformed guards.

If the robbers were to melt in with the background, there would be no need for them to do it inside the bank – it would have to be out in the building's lobby.

I take a good look around out there at different times of the day and see the same fixtures: elevator operators, lobby security, maintenance crew, magazine stand, the occasional appearance of a genuine armored truck, a car-parking guy, and all the other usual things you would expect to see there. The real puzzle seems to be how they got away with their loot.

I ask the office to try and get some security tapes from the lobby of each bank. I want to see the action near those bank exit doors, to see if anything out of the ordinary happens. I also make a request to see the logs from those lobby security guys who sit behind their counters and view an array of about ten little television screens.

It's now a few days later and I've just received a big package that contains copies of security videotapes from the three lobbies, but only footage shortly before and after each robbery. Also included in the package are copies of the three lobby security guard incident reports. Everything gets scanned in to the computer at thirty-five dollars an hour, with the computer instructed to only seek out items that occurred in all three lobbies on the day of each robbery.

The list gets printed out and includes several items, but only one looks too odd to be a coincidence – and it was the same series of events each time. A woman enters the lobby with a large Rottweiler dog on a leash. When a security guard approaches to inform her that no animals other than seeing-eye dogs are allowed inside the building, she begins to argue with the guard and the dog strains at his leash, trying to attack the guard. This commotion in the lobby causes the other guards to run over. The woman is told that she must leave the building immediately and she does. The incident draws the attention of everyone in the lobby.

I may not be a trained detective, but if that dog act isn't a diversionary tactic, then I'll hang up my amateur detective badge. I also appreciate the fact that the purpose of any diversion is to take attention away from some other activity that is going on at the same time.

The incident reports indicate that each dog act took place at about the same time as the bank robbery concluded, so it looks like she was trying to give the robbers a chance to exit the bank and enter the lobby without being noticed. At that point in time, they would still have the money with them.

Each dog incident lasted less than two or three minutes. Because we already know that the gang didn't go into an elevator or exit the building with the money, the diversion must have been for the purpose of giving them a chance to stash the money somewhere. It wouldn't serve any purpose to have the dog lady's face scanned into facial recognition software, because she always wore a hat that has some dark veil hanging down in front. And even if we could identify her, there's no way to tie her into the bank robberies.... yet.

Fortunately, all the security videotapes have that stop-watch-like time code running at the bottom of the screen, so it's not hard to figure out the timing. By comparing the lobby tapes with the bank tapes, it looks like all the inside guys needed was about ten seconds to dump the money - but where? And if they do dump it somewhere, how do they retrieve it?

They've obviously got a pretty good plan working, and with their current success rate, there's no reason for them to stop now. They're too young to retire, so I would think they're going to pull another job or two - and with the information I've already got, I think there might be a way to catch them.

A big map of the west side of town shows the location of all three of the bank jobs. They appear to be in a small area, so it seems reasonable that they would stay in the neighborhood. I drive up and down the neighboring main streets and locate another eight or nine large buildings that have banks located on their main floor. The next job will be the setting of the trap.

I grab a handful of some special business cards our computer printed and start out with the first bank and go directly to the person in charge of lobby security. He introduces himself to me and invites me into his office. I hand him my card and try out the spiel that we rehearsed earlier at the boat. The dog believed it, so I see no reason why the security chief shouldn't.

"Chief, as my business card indicates, our practice is limited only to the civil prosecution of dog bite cases. I know that sounds strange but as you probably know, there are a lot of dogs here in Southern California."

Long ago, I learned that if you utter four magic words, they make any person's head nod up and down in agreement with whatever you're saying, so always try to use them, and they are: 'As you probably know...' Now that he's agreeing with me, I press on. "We've had some small children injured by a woman's large Rottweiler. Our problem is, we don't know how to locate her. Several of the clients are quite well-off, so they've authorized me to offer a reward for any information that leads us to her."

At this point the chief tries to straighten me out. "Mister Goodwin, I appreciate the fact that you're trying to locate this dog-lady, but all we do here is building security – we don't go out looking for people with dogs."

"Chief, you're absolutely correct, and that's why I came to you. We've got some information that her husband runs a business in one of these large office buildings and she occasionally comes to visit him. We also understand that she may have bribed some lobby security guards because she's allowed to bring the dog into the building and elevator when she goes up and visit with her husband."

The Chief strenuously denies this. "No way, Goodwin. My guards are above reproach. There's not enough money in the world that'll make them break the rules and let a big Rottweiler into this building, let alone into an elevator."

"Okay, Chief, I believe you. Tell you what, here's what I'd like to offer you. On behalf of my clients, if your staff have any reason to stop a woman with a large barking Rottweiler and ask her to leave the lobby, I'm authorized to pay five hundred dollars in cash to the charity of your choice, if while in the line of duty, one of your guards discreetly follows her outside and gets a description of her vehicle and its license number. And if that member of your staff wants to go above and beyond the call of duty and follow the vehicle to wherever her next stop is, my client will pay an additional five hundred dollars for that address."

The Chief looks at me and rubs his chin. I go on. "Chief, we have a feeling that if she's going to come into your lobby at all, it'll be within the next week or so. What do you say? Can we count on you and your fine staff to help us out, so that we can recover some money for the injured children?"

He takes my business card and thinks about it. "Well, I guess that finding out who tried to break our security rules would be a reasonable extension of our duties here. Let me talk to the staff. I think I can work it out... and it'll help the children, right?"

It worked like a charm. Not only did he agree to go along with the plan, but as my business card indicates, I am now officially 'Archibald Goodwin, private investigator,' under the supervision of one 'N. Wolfe.'

I go through the same procedure at the rest of the banks picked out as likely targets and wait for a phone call from one of the building security chiefs. Just in case some good info comes in, I have the office prepare an envelope containing a thousand dollars in C-notes.

They're going to strike again and we want to be ready. After their next job we may know who some of the players are, so that we can stake them out and follow them to another job. This is really a job for the authorities but they would never believe me if I brought this story in, so I'll just have to do their job for them.

This is exciting for several reasons. First, I may get some information as to how the Drago and Blitzstien cases are connected. Second, as Archie Goodwin, I may actually solve a crime and break up a bank robbery gang – and third, there's a ten percent reward out for information leading to the arrest and conviction of this gang, so if my plan works I'm in line for a nice payday. They've already stolen several hundred thousand dollars, so by the time I catch them my bounty should be enough for a new yellow Hummer... that is, minus the kid's cut.

After a couple of days go by I start to get antsy. Harold's trial date is coming up sooner than I'd like and there have been no calls from the lobby brigade. My waiting ends. The early afternoon local news show reports that another bank has been robbed. It was on our list of possible targets.

Sure enough, the answering service we hired specifically to receive calls for Archie Goodwin lets us know that a message came in. It's from the security chief of the building where the most recent bank robbery took place, and he's got the whole package for us – license plate, description and her destination.

I grab the envelope of cash and drive over to the building. By the time I get there, it's crawling with cops and feds. My old friend Special Agent Snell is there. Not wanting to blow my 'Archie Goodwin' cover, I wait until he's busy in the bank before I approach the security chief.

"Chief, I understand you have something for me."

He smiles. "Sure do Mister Goodwin, do you have something for me?"

I take the envelope out of my pocket and hand it to him. He tells me to wait a minute while he goes to his office for my package. I'm sure that being in the security business he wants to count the money first. When he returns to the lobby, he hands me an envelope. I have one more request. "Chief, do you mind if I ask the member of your staff a question about the lady?"

Not surprisingly, I'm told that he didn't want to trust the assignment to anyone, so he did it himself. "Wow chief, that's some job you did. Let me ask you, did she go right to her car and then drive home?" His answer confirms my suspicions.

"Not really Goodwin. She walked the dog back out to the car and then drove around the block a couple of times. After each time around the block, another guy got in her van, from a different part of the block."

I praise him again for the fine job he did, thank him and leave. What a great security chief he is. He follows the lady, sees her pick up all the members of the gang who just robbed his building's bank, and he doesn't have a clue. All he knows is that he's got a grand in his desk, and he's happy. I don't want to push him too far about whether or not any of her passengers were carrying any bags, because there's a possibility that his ignorance actually has a bottom limit and I don't want to stir him into any action that's beyond his capabilities. The heavy lifting on this case should be left to my new organization – Goodwin & Wolfe. Wait 'till I get back to the boat and tell Wolfe about the results – I'm sure he'll drool with anticipation.

That thousand dollars was well spent because it confirmed my suspicions about the dog act being a diversion. Information on the dog lady's vehicle shows that it's registered to a man who lives at the address where she ended her trip that afternoon. This means that I've actually located the gang's hideout. I'm starting to feel a little like Elliot Ness. I know who the players are and where they start out and end their jobs, but I have absolutely no experience in what to do next.

The easiest thing for me to do would be to call the Feds and let Snell and his boys bust down their door. They'd probably find the stolen money, but that would leave me out of the action completely and that's unsatisfactory. I've broken this case with real detecting and brainwork and nobody's going to steal my perps from me.

What I want to do now is figure out some way that I can bring this gang's career to an end. I want to be able to catch them in the act of robbing a bank. I want to be able to put on my cape and be Captain Crimefighter. I want to have my head examined. Am I crazy? This is insane, trying to bust up a robbery gang. I could get killed. These people have guns. There's got to be a safer way for me to play the hero.

Actually, I think this whole stupid gangbuster urge is probably just to impress Myra. I have no doubt that she'll be the next district attorney of this county and I don't want to just be 'the guy who used to be married to the D.A.' If I can pull this off, maybe I can get back some of the respect she used to have for me. Who knows?

After about an hour of serious conference time with my canine partner 'N. Wolfe,' he decides to slurp some water from his bowl and take a nap. It's so hard to find good associates. However, we did manage to come up with a plan.

With the help of some other members of our staff, we can stake out the gang's house and follow them to their next job. If things go according to schedule, the dog lady will probably do her exit strategy in reverse. If I was planning it, I'd go around the bank building's block a couple of times, dropping off the 'inside' guys at different places. Then I'd pull into the parking lot and casually walk the dog towards the lobby, keeping my eyes on the bank's doors that exit to the lobby.

If that's the way it's done, then once she starts to circle the bank building, we'll have from five to ten minutes to get in place – whatever that means.

The other problem is that I haven't figured out how they get the money out. A light bulb just went off over my head. In excitement, I scream out a yell of success that wakes my associate. When he decides to approach me, I tell him how it's going to go down.

First, with the help of the four Asian boys, Jack Bibberman, Vinnie, and Stuart, we stake out their house. This doesn't have to be an around-the-clock operation because all the jobs they've pulled so far were in the afternoon. They usually wait at least a week in between jobs, so all we have to do is post someone down the street from the house starting at noon every bank day, starting in about four days.

As soon as they're on the move together with the men and the dog all in the van, we'll have our stakeout person call us and then start to follow them. We'll do it like the real cops, with at least two vehicles on their tail: one a private car and the other a taxicab. Someone being followed might notice a car on their rear for a while, but taxicabs are almost invisible – they disappear into the street scene.

We'll keep in constant cell-phone communication with the tailing vehicles so that we can be waiting at the location of their intended job. When the van starts to circle the block, we'll get inside and post surveillance at the bank exit leading to the lobby. One of our team will wear a bright print Hawaiian shirt, a pair of Bermuda shorts with street shoes with black socks and have a camera hanging around his neck. This will be one of the Asian boys and he'll look like a typical Asian tourist. His job will be to pretend like he's shooting some video of his wife, one of the waitresses recruited from the Chinese

169

restaurant. This will give us a good record of the gang exiting the bank, and hopefully we'll see what happens to the money.

My job will be to talk to the Chief of the building's security. No doubt he's one of the guys I've already talked to, so he'll know who I am. This time I'll tell him the truth, which is that I'm working in conjunction with Senior Special Agent Robert Snell of the FBI's bank robbery task force. That's not too far off. I intend to turn everyone over to him. I'll tell him the real truth about what's going down at his bank. If he doubts me, I'll show him copies of the dog incident reports from the other lobby guards. I'm sure that in less than sixty seconds I'll have him convinced to join the program.

Our vehicle team will verify that they've still got the same license plates on the van because that will be crucial when we call the feds.

Just to play safe, I have Vinnie call two of the huge guys who used to work security for him when he was shooting porno movies. It's always nice to have a little muscle around. I'm especially happy to find out that they are actually reserve deputy sheriffs, which means they can legally carry guns. I'm not planning on turning the lobby into the OK Corral, but it's always nice to play it safe. To cut down on expenses, the porno security guys are placed on call and told to be ready to meet us wherever we say, with only five minute's notice.

We're all set. The next few days go by with about seven false alarms. Every time the dog lady leaves the house to go shopping or have her hair done, we get a call that she's on the move. Everyone is jumpy because we know it's just a matter of time before the real thing starts to happen. And then it does. On the fifth day of waiting, we get a call that the whole gang is in the van and they're on the move.

Everyone springs into action. The porno security guards are called. They get into their vehicle and get ready to meet us. Our Asian tourist and his wife are part of the vehicle team trailing the van that day, so they'll have time to get inside the lobby while the van is still circling the building.

The reports are that they're now approaching a bank building on Wilshire Boulevard and starting to circle the block. This is great. It's less than a mile from Snell's office in the Federal Building.

We tell our reserve sheriffs where to meet us. Their main assignment is to guard the Asian tourist and his wife, just in case anything goes wrong.

I speed over to the bank building and run into the lobby, straight to the security chief's office. Just as planned, he's on the same page as us in less than a minute. At this point, we haven't notified anyone in the bank. No need to cause a panic.

A quick look in the lobby shows that everyone is in place. The Asian tourist is videotaping his wife. Our huge sheriffs are standing by – one by the husband with the camera and the other by the wife. I take a position by the doors leading to the parking lot, so I can give the security chief a heads-up as to when the lady and the dog are approaching. I look over through the glass doors leading to the bank and everything looks normal. The robbery is probably already in progress.

Looking through the lobby's glass doors I see the lady with the dog. She's paused on the steps outside the lobby with a cell phone to her ear, obviously waiting for her signal to start the show. I signal our crew in the lobby that it's about to go down.

Just as planned, the lady and the dog enter the lobby. At this point, I don't want to be in that group of people who have their attention diverted by her action, so I walk over to the doors leading to the bank. Behind me, I hear the dog barking. Everyone turns around but the Asian tourist and me. Even our girl playing the wife looks over in that direction. Like true soldiers, our two sheriffs don't take their eyes off of their wards. I see two men walking casually from the bank towards the lobby. They're both wearing large sunglasses. As they come through the doors, I turn away and look towards the dog act, so as not to be too obvious. Our Asian tourist pretends to be looking toward the dog act, but all the while keeps the camera pointed at the bank's exit door.

The sheriffs look at me for some signal, but I let them know to stay cool and let the guys with the guns go by. And then it happens. I'm standing near a large glass window and I see a reflection of what's happening. Both robbers take off their sunglasses and along with the bank loot, toss them into a large garbage receptacle near the door. They then continue through the lobby, separating into two directions, each toward a different street exit.

I've already pre-programmed Snell's number on my cell-phone's speed dial, so I call his office with an urgent message and get right through to him. "Agent Snell, this is attorney Peter Sharp. I thought you might like to know that a bank has just been robbed down the street from your office." He gulps.

"What bank? We haven't gotten any silent alarms from anywhere."

Finally I get my chance to play the hero. I give him the bank location, the license plate and description of the van and the address where he can pick them up. I don't even get a thank you. He probably thinks I'm part of the gang. The Feds are all paranoid – it's part of their training.

The bank robbery is complete. In accordance with our instructions, everyone stays in position. We've got another couple of minutes before the whole gang is in the van. Just then, to my great surprise, here comes a maintenance man, complete with gray striped jumpsuit and some large embroidered patch on his back. He's carrying a large empty plastic garbage bag and just like every other maintenance man in the world, he walks over to the receptacle where the gang dumped their sunglasses and money, pulls out the trash liner and replaces it with a new one. He then starts towards the other side of the lobby. I signal everyone to stay in place.

The maintenance man goes all the way to the rear exit and walks out of the lobby towards the parking lot. He's probably the last one that the dog-lady picks up after she's gone around the block several times and picked up the other gang members.

Agent Snell and his gang run into the building. He sees me and comes over. I look at him and in true old-style western movie drawl, point and tell him "they went that-a-way." By the look on his face, I can tell that he's making his mind up whether to shoot me or thank me. Fortunately for me, he signals his men to go outside after the van.

Also according to plan, the press has been contacted and I'm ready to make my announcement on the steps outside the bank. This wasn't arranged just to satisfy my ego, it's sort of an insurance policy so the Feds don't take all the credit and cut my gang out of the reward.

Many years ago I learned the hard way that you get more bees with honey than with vinegar, and now is a good time to use that knowledge. There will be numerous press conferences and interviews with Special Agent Snell and I don't want to put him into a position where he's forced to give me all the credit. I'm not looking for credit – all I want is the reward money, so I think that the best way to go is to make it easy for the authorities to appreciate what I've done. I've also learned that if you want someone in the public eye to be on your side, all you have to do is praise them – and that's exactly what I intend to do. Once you've publicly said how great someone is, you make it very difficult for him to then try to destroy your credibility. It's showtime. Here goes... the cameras are on me.

"Ladies and gentlemen, before we get into any details of the robbery and how the gang was caught, I'd like everyone to know the great respect I have for the Bureau's Special Agent Robert Snell and his task force. When I called them for help, they came out in full force and did their jobs professionally. The bank robbery gang is now in custody and I have every hope that much of their loot from the last few robberies will also be recovered at their hideout."

The feeding frenzy starts. Most of the questions they shout out ask why I'm here at all making a statement.

"The reason that I'm here today is that the FBI, because of regulatory and budget restrictions, can't do all the things that a private citizen can do. And they shouldn't. In this case, my law firm happens to be representing a bank against a slip-and-fall victim. The bank was robbed later that day. I'm also representing a person who is charged with murdering that slip-and-fall victim. Because of the possible links between these two cases and the robberies, and with the cooperation of Agent Snell and the local authorities, I organized a group of my associates and we set a trap for the robbers. Our plan could only go so far because we have no training or authority to arrest people, so Agent Snell had to come in and pull our bacon out of the fire – and we can't thank him enough for that."

If I wanted to, I could probably stand there for another couple of hours and the questions would still come in fast and furious. Agent Snell's trained eye notices the cameras and if there's anyone that the FBI won't let escape, it's a curious news reporter. I see him walking toward us and decide to give him a fanfare. "And here he comes now ladies and gentlemen, the hero of today's events, FBI Senior Special Agent Robert Snell." I step back and let him walk into the spotlight of attention. While he's making his own self-serving statement, I take the opportunity to gather my crew so we can get the hell out of here.

18

Back at the boat the champagne is flowing. To be truthful, it's not really champagne, but we're treating our wine coolers like they're the expensive bubbly stuff. The kid made arrangements for the 'wrap' party, but she had difficulty convincing the guy at the liquor store that she was twenty-one, probably because she couldn't see over the counter. So, we're drinking coolers, from Laverne's boxed wine collection. I'm sure she'll be looking for her pound of flesh as repayment later tonight... and I always pay my debts.

As promised, whatever reward comes in will be split up between everyone. Being the brains of our coalition forces, our firm will take the usual lawyer's thirty percent and the rest will be divided evenly between everyone else. According to the newspapers, the robbery gang averaged almost three hundred thousand from each of the five jobs, making the total somewhere in the neighborhood of a million and a half. If the reward is ten percent, our group will be cutting up one hundred fifty thousand, and my third should get me the yellow Hummer that Budget Rent-a-Car is now trying to get rid of.

We turn on the evening news and see ourselves on camera. The story is not only on the local news, it makes the network broadcasts too. The wonderful saga about a group of civilians helping the FBI break up a bank robbery gang is just too juicy an item for them to ignore. And we see that my strategy paid off. Whenever Agent Snell is interviewed, he's always asked about the contribution that the concerned citizens made to help him break the case and true to my plan, he answers "Yes, they did a fine job of surveillance and putting things together for us – things that our budget wouldn't allow us to do. We owe them a debt of gratitude for giving us the information that led to the arrest of this gang." Those remarks of his are also probably intended to help the FBI's next budget request.

The party starts to wind down after an hour or so, and before going to Laverne's houseboat to pay my debt, I can't help but ask myself what we really accomplished today. Sure, the bank robbery gang was caught and we've got some reward money coming, but does it really help me out with my questions about the Drago and Blitzstien cases? Not by a long shot. I still think that everything's tied together and solving the robberies is just the first step in completing the whole puzzle.

There's nothing like the bright southern California sunshine to clear your head and let you face the new day with a new outlook. As usual, Laverne left early in the morning and I'm now finishing the greasy French toast she left out for me. Today I plan on looking at the security tapes from the hospital again. Maybe there's something I missed. I intend to view all the tapes - not just the one cassette with the murder on it.

After hours and hours of viewing the tapes, I finally see something that probably is just a defect on the tape, but just to make sure, I call the lab and tell them the frame I'd like an enlargement of.

Modern technology is great. In the old days, which in technospeak is about three years ago, to get the enlargement I want would take up to a week, taking the process and mails into consideration. Now, the picture is waiting for me in my incoming email folder and the kid's photo-quality printer will have it ready for me in about fifteen seconds.

Looking at the picture, I see something I absolutely cannot figure out. The shot depicts Harold with his back to the camera standing next to Drago's bed, which has a privacy curtain blocking any view from the room's open door. This point in time is before Harold used the pillow to smother Drago. What catches my attention is something in the hallway, low down near the floor. It's slightly blurred but I'm amazed at what I think it is. It looks like the white tip of something furry – like a tail.

I have to sit down for a minute. This can't be what I think it is because they don't allow animals in the hospital... or do they? Just to satisfy my curiosity, I press the button on our electric can opener – the one that's used every day to open the large can of dog food that my associate eats. Hearing the whirr of the can opener brings the Saint Bernard running from the forward stateroom and I have a chance to see his tail. The rear portion of it is white.

Not wanting to see a look of disappoint on that huge face of his, I toss him a dog biscuit. He's been paid for his trip, so he retreats. I sit down with my head in my hands. I know that the kid does her dog act at the hospital, and I also know that the children's ward is on the same floor that Drago got killed. Does this mean that the kid and the dog walked by Drago's room while the murderer was in there? It's possible, if that's the dog's tail. And anywhere that the dog was, the kid was too.

I have to get some facts in order, so I call Jack Bibberman and tell him to check with the hospital for the exact days and hours that Suzi was at the hospital doing her volunteer turn at the various wards there. I know that if I try to speak to her, the conversation on her part will probably be extremely brief, so I want to know what I'm talking about before trying to ask her any questions.

It took Jack B. only two hours to get the requested info together and just as I suspected, the timeline fits. The dog was on Drago's floor at the time of the murder. Does this do me any good? I really don't want to get the kid involved in this case, especially because she's not a truly independent witness – counsel for the defense is her legal guardian.

Putting Suzi on the witness stand would also be a terrible situation for Myra, who would then be forced to aggressively cross-examine her and try to destroy the credibility of a little girl she's really fond of.

Even if she did walk by the room while Harold was in there, I can't imagine anything she could have seen that could possibly help me with this case. Even though the door to Drago's room was open, Harold did his smothering work behind a privacy curtain so that whatever he was doing

179

wouldn't be visible to someone walking by out in the hall. There was no window next to Drago's bed, so Harold's actions didn't form any visible silhouette on the curtain.

I'm going to leave this alone. It was a pure fluke that I happened to notice the tip of what I'm sure is the dog's tail in that picture. Anyone else looking at the footage probably wouldn't spot it - and even if they did, they'd never be able to figure out what it was. Case closed. She's not being brought into this.

All this does is leave me with more questions than answers and Harold's trial is coming up soon. I still have absolutely no strategy for his defense but I've got to keep working on the case, so I figure that another visit to him couldn't hurt.

Harold looks worse than ever as he walks into the jail's interview room. He looks at me with an angry glare. "You caught those bank robbers, huh?"

"I did have something to do with it, but the FBI made the arrests. All I did was point them in the right direction."

Strangely enough, this looks like the start of our first real conversation. He's finally talking to me but unfortunately it's not about his case.

"You gonna get a reward for that?"

That's strange – his asking me about a reward. I'm starting to sense some other agenda on his mind, so I let him go on. "You think you got the whole gang of 'em?"

"Yes Harold, it looks that way. They were all arrested together in a van shortly after finishing their last job. From what I see on the news, the feds found bags stuffed with money from all the other jobs when searching the house they all worked out of."

"You didn't tell me if you're gonna get a reward."

"I don't know for sure. Usually in cases like this they pay something to people who help get their money back, but it remains to be seen if I'll actually get anything out of it. I had a group of about seven people working on that case with me, so even if there is a reward, it'll be cut up a lot of ways."

He goes silent again, obviously thinking about something. Then he starts to question me again. "You think they'll pay more money for information about others in the gang that ain't been caught yet?"

So that's what it is. He's had his ears open while he's been here in jail and must have heard some other inmates talking. As cold as it will sound, I have to ask the question. "Harold, let's face the facts here. You've already admitted to me that you killed Drago. I even had to fight to get you to not plead guilty at the first arraignment. What's the difference if they'll pay more money for information on other gang members or not, you'll have no need for any reward money – you'll be in prison.

"Yeah, but my ex-wife and kids won't, and they can use the money."

Come to think of it, I remember that when the background checks came in on him and Drago, there was some mention of him having a family somewhere. "Where are they Harold?"

"They live in the high desert – between Palmdale and Lancaster."

I get his family's address and tell him that I'll look further into whether there's any more reward money to be had. He looks weak as he leaves the interview room. He's a cold-blooded killer, but I still feel sorry for him.

Back at the boat, I call Agent Snell's West Los Angeles FBI office and ask him about additional reward money for members of the gang not yet caught. He tells me that there is some more money available. They have an arrangement whereby the banks authorize them to pay out reward money on either a 'head count' or 'dollars recovered' basis. We're already entitled to a pretty nice sum on the dollars recovered and now I learn that we can also collect on the head count basis for other members of the gang, but there's a string attached. In order for someone to collect on gang members still at large, there must be proof that they also participated in the robberies that took place. Just being members of the gang who might pull off new jobs doesn't qualify for reward money.

I now know the rules but I don't know how it'll help Harold in any way. Even if he gives me some information on the names of remaining gang members, I'm not going to spend a great deal of time and money putting together another master plan. I try to limit my hero playing to just once a year. Another reason I'm not inclined to get involved further is that if I decide to continue doing criminal defense work, it wouldn't help my image to be looked at as the guy who sends people to jail, instead of getting them out.

I write a nice letter to Harold telling him that yes, there is more reward money available and that the best way to go would be for him to convey his information to the Feds and let them know that any reward is to be paid directly to his family.

Next time I visit with Harold he tells me that my idea stinks. First of all, he doesn't want to be labeled as a 'snitch.' That can be very dangerous for a person serving time. Second, he doesn't trust the authorities to pay the reward money out to his family... he wants me to do it. I tell him that I'll think about it, but I can't do anything about it until after his trial is over. He's not too happy to hear this but that's too bad. I've got to keep my priorities in order. First things first.

Only two days until Harold's trial. I call the autopsy place to find out what's holding things up. Victor Gutierrez, the main guy there, tells me that they had to re-schedule it twice because Myra's coroner guy kept canceling out due to prior commitments. I tell him that the trial is in two days and I've got to have the information, so he should go ahead with it immediately. They've already got Drago's body there, so it shouldn't take too long. I get a message off to Myra letting her know that her guy flaked out on us twice and that the autopsy's going on with or without him. She understands that anything she does to prolong this post-mortem might make her look like she's interfering with the defendant's right to a speedy trial, so she backs off and tells me to go ahead with it.

I spent yesterday and today preparing what will be done in vain – a closing argument. Fortunately there won't be any jury in this case, so my embarrassment will be limited only to the people in the courtroom. The trial will go on tomorrow, as scheduled and I feel like a guy being walked to the gallows. The phone rings. My caller ID display shows 18002886779, which I recognize as the numeric equivalent of the Autopsy place, so I know who's calling. I grab the phone "Yeah, Peter Sharp here, what have you got for me?"

It's Victor Gutierrez, the autopsy place's supervisor. "Hello Mister Sharp, it's Victor here, at one eight hundred autopsy."

"I know that Victor – have you got the results yet on Drago?"

"Yes we do, Mister Sharp." He stops talking.

"Well, what is this, a quiz game? What have you got? What's the official cause of death? Asphyxiation?"

"Not exactly."

"Not exactly? What are you telling me, that he wasn't smothered to death by a pillow?"

"That's what I said Mister Sharp, he died of natural causes."

19

Impossible. "Are you crazy Victor? I've got video footage that shows the murder actually taking place. Drago was lying in the hospital bed when my client smothered him to death with a pillow."

"Well Mister Sharp, maybe someone pushed a pillow down on his face while he was laying in the bed, but the guy was smothering a dead man."

I have to stop for a minute. This is too much for me. My mind is racing. Could Harold be innocent of the murder? I don't realize how long I'm quiet while Victor is waiting on the line.

"Mister Sharp, you still there?"

He shakes me back to the reality of our conversation. "Okay Victor, tell me what you think the actual cause of death was."

"Mister Sharp, the deceased's death was as a result of internal hemorrhaging, caused by a broken rib that punctured an arterial wall. The rib looks like it was broken shortly before his death, and there was constant internal bleeding that went undiagnosed. He finally died from his injuries before anyone pushed a pillow down on his face."

"You're serious about this?"

"Mister Sharp, we don't joke about death... it's our bread and butter."

I'll give him the benefit of the doubt and believe that he's serious when he says that. I don't know where to start, but I've still got some unanswered questions. "Victor, do you have any idea how long he was dead before the pillow incident?"

"There's really no way to tell, but it must have been less than a minute before the guy tried to smother him."

"How the hell can you be so sure about such a short period of time?"

"Simple. He was hooked up to a monitoring device that sent a signal to the nurses' station. As soon as his heart stopped, the device sent a flat-line signal and the rescue team ran into the room. It couldn't have been more than a minute, because they started resuscitation procedures. If there was someone working him over with a pillow, he must have almost bumped into the medical team as they ran into the room."

He's right about that. Harold hid behind a screen, making his exit after the team was busy working on Drago. "Victor, the trial starts tomorrow. As we've already arranged, I want you on one-hour call, so when my defense case gets started, so you can be there with your report. Got it?"

"Yes sir, Mister Sharp. I'll be there. I just want to remind you that the witness fee isn't included in the autopsy price."

"Yeah Victor, I know – there's no free lunch."

This is coming together too fast for me. So many thoughts are racing through my mind, but strangely enough the one that seems uppermost is that if I beat Myra on this case, we're having dinner at the Lahaina Yacht Club and I'll be back in the saddle again.

Boy, what a dog I am to be thinking of nailing Myra again, while I'm getting ready to go in on a capital murder case. Okay, back to business. There are some downsides to this too. In order to get her into the sack in Hawaii, I've got to destroy her in court, which will mean that by losing what looked like a slam-dunk case, she'll probably have no chance of getting elected as District Attorney. That won't make her happy and will probably turn our romantic weekend in Hawaii into a replay of our last couple of days cohabiting - just before she finally threw me out.

It looks like the only winner in this whole situation is a guy who can't even murder someone in a timely fashion – Harold Blitzstien.

The bailiff calls the court to order and Judge Axelrod takes the bench. Once the case is called we each stand up and state our name and representation for the record. There are only a few members of the press sitting in the spectator seats. Myra seems very relaxed because she still thinks she's going to win. She's got a copy of the autopsy report because I told Victor to fax it to her, but she probably didn't even take the time to read it. Why should she? She's still positive that Harold did it. Myra starts her opening statement. "Your Honor, the People intend to show that the Defendant entered the victim's hospital room and smothered him to death with a pillow. This fact will be proven beyond a reasonable doubt by the introduction of videotape evidence that shows the defendant committing the crime." She sits down. That was probably the shortest opening statement on a murder case in history. Now it's my turn, and I hope that the paramedics are nearby because what I have to say may put Myra into shock. I'm not worried about how it'll affect Harold because he's sitting here like a zombie.

I stand up. "Your Honor, we intend to introduce evidence to the fact that the deceased died from natural causes as the result of a slip-and-fall accident that occurred a day earlier than the incident which is the subject matter of this trial. The

Defendant, Harold Blitzstien, did in fact attempt to murder the deceased, but his efforts were wasted on a man who was already dead." I sit down.

This statement is the shortest opening I've ever given, but it had the most impact. The judge is staring down at me with one of those 'are you kidding?' looks on his face.

Harold comes out of his trance with a questioning expression on his face. The few reporters in the room jump up and run out to the hallway, dialing on their cell phones as they run. Myra sits there silently looking at me, in a state of disbelief.

The judge breaks the silence. "Mister Sharp, in your opening statement, you alluded to the fact that you would be introducing evidence to support your contentions. Have you informed the prosecution about this?"

"Yes I have, Your Honor. The evidence is in an autopsy report that was faxed to her office yesterday. We have the person who did the autopsy and prepared the report on one-hour call. If you'd like him here, we can page him."

Myra is in the first stages of becoming ballistic. "Your Honor, we strongly object to this new evidence. It just came in to our office yesterday, less than twenty-four hours before the trial. We've had no opportunity to have our medical examiner go over it. We'll have to ask for..."

I cut her off mid-sentence. "Your Honor, the private autopsy that was agreed to by the People was re-scheduled several times because the People's representative kept canceling out. When it appeared that no one from their side was going to show up, we couldn't wait any longer and notified them that due to the rapidly approaching trial date, we had no other choice but to proceed without them."

Myra starts to argue again for a continuance, but the judge won't have any of it. "Counsel, it looks like you're both a little right. I'm going to put this matter over until tomorrow morning to give the district attorney's coroner a chance to look over the results of that report. The People will take a couple of days to put on their case, so it won't be until next week when you start your defense and call the autopsy guy to the stand. By that time, if the People want, they can have the body examined in their own facility to confirm or deny your results." With that, he bangs his gavel, says "see you tomorrow morning at nine," and heads for the golf course.

The reporters who ran out into the hall come back into the courtroom and are informed by the clerk that life continued, even without them there, and that the case has been put over until tomorrow morning at nine, at which time I'll bet there isn't an empty seat in the room. Too much is riding on this case for the press to leave it alone. A slam-dunk case might get snatched right out from under the nose of the county's most popular prosecutor, whose chance for election as District Attorney is now in jeopardy - all of this being brought about by her ex-husband. This is definitely screenplay material. Too bad Spencer Tracy and Katherine Hepburn aren't around to play our parts.

The vultures are gathering in the hallway outside the courtroom. The reporters present all probably called for backup, so the camera crews are waiting for us as we step out of the room. Both of us make the same decision to avoid the press, so like running backs, we push our way through the news crews, make it to the exit door and hurry to our respective cars.

That night the story leads on all the local news shows and also gets mentioned on the network broadcasts. They can't seem to let go of the fact that Myra and I were once married and now they say that I'm out to destroy her. They keep reminding the viewing public that Myra isn't the only celebrity in the courtroom – they point out that I was the one who single-handedly broke up a big bank robbery gang. I'm sure my coalition forces get a kick out of hearing how I did it all by myself.

This may be good for Harold, but it certainly isn't doing Myra any good. And since she's friendly with the kid, I'm cooking for myself this week because the kid's mad that I'm going to make Myra lose. Gee, maybe she doesn't notice that if Myra loses, I win. Goes to show you how the loyalties go. Those females sure stick together.

The phone is ringing constantly, so I shut off the ringer. No sense in answering. If they want me on *Nightline*, they'll have to arrange it by email.

Just to make sure I'm not dreaming, I call Victor at the autopsy place and we spend about an hour going over what I'll be asking him and what Myra will probably do to try to discredit his report. He stands by his autopsy results and assures me that any competent medical examiner would make the same findings.

The thing that bothers me is the timing. Everyone knows that Harold was in the room at about the same time that Drago died, but how do I go about convincing the court which event came first, the death by natural causes or the smothering? They both must have happened at almost the same point in time, maybe just seconds apart. This is starting to look like what the racetrack calls a photo finish. I wish there could be some instant replay. Wait a minute, there is… the videotapes.

I've seen that five minutes of tape so many times, it's permanently etched in my memory. It doesn't help at all. If I'm going to win this case, I've got to figure out some way to combat Myra's argument, which will probably be that if the report shows smothering wasn't the cause of death, that the forcible use of the pillow caused the broken ribs to pierce the blood vessels and bring about the hemorrhaging that caused the death. If she's successful with that argument, then it's all over. Harold goes down for the murder.

Contrary to common belief, judges are human too. I have to admit that if it was me sitting up there on the bench hearing this case, and I saw a defendant try to smother a guy with a pillow, I might be inclined to believe that the death was caused by the defendant's acts. All the laws say that you're supposed to give the defendant the benefit of the doubt, but the margin of doubt in these facts is so slim that it's almost invisible. I'd like to think that we have a chance, but all that the autopsy did was give me something to argue about that I didn't have before.

This morning the crowded courtroom looks like a place where they're giving away free money. If I weren't such a well-known crime-busting attorney, I probably wouldn't have gotten through security and into the courtroom. Reporters are here from every station, both local and network. They all sense that this is going to be a battle of arguments between the attorneys. To make things easier for all of us, Myra and I go into chambers before the trial starts and we both stipulate to the admitting into evidence of the videotape and autopsy report. That will save about a day of trial and eliminate the necessity of qualifying the witnesses, establishing a continuous evidence chain of custody, direct examinations, cross-examinations, etc.

I can't get over how terrible Harold looks. When he's led into the courtroom he sits down at the counsel table and with eyes closed, bows his head as if he intends to sleep through the trial. He must have nerves of steel.

Once the judge takes the bench the show begins. Myra bases her entire case on the videotape evidence that shows Harold pushing that pillow down on Drago's face. Copies of the tape were made and sold to the press by some hospital employee, so the public has already made their mind up. It's a good thing this isn't a jury case because it would have been impossible to get a jury of twelve people who haven't seen the murder over and over again on television. To get a fair panel, you'd have to find a dozen Al Qaeda members who've spent the last month in a cave somewhere without a television set.

Myra calls only one witness, the Coroner of Los Angeles County. I know exactly what he's going to say and he doesn't disappoint me. Notwithstanding the fact there's no apparent sign of asphyxiation having caused the death, it's his expert opinion that the decedent's hemorrhaging was brought about as a direct result of the defendant's exerting force upon the decedent's body.

No surprise there. He's sticking to the prosecution's contention that Harold is guilty. His argument is so convincing that I'm almost starting to believe him. I don't even waste the energy to ask him any questions on cross-examination, other than just one: "Doctor, is it possible that Drago was dead before the defendant put the pillow on his face." He tries to wriggle out of it, but I finally pin him down to a 'yes' or 'no' situation, and he agrees with me that it is in fact possible.

This case has been like a roller coaster ride for me up to now. From not having anything at all to work with, to having a favorable autopsy report, to having my report torn apart by a credible witness with a believable argument. I wish there was some way I could get off of square one.

After the doctor strikes his dagger into my case, Myra decides to leave it in and twist it a little. Not only does she have a fifty-inch flat screen plasma display television screen rolled into the courtroom, she's also brought with her a high-end video deck that will play the crucial footage in slower than slow motion. She's going to show it one frame at a time.

Myra is going to make this look like a slide show presentation being made to capture a new advertising account. As the frames go by and the action jerkily moves on the screen, Myra is doing her voice-over description, like a play-by-play sports announcer.

The footage she chose was the very short section that shows Harold lowering the pillow down onto Drago's face and then lifting it up and moving away from the bed.

I've got the still photo enlargements we had made sitting in front of me on the counsel table, complete with dog drool marks on one of the photos. To keep my mind off of the fact that I'm being destroyed, I concentrate on the small portion of one photo that the dog ruined for me. In another couple of seconds, it will be appearing on the screen. Here it is now. I see the portion of the screen that shows something that I didn't notice before because it was marked by the dog. I jump up in my seat and do something I've never done before in my entire twenty-plus years of trial work. I shout "Whoa" out loud.

Every eye in the courtroom is on me. I'm so embarrassed, I wish there was some small portion of the carpet to crawl under. I don't know what happened to me – it just came out of my mouth. As I heard the exclamation, I was saying to myself "what idiot just shouted that out?"

The thing that shocks me out of my senses is a portion of the screen that shows a monitoring device over the bed. I run over to the display and write down the exact frame that's on the screen and then apologize to the court. It doesn't matter what I say. Everyone in the courtroom thinks I'm crazy, but at this point I can't care less. I think I've just won the case. I return to my seat and let Myra continue.

Every member of the press is surprised by my actions but they know me well enough to realize that whatever it is that causes me to react like this must be important.

Myra finishes her presentation and the prosecution rests. It's my turn now and I intend to put the video on cross-examination.

I address the court. "Your Honor, we can now prove beyond any reasonable doubt that Harold Blitzstien is not guilty of the crime with which he has been charged."

At this point, the reporters are scribbling notes feverishly. I take a pause. I don't want them to miss one precious word of what I'm going to say.

"Your Honor, we would like to have the video person freeze a portion of the tape that the People admitted into evidence... more particularly this frame." I hand my scribbled note to the techie, who proceeds to bring up that frame. When it's on the screen, I continue. "As shown by the prosecution, this exact frame of the video is prior to the attempted smothering of Mister Drago. The pillow is being lowered onto his face, but has not touched his body yet. Myra jumps up to make an objection. "Your Honor, we've gone over all of this before. If defense wants to..." The judge cuts her off with a quick wave of his hand and overrules her. He signals for me to continue. Good. Not only have I got every reporter in the room sitting on the edge of his seat, I've got the judge captured too. Now it's time to 'thrust ho.' "We would ask the court to take notice of one particular portion of the upper left corner of the screen."

Pointing to the corner of the screen I want him to concentrate on, I go on. "Your Honor, this device is an electronic monitor that detects the heartbeat of the patient and sends it to the nurse's station, down the hospital corridor. As you can see, at the exact time that the defendant is lowering the pillow down towards Mister Drago's head, the monitoring device is showing that the heartbeat line is flat. This is an indication that Drago was dead at the time of the alleged pillow-smothering event. Rewinding the tape several frames will surely indicate that the alleged victim's lifeline must have gone flat a few seconds earlier.

"Furthermore, we would argue that if the computer print-out of the nurse's station is brought in as evidence and compared with the time-code on this exact video frame, we can establish beyond any reasonable doubt that Mister Drago was dead prior to the defendant's actions."

The courtroom erupts. All the reporters get up and run out of the room. The judge is banging his gavel demanding order in the courtroom, but he's hardly heard over the noise of the reporters shouting into their cell phones as they rush outside to reach the news vans to make satellite transmissions of this story to their stations.

With all the commotion going on, nobody notices poor Myra sitting there quietly. She knows she's been beat. I walk over to her table.

"Sorry kid, but it's right there on the screen. I had to do it."

"Yeah Peter, I know. You won fair and square. I've got no complaint. To be truthful, I wasn't even thinking about this case. I'm too busy thinking about my not-too rosy future as a lawyer."

"Whattaya mean, not too rosy? You're a great lawyer. I just got lucky, seeing that portion of the screen. You had me beat every which way up to that point. No one can fault you. They should be lining up the block to get you as their lawyer."

"Yeah, but it's not the clients I want lined up… it's the voters. I don't think I have a chance now."

"Listen to me. I'm going to make a promise to you. First, we're going to have dinner at the Lahaina Yacht Club in Hawaii. Then, I'm going to pull another ace out of my sleeve and get you elected to the office of District Attorney of Los Angeles County."

"And just how do you plan on doing that?"

"Never you mind, beautiful. You just go home and pack your bags for our trip to Maui next week. I'll take care of everything."

I turn back to the defense table. Harold is sitting there with his head still bowed. What a wonderful thing I've just done, getting a cold-blooded murderer off scot-free. I wonder who he'll kill for money next. I figure he might at least want to shake my hand, so I sit down next to him. "Harold, you're a free man now. I know what you tried to do. You tried to kill a man in cold blood. It didn't work. The angel of death beat you to it. I'm glad I won the case because as it turns out, you didn't really do it. But I want you to know that this hasn't been a nice experience for me, so I hope you're not too offended when I tell you not to waste your time expecting to thank me and shake my hand. I hope I never see you again." Having said that, I walk past him and bend down to pick up some of the boxes of paperwork I left under the counsel table. In doing so, I brush up against him. He slowly starts to lean over and then falls over onto the floor like a limp rag. He's dead.

20

He must have died some time during the trial, but because everyone was so wrapped up in my brilliant defense presentation, nobody noticed. I wait for the ambulance to come and take him away. The paramedics don't even try to revive him. They can spot a cadaver when they see one.

I sure would like to know what caused his death, but I shouldn't have to wait too long to find out because there's no way the county will avoid doing an autopsy on Harold, especially when he died in one of their courtrooms.

When the paramedics arrive, the press smell another story and they once again fill up the courtroom. When the judge isn't on the bench, the court isn't officially in session, so lights, flashbulbs, and video cameras all join in with the reporters.

They're so busy following the gurney out to the ambulance that they don't see Myra and I sneak out.

While we're walking out the rear courthouse exit completely unnoticed by the press, Myra asks me why I'm missing this opportunity to do one of my 'courthouse steps' performances. I let her know that in my mind there is no news here. The only purpose the local press serves is to make us aware of crime on the streets and to relay the hype that the advertisers and politicians want us to see. The only time I stage one of those outdoor performances is when I want to do the same thing that everyone else does – manipulate the news to my own advantage. This time I won and true justice lost. There's no need for a statement. It's over.

Now I'm really up the creek. Aside from the fact that I've just had an incredible victory in a criminal case, by proving that the slip-and-fall claimant died as a result of his accident in my client's bank, I also destroyed my insurance defense career at the same time,

There's no sense in trying to stall off telling Indovine – if he's watching television, he'll see how I elevated the bank's liability from a nuisance slip-and-fall situation into a loser of a wrongful death case. Thanks to my brilliance in the courtroom, instead of having a chance to settle for a thousand dollars, it will now cost the insurance company over a million. I'm also sure that Drago's attorney will be watching my demise on television tonight. This might mean a payday of several hundred thousand dollars for him. He owes me big time.

What a fine mess I've gotten myself into this time. Myra is destroyed, the kid is not happy, and my insurance defense career is over. There's a message on my answering machine telling me that email has come in for me. I'm so far down in the popularity department that the dog won't even deliver a message to me.

I check the email. Indovine's office would like me to submit my final timesheet. I've been fired. This is wonderful. Not only is my civil practice in the dumper, but ever since I busted the bank robbery gang, the criminals don't like me either.

Another message is waiting on my machine. It's the administrator at County Jail. They want me to come down there and pick up Harold's personal belongings. I pawn this chore off onto Jack Bibberman.

Amazing as it sounds, the County has decided not to perform an autopsy on Harold. The news broadcast says that he obviously died from the stress of the trial, and they're ruling it 'natural causes.' They don't believe that anything else could have been instrumental because he was sitting in open court.

This sucks. I really want to know what happened to him, so I call Victor the autopsy man and leave a message on his machine that I've got another assignment for him. I don't care if the office won't pay for this – it has to be done.

No more than five minutes pass by when my phone rings and I see it's 1-800-autopsy calling. "Hello, Victor?"

"Yes Mister Sharp, what can I do for you today?"

"I've got another assignment. As you've probably seen on the news, my client died in the courtroom and the county has decided not to perform an autopsy."

"You think there was foul play?"

"No Victor, I don't think there was any foul play, but I really would like to know what he died from. I may be talking to his wife and kids soon, and I want to be able to have some answers for them."

"Well Mister Sharp, I'd like to help you out, but our van is really busy this week. There was a bad freeway crash down in San Diego and our mobile lab was called down there to help out. Can this wait another week or two?"

"I don't think so. The county isn't in the body warehousing business and if I don't get Harold's body out of their morgue they may dispose of it, because nobody else has claimed it."

"Well maybe if you call a funeral home, you can get them to pick up the remains and bring it over here. They'll probably charge a couple of hundred but at least the body will be picked up for us."

"Okay Victor, I'll make some arrangements to get it over to your place tomorrow, so please clear some room for it."

After hanging up I make some calls to various funeral homes, only to learn that the only way they'll do a pick-up is if they get the funeral too. It's bad enough that I'll have to pay a couple of grand for the autopsy – I don't want to have to spring for another five thousand for a funeral too. If I'm lucky, the court's payment to me for handling Harold's case will probably give me just enough for the autopsy and some Myra jumping in Maui. I don't want to go into debt just to be a nice guy. There must be another way to get Harold to Victor's place.

Every once in a while, a brilliant thought comes along. Harold's body will easily fit in the back of Stuart's air-conditioned armored van. It's perfect for transporting a body. Now all I have to do is talk Stuart into having Vinnie do the heavy lifting. I dial Stuart's number and after a minute of small talk, I try to lead into the real reason for my call.

"Listen Stu, I was wondering if you and Vinnie could do me a small favor. I need a box picked up downtown and delivered out near Pasadena. Would that be possible? I'll be glad to pay fifty bucks for the driver's time."

"Sure Pete, I think that can be arranged. What's in the box? Nothing illegal, I hope."

I was afraid he'd ask about that. I don't want to lie to him but at the same time, I'd rather not let him know that I'm turning his beautiful armored van into a hearse. "Stu, I'd like to tell you but it might be a violation of the lawyer-client privilege, so if you don't mind, I'd rather not say anything until the case is over. Then, I'll tell you all about it."

He bit. "Okay my friend, I understand. I'll call Vinnie and tell him he's making a non-funeral run tomorrow morning. Email me the pick-up and delivery info and I'll get it done for you."

Great. And I didn't really have to lie to him, because I still am working on a case with Harold involved.

Next afternoon the phone rings and my display shows that it's Stuart calling. "Hello Stu, what's up?"

"Pete, you really should have told me what Vinnie was picking up for you."

"Why? What's the difference?"

"The difference is that if I would have known what it was, maybe Vinnie wouldn't be in jail now."

If I live to be a hundred, I'll never understand how a guy like Vinnie can manage to get thrown in jail so often. I haven't heard the story yet but I have a feeling that it'll be unbelievable. Per Stuart's request, I drive to the Valley Services Division of the Los Angeles Police Department in Van Nuys. When I get there, both Stuart and the station's watch commander, Lieutenant Evans, are waiting for me.

After explaining to Evans the whole story about how Vinnie was doing me a favor by delivering Harold's body from one morgue to another, he surprises me with a question. "Hey, aren't you the guys who broke up that bank robbery gang?" Fame is wonderful. The cop recognizes us.

"That's right Lieutenant and if I can get our crime-fighting partner out of your lockup, we can finish up working on this case."

"Will it be something going down here in the Valley?" He must smell a big bust in the offing.

"You never know, but I'll tell you what: if I have to call for back-up, you're the one I'll ask for. So start wearing your best uniform to work each day for the next week, because you'll want to look good for the television cameras."

He must have believed I was going to make a hero out of him, because less than five minutes later Vinnie was out in the lobby waiting for us – with his girlfriend Olive – and she was definitely not a happy camper. He tried desperately to explain to her what happened, but she wasn't having any of it. As soon as she was out of jail, she was out of there. I heard her calling for a cab on her cell phone as she walked right on past us and out of the building. Vinnie couldn't wait to tell his story, but first he wanted an apology from me. Stuart interceded and explained that it was some attorney-client privilege 'stuff,' so Vinnie backed off, deciding to tell me his story instead.

Olive always liked guys in uniform, so when Vinnie finally became one, she fell hard. And driving a big armored truck helped accentuate the attraction she felt for him. She kept pressing him to take her for a ride in the truck, but there never seemed to be a day off without a funeral until today – so he invited her to join him on his pickup and delivery. As Vinnie explains it, I struggle to keep a straight face. From what he tells me, it sounds like a foreign, Jacques Tati film.

Neither one of them knew what the cargo was, so they had a grand time chatting about their future and didn't pay any attention to the sheet-covered gurney that was being loaded into the back of the truck.

Along the way, they decide to stop off at a Burger Queen drive-thru place to get some cheeseburgers. Before getting to the fast food place, Olive asks Vinnie if he would please stop off at a gas station so she can take a leak. Not being anything like her boyfriend, she prefers toilets to trees. Vinnie, being so proud of the grand vehicle he's driving, tells her not to worry... the truck is equipped with it's own private toilet. All she has to do is go through the door behind the seats and make herself comfortable. Olive does as told, sees the port-a-potty and sits down to take her leak.

While she's sitting there minding her own business, she sees that directly in front of her is some sheet-covered thing on wheels and notices that there's a strange odor coming from it. At the same time, Vinnie spots a drive-thru fast-food place, so he pulls in, orders some food, and then pulls up to the cashier's window to pay for and pick up the food.

Unfortunately, he misjudges the narrowness of the drive-thru lane, which wasn't designed for vehicles as wide as his truck. The result of this slight error in his judgment results in one of the truck's front wheels hitting and then going up onto the driveway's curb.

Ordinarily this wouldn't be a very damaging incident, but in this case, it tosses poor Harold's body off of the gurney and onto Olive's lap.

I don't know how the average person would react, taking a leak in the back of a truck and having a corpse jump on you, but Olive is slightly upset. Well, maybe slightly upset is in understatement. She comes unglued, jumps up in a panic and rushes for the back doors of the truck, to escape from the stinking corpse that has just attacked her and is still in her lap.

Unbeknownst to Vinnie, Olive and Harold, the fast-food drive-thru place also sells coffee and donuts, so directly behind Vinnie's truck is a black-

and-white L.A.P.D. police car with two uniformed officers.

I can only imagine their surprise when they see the back doors of the truck in front of them fly open and Olive diving out onto the hood of their police car, complete with Harold on her lap and her panties still down beneath her knees. I've heard that the Los Angeles Police Department has a very thorough training program, but I doubt if a situation like this one is in their books... although from now on, it probably might be.

This must have really been a Kodak moment, but there's never a camera around when you need one – unless the fast-food place had some electronic surveillance mounted on the outside of the building. I'll have to send Jack B. out there to scope the place out.

Making the situation stranger was the fact that Vinnie had no idea what had taken place until one of the police officers walked over to him with gun drawn and asked him to 'please exit the vehicle.'

If I ever have grandchildren, someday when they're old enough, I'll tell them this story. Right now, it's tough enough not to break up.

After the story is told, Vinnie lets me know that the only way he wants to be around a dead body is if it's in a hearse and at least three car lengths in front of his truck. I apologize to both he and Stuart. It's a good thing that the police did the public a service by delivering Harold to Victor's place, because there's no way Vinnie was letting it back into the truck. I'm sure Victor will take care of further transportation when the autopsy has been done.

Vinnie and Stuart finally calm down and I've come back to the boat, where I find Jack Bibberman is waiting for me. I can't resist telling him about Olive's adventure and we both spend several minutes having a good laugh about it. I also think there's a giggle coming from the forward stateroom.

The reason Jack came to the boat is to finish up the errand I sent him on – to pick up Harold's personal belongings from County Jail. Harold probably knew he'd be arrested because there was nothing there but some articles of clothing and an envelope – addressed to me.

His writing style is as brusque as his conversational skills. The letter is short and to the point, and answers some questions that were bothering me. It's scribbled in pencil.

Lawyer:
Thanks for your help. I was in the gang too. If there's any more reward money, send it to my wife and kids.

So that's what it was. He was part of the robbery gang. Now I know why he was so interested in whether or not there would be some extra reward money, but I still can't figure out why he tried to kill Drago. He told me that it was 'for the money,' but who would pay him for a job like this? Our background information didn't come up with any prior criminal record. I can understand how a previously honest person might get tempted to join a gang to rob banks. Ever since that crime was glamorized in the Warren Beatty film 'Bonnie and

207

Clyde,' I'm sure a lot of unsuccessful people have fantasized about it, but that doesn't necessarily mean it could lead to a cold-blooded murder for hire. There's more to it that I don't know about yet.

Now that Harold's murder trial is over, there's no danger of little Suzi getting dragged in to testify, so I feel a little better about trying to find out if she actually saw anything in Drago's room that day. Knocking on her stateroom door and asking her straight out is not my style with this kid, so I send an inter-office email addressed to any member of our staff who may have been in the hospital that day. I'm hoping this may get a slight rise out of her. If she takes the bait, I might even get some information out of her.

As usual, she proves that she's much smarter than I am. A message is delivered by dog-mail. It only asks one question. "What took you so long to recognize the tail?"

She did it again. She's so many steps ahead of me, I'm probably not even in the race any more. If she decides to practice law some day she'll be dangerous in a courtroom. I'd hate to be on the other side of any case she's on.

To my amazement, the door to her stateroom opens and she actually comes out to speak to me.

"Thank you for not getting me involved in the case. I really didn't want to go against Myra. I didn't see anything in the hospital that day. As I walked past the room, all I saw was that man hanging his coat up in the closet."

That having been said, she promptly turns around and they both exit. The Saint Bernard had no comment.

Did I hear her right? She said that Harold was hanging up his coat in the hospital room closet. Something in my brain doesn't compute. I must have watched that hospital footage more than fifty times, but I don't remember seeing Harold in a coat. It's back to the VCR. I get the videos out and start watching them again.

After the pillow incident, Harold appears on the hallway camera wearing a trench coat. I go over the earlier tapes. He wasn't wearing a coat when he came into the hospital room. She was partly correct. He went to the closet all right, but not to hang up his coat – to take Drago's coat. But why? Why would he want to steal Drago's coat?

I call Jack Bibberman and tell him that his job is to find out the names of the paramedics who picked Drago up at the bank after his slip-and-fall. I want to interview them. Now I'll take a look at the bank's videos, to see what Drago was wearing that day.

Sure enough, the bank's cameras show Drago wearing that same trench coat. Nothing more to do now until Jack B. gets me those paramedics to talk to.

The phone rings. It's Stuart.

"Yeah Stu, what's up?"

"Vinnie put in a workman's comp claim against me."

"You must be kidding – why would he do a thing like that?"

"Because I told him to. He was so upset about that incident with Harold and Olive, he hasn't been sleeping very well and he's really been acting edgy. I think the corpse thing really got to him, so I told him that if he puts in a claim the insurance company will pay for some therapy."

"Okay, I'll go along with that. Is it helping any? Have you noticed any change in his behavior?"

"Yeah, he's calmed down a bit... and he got back together with Olive, so he's a lot happier now. But he still won't go to a funeral unless he's driving the truck. He never did like them, you know. His uncle died last year and Vinnie wouldn't even go to his funeral – he was afraid he'd see the guy in an open casket and he just wasn't ready for that."

I never realized how much Vinnie disliked dead bodies. I can't help but laugh every time I think about it, but I also feel bad he was traumatized like that. I guess if you're a person who doesn't care to be around stiffs, an experience like that can really shake you up. It's nice to know that he sought out some professional help – it takes guts for someone to do that. Maybe it'll stop him from peeing on trees, too.

Jack B. comes through for me again. He got the names of the paramedics who brought Drago to the hospital. They both work out of a fire station not far from the Marina, so I go over there to ask them a few questions. When I ask them about Drago's clothing, they tell me that they remember he was wearing a dark trench coat.

"You guys must see almost a hundred people a month. How can you remember what a guy was wearing a couple of months ago?"

"Simple Mister Sharp, other than Peter Falk playing Lieutenant Columbo, not too many people wear a trench coat on a warm day when the sun is shining."

They're right. This trench coat is becoming more interesting every day. Just another question and I'm through. "Did you guys take him to the hospital with the trench coat on?"

"No, we usually remove outer garments, so that we can loosen up shirts, ties, and belts. But I'll tell you one thing."

"What's that?"

"The trench coat was heavy. When we took it off and tossed it into the back of our vehicle, it made a clunk when it landed."

"Did you check to see what made the noise?" They both answered, almost in unison "No way. If he had a ton of coins or something on him from the bank, we didn't want any part of it. Better to let the FBI go through his pockets... we don't get paid to investigate, all we do is resuscitate."

I remember going through the police reports. They specifically mentioned that Drago didn't have anything on him that indicated he was a bank customer. No deposit or withdrawal stuff, no nothing. If they found out what he didn't have, why didn't they find what he did have? Maybe it's because they didn't do their investigation until after Harold took the coat.

The police report is somewhere in the file, so I hunt for it and drag it out. All they mention going through are his suit and pants pockets. No mention of a coat. Harold must have beat them to it.

I call Victor at his autopsy lab. "Victor, let me ask you a question. Do you ever take fingerprints off of the bodies you examine?"

"Sure, Mister Sharp. Any time it's a case where the deceased was involved in a crime."

"Drago wasn't involved in a crime. Did you happen to take his?"

"Sure he was involved in a crime. At the time he was brought in here, everyone still thought that he was a murder victim. Nobody asked me to, but after working in crime labs for so long, I sort of do it out of force of habit. Let's see... I've got the fingerprint card laying around here somewhere. Do you want it?"

This is great news. I tell Victor to scan it into the computer and email it over here. I then call Lieutenant Evans in Van Nuys and tell him that I need a favor and if anything pans out from it, he'll get the credit.

He jumps at the chance to join in with Captain Crime Crusader. The fingerprint card is sent to him electronically and he runs it through the system for me.

Two days later, I get a call from the lieutenant. "Mister Sharp, we have something very interesting for you. Your guy Vlad has been a very bad boy."

"Did you say Vlad? My guy's name isn't Vlad... it's Mike Drago.

"That's what you think. The fingerprints you sent me match up with a guy named Vlad Drago, who is wanted by Interpol for crimes of violence in several countries. He came here from Croatia and has a rap sheet a mile long. Do you want me to round him up for you?"

"Sorry to disappoint you Lieutenant, but we've already got this one. Those prints were lifted off of a dead guy."

"You mean there's no one to go out and arrest?"

"Not today Lieutenant, but stay tuned... we're still working on the case."

If the victim wasn't Mike Drago, then who the hell was he? That last name isn't a really common one, so they're no doubt related. If I have to make an educated guess, I'd say that Vlad is Mike's brother. I tell Jack B. to check the immigration records to get their family's history in this country. There are very few reasons to assume someone else's identity, and if you aren't doing it to get some new credit cards on someone else's dime, then you really must be up to no good.

I check out Interpol's website and learn that they're the largest international police organization in the world, set up in 1923 to facilitate cross-border criminal police cooperation. They now have 181 member countries spread over five continents. They support and assist all organizations, authorities and services whose mission is to prevent or combat international crime, and now that I'm an official Crimefighter, I suppose that Interpol will help me out on future investigations.

Jack B. is a pretty smart guy. He contacted Special Agent Snell at the FBI. Snell knows we're probably working on getting more members of the gang and wants to get on television again. Jack convinced him that it would be in everyone's best interest if the feds would check with immigration. It would be much easier for them to do it than someone outside the government.

Bingo. The immigration check comes back with some information for us. Vlad and Mike were just two of five Drago brothers who were brought to the U.S. when they were children, because their parents wanted to get out of Serbia. Vlad had a string of brushes with the law, but his brother had a clean record with only one minor problem He was killed by a stray bullet during some gang shoot-out that no doubt involved his big brother Vlad.

Vlad probably figured that assuming Mike's identity would give him a clean slate, so that if he got arrested again no priors would show up on his record. I guess he forgot about fingerprints, but there aren't many career criminals who are members of MENSA, so it's understandable he'd make one or two mistakes along the way.

Now that we know who he is, I think my hunch about the heavy thing in his coat is probably right on the money. Drago was carrying a gun when he slipped and fell in the bank. I have another phone call to make.

"Victor, it's Peter Sharp. I have a question to ask you about Drago and those ribs he broke when he fell in the bank."

"Ask away Mister Sharp, I've seen the video footage of his fall, and I've got some questions of my own about those broken ribs."

"Okay Victor, here goes. Is it possible that his ribs were broken by something big and hard that was inside his suit coat?"

"That's what I was thinking, but the police didn't find anything. I still say that broken ribs like that shouldn't have happened. I saw his fall on videotape and it looked like he landed on his ass. Our autopsy confirmed a bruised coccyx, so there must have been something else that put pressure on the ribs when he fell."

"Same thing I was thinking. What if he had a big handgun in the inside pocket of his suit jacket... could that have done the rib damage?"

Victor confirms my hunch. Drago was armed when he was in the bank. Now I ask myself, if a person goes into a bank where he has no account, no money to deposit, no checks to cash, and no loan to apply for, why does he go in there armed with a big gun?

Even the dog should be able to figure this one out. Drago was there to rob the bank. He's part of the gang, along with Harold – and what looked like him writhing in pain on the floor of the bank after his fall was actually a struggle to get the gun out of his suit coat pocket and into his trench coat pocket, where it would be less likely to be discovered later.

The pieces of the puzzle are slowly starting to come together. They were going to take the bank down that morning until Drago slipped and fell. That threw them off of their plan for a while but they didn't want to give up the score, so they went back later and finished the job. An hour after I got the case assigned to me and visited the bank.

I've got to hand it to Blitzstien. He confessed to being a member of the gang but wouldn't rat out Drago. That's loyalty, but of a strange kind. I guess in the twisted minds of those criminals it's okay to try and kill someone, but snitching on them is a no-no. Now I can understand why Harold wouldn't talk directly to the feds. He told me he didn't want to have a reputation of being a snitch.

More questions have been answered, but I still don't know how to put it all together. All I know for sure is that Drago's status has just dropped from invitee to trespasser.

With respect to land occupiers' responsibility and liability to people who come onto their property, the lowest classification of visitor is the Unknown Trespasser. Now that I can probably establish that Drago is in that bottom category, there's a possibility that the bank's exposure can be minimized to practically nothing.

But what the hell am I even thinking about this for? Indovine's fired me from the case. Nevertheless, I feel duty-bound to at least call and let him know this new information. Maybe this will rehabilitate me in his mind and he'll hire me back. The odds are slim, but I've got to try. I call his private line. He answers the phone and it sounds like he's in the men's room of the Titanic, so he's obviously on the speakerphone.

"Hello, Indovine here."

"Mister Indovine, this is Peter Sharp and I've got some new information on the Drago case that may help your client."

"Well, well, of it isn't the crime-fighting lawyer. Too bad you didn't study law as hard as you read detective stories. As a matter of fact, our client is here in the room with me right now and we're really not interested in anything you have to say about the Drago case. Thanks to you we're in the process of making a seven-figure settlement with his family's lawyer, so please don't call this number anymore."

"Wait Charles, don't hang up, I'm begging you not to settle. If the information I have is correct, your client may not have to pay out any money at all on this case."

"That's enough, Sharp. Neither my client nor I are interested in your desperate attempts to be re-assigned to this case. The grown-ups are handling it now, so I'll bid you a good day."

With that bit of humiliation, he hangs up the phone and all I'm left with on my end is a dial tone. He shouldn't have done that because now I'm really going to make an effort to show how wrong he was. Ignorance alone is a bad enough trait, but when combined with arrogance the result is really terrible – and Indovine did one of the best jobs of combining the two that I've seen in quite a while. Well, what goes around comes around.

The only small tasks I'm left with now are getting Myra elected as the new District Attorney, proving that Drago and Harold were part of the gang, earning some extra reward money, and getting that million-plus back for the insurance company. No problem.

21

Myra has only two declared opponents in the upcoming race for District Attorney. One is a guy named Seymour, with the same seniority and experience that Myra has. He's been the acting District Attorney since his predecessor was forced out of office not too long ago. The other candidate is some pony-tailed activist who promises to legalize drugs when he gets elected.

I've never been up against Seymour in court, but word has it that he seems competent. Not too quick on his feet, but competent. I really think that Myra would make a better D.A., so getting her elected won't give me any pangs of conscience. The other attorney running doesn't stand much of a chance, because the people who would like to see drugs legalized for the most part have already had their right to vote taken away because of a felony conviction.

Seymour's starting to run some negative campaign ads on local television stations, and his main thrust is that Myra lost the Blitzstien case. What a putz this guy is turning out to be. Harold may not have been a nice guy, but he was one hundred percent innocent and any prosecutor with an ounce of ethics would have done the same thing that Myra did. She got out of my way and let me prove it to the court. No excuses afterwards, no blaming her loss on unfair trial tactics, surprise, or technicalities, she just kept her mouth shut and accepted her loss like a real pro. I admire her for that, so I intend to make up for all those times I destroyed her by getting her elected. I just don't have the slightest idea how.

At least I'll have a good laugh along the way, because Jack B. tells me that he drove by the fast food place, and that they do in fact have some security cameras mounted on the outside of the building, pointed directly down at where the famous Olive-Harold incident took place. I drive over there to try and talk them out of some copies of the videotapes.

The manager has a typical fast-food place complexion and starts out being pleasant. I explain to him what I want, and his first response is the typical "no way." I decide that some creativity is required here.

"Listen, I'm working with the police on this matter. As you probably remember, there was a squad car involved in the incident and the behavior of the officers is being called into question. Now you wouldn't want to see some of your customers get a bad rap would you?"

"If they're cops, I couldn't care less. In the past couple of months they've stuck my wife's car with over a dozen parking tickets and I don't think it's fair."

At this point I don't think it would do any good to try and explain that uniformed officers in squad cars don't usually write parking tickets, but I'm not here to educate him, I'm here to get those tapes.

"Okay, you're right. It's probably not fair. Tell you what... why don't I take those parking tickets with me and show them to the parking ticket boss and explain how unfair it is. If I can get him to wipe out those tickets, would you let me borrow that tape to make a copy?"

He thinks about this for a minute. "You mean it won't cost me anything? The tickets will be taken care of, one way or another?"

I assure him that they'll be taken care of 'one way or another.'

Thirty minutes later I'm at the Van Nuys courthouse standing in the ticket-paying line just off of the first floor lobby. Four hundred and twenty dollars later, the tickets have been taken care of - one way or another. I go back to the fast-food place, show him the dismissal receipts and pick up the cassette starring that famous team of Olive and her trained corpse.

Watching the video confirms my hunch that if it wasn't for the fact that Olive's underwear was around her ankles, this footage could definitely win some award on a reality-type of television show that solicits video footage of zany events from viewers.

If I'm going to have some meat, it's not going to be at a fast-food place. I like high-class restaurants and my definition of high-class is any place where the napkins are not on the table in a dispenser. To reach five-star level in my mind, the napkins should be cloth, the booths should be upholstered, and there should be a rug on the floor. If there's no spoon in the place setting, then I know the place is out of my price limit. Only the stratospheric joints leave out the spoon... you're brought whatever type of spoon is required for the type of food you're eating.

This is much better than watching video of people falling or getting murdered. This is enjoyable.

I think I'll offer it for sale to Christopher Guest or Larry David, to include in one of their next projects. Aside from me, they may be the only two guys I know of with a weird enough sense of humor to find this incident amusing.

Strangely enough though, there's more interesting stuff here. I also enjoy looking at the characters that use this drive-thru facility for their nourishment. You can actually see how popular French-fries really are. It's amazing how many people enjoy shoving that fried grease down their throats. It's also enjoyable seeing the people in the cars and how they relate to each other. The guys asking their female companions for money, the looks they get when it's given to them... wait a minute, there's a kiss going on in a car parked two or three spots in line behind the squad car. That's nice. Love in bloom. Oh-oh, another minute or two later, as the cars pull up to pick up their food from the cashier, I see that the kiss took place between an older guy and a younger man. Well, it takes all kinds. That's their business. It was probably a father kissing his son. I like to give everyone the benefit of the doubt.

Good news. The reward money has come in from our now famous cracking of the bank robbery cases. I'll be getting my yellow Hummer, the four Asian boys will finally be getting their own one-bedroom apartment with indoor plumbing, Jack Bibberman is going to start night law school, Stuart is planning a cruise, Suzi is not telling anyone what she's doing with her share, and Vinnie is getting married to Olive.

That therapy must have really helped him, because Olive finally said yes. Of course the reward probably didn't have anything to do with it.

Stuart tells me that they're going to have the ceremony at a little church in North Hollywood, with the reception later that day at our favorite Mexican place, Pollo Meshuga. Patròn margaritas, here I come!

I call Myra and let her know about it and talk her into being my quasi 'date' that day. We might as well spend a little time together, because we haven't got much of it left. After we get back from Hawaii, she'll be busy running for District Attorney, and after that it will be awkward for us to be seen together if I continue to practice criminal law. It just wouldn't look good for the District Attorney to be seen socially with a criminal defense attorney – especially one that she used to be married to. There'd be too many chances for people who oppose her policies to take potshots at her because of her social life. Maybe we can sneak around a little.

In between calls from Stuart, who's constantly in a state of desperation trying to help make plans for Vinnie's bachelor party and wedding, I try to do some research on Drago's case and discover that it's a lot harder to do legal research when you're not getting paid for it.

If I'm going to be able to do any good I've got to put a stop to the settlement before it reaches the final disbursement point. If it goes through, the probate court will probably want to be responsible for distributing the funds, making sure that debts of the estate like medical and funeral expenses are paid.

That should give me at least a couple of weeks to get the goods on him, so that the court can freeze the funds and possibly return them to the insurance company. As a last resort, I can put a kibosh on the entire probate procedure by proving that the deceased isn't Mike Drago, but is actually his relative, Vlad. That would not only stall the entire probate, but might also give the insurance company a reason to allege fraud in the claim – especially if that lawyer knew that it was Vlad and not Mike.

Before getting too involved in getting the insurance company's money back, I'd better talk to Special Agent Snell again. The last time we spoke, it was to discuss the possibility of some additional reward money for establishing the identities of other members of the gang who haven't been arrested yet. I didn't get into too much detail with him then because at that time I wasn't aware of the fact that both Drago and Harold were members of the gang.

Now that I know who the other two gang members are, I've got to make some arrangement with Snell so that even when he finds out that they're both dead, my reward claim will still work. I call him up to discuss it and tell him I know the identity of the other two, but my main concern is the part that says 'information leading to arrest and conviction.' I don't want my reward money depending on the authorities' ability to arrest and convict. Snell agrees that if the other two are outside the United States, it might be difficult to find them, even with Interpol's help. I decide to offer him a deal he can't refuse.

"Agent Snell, I'll tell you what. If we can agree on a fixed amount right now, I'll provide you with the names of the other two members of the gang, along with their pictures and a local address where each one can be found. And if the current address isn't correct and you can't see each one of them, then I'll give up any right to a reward."

"You're serious about that? You'll give us addresses to go and pick them up?"

"I'll give you the addresses. You'll have to make your own decision whether or not you want to pick them up."

"How much money are you looking for on these two?"

"Well, considering the fact that this will make you an even bigger hero for closing the file on that whole gang, I think that twenty-five thousand for each isn't unreasonable." There's silence on the other end of the line. He doesn't know that I'll jump at anything over five grand for each of them.

"That's a little high for a head-count reward, but I think I can swing twenty-five for both of them. That's twelve-five for each. I'll fax the agreement over to you first, so you can feel safe about the terms."

"That's okay, I'll fax *you* an agreement to sign... and the twenty-five K total will work for me. What do you want first, the addresses?"

"That all depends. Are they on the move?"

"Not at all. In fact, I can tell you with complete certainty that they haven't the slightest idea they're under suspicion, and that they are definitely not on the move. They'll be at their present locations for a minimum of another month or so and they never go outside."

"They're really lying low, aren't they?"

"You could say that."

"Okay, first we'll need their photo-graphs…"

I cut him off on that one. Once he's got the pictures, the game is over. He'll know that they're both dead and I'll be screwed out of the reward money. I've got to change the ground rules here. "Oh yeah, the pictures… they're not immediately available, but I guarantee you won't have any trouble picking up the wrong people… I'll give you complete descriptions of them.

"And while I've got you on the phone, you should know that ever since the publicity we got last time for giving you that gang on a silver platter, my criminal practice has suffered. I'm afraid that if it gets out that I helped you discover another two members of that gang, I'll completely lose any remaining integrity I have with the underworld and no crook will ever trust me. It'll look like I'm too close with you feds. I'm going to need you to do me a favor. Keep my name out of it. Once it's known that you found out about more gang members, you'll be in the spotlight again - and that's okay. You take all the credit. All I want is the reward money. Can you assure me that you'll keep my name out of it?"

"Okay Sharp, I think we can do that. Discretion has always been one of our strong suits. You can take my personal word for it that I won't mention your name once – to anyone but the person making out the checks for the reward."

Vanity rears its ugly head. He goes for the chance to take all the credit and lets me draft the reward agreement. I word it so that there's no mention of arrest or conviction. It relies entirely on my proof that they were both members of the gang and participated in at least one of the bank robberies. We exchange corrected copies back and forth by fax and the deal is sealed. I promise to deliver the location info on the other gang members to him by the end of the week.

I have the goods on Drago, but also know that they won't accept Harold's written note to me. Come to think of it, I don't think that the note can be given to them. It was written to me while Harold was still alive, so it probably falls under the client-privilege category of communications.

I know that all the banks and lobbies were loaded with security cameras. If they were both part of that robbery gang, at one time or another they were inside one of the banks, lobbies, or both.

Most of the local cops eat at the Chinese restaurant where the kid reigns, and one of her fans is the cop in charge of the police computers where that expert loaded that facial recognition program that nailed Harold. If they've still got that software, maybe she can use it to scan for the appearance of Drago and Harold somewhere in the bank and lobby security videos. I send her a memo and mention that the firm has a chance to get another twelve large in reward money if we can use that software. There's a quick response by dog-mail: "give me the pictures." I like doing business with her. Whenever there's money involved, she's extremely cooperative.

Jack Bibberman helps me organize all the pictures we have in our digital file, going back to when I was first assigned the Drago case. There are quite a few more than just Drago's and Harold's but I don't know how to work the Photoshop program well enough to separate out just the two we're interested in, so I give Suzi the entire file. She tells me that it might take a couple of days.

Vinnie's wedding day is tomorrow and we'll all be at the little church in North Hollywood, watching Vinnie and Olive get hitched. Myra and I make plans to get together. She wants to ride in my new yellow Hummer, because everyone looks at us. It must be because of the way that the dog rides with his head sticking up and out of the open sunroof. Suzi got some special aviator-type dog goggles for him to wear as eye-protection, and with his big ears flopping in the wind, he looks like a World War I air ace.

The phone rings. It's Victor from the autopsy place and he's got a transportation problem. His car's transmission is on the fritz and he wants to know if I can pick him up. I tell him that I'd like to, but I've got to go in the complete opposite direction to pick up Myra in quaint Brentwood Glen, at the house we used to live in, and with presents we're schlepping for everyone, plus the kid and dog along, we're really filled up.

He understands and says that he has a back-up vehicle to use. We agree to see each other at the church.

Today's the day. I've got my best suit on, and I'm driving the Hummer to pick up Myra. Things couldn't be going any better. Myra and Suzi are pleased to see each other, and all the way to the church I'm completely ignored. The dog gets petted during their conversation. I get ignored. It's amazing how much the kid talks to everyone but me. They both yap all the way from Brentwood to North Hollywood, catching up on some of the most meaningless items. The only time my name is mentioned is when Suzi tells Myra about my new pasta recipe, which includes the usual eight ounces of large elbow macaroni, topped off with a small can of creamed corn and a small can of sweet peas. Myra winces at the thought of it, but Suzi tells her that it really doesn't taste that bad. I finally get a chance to take part in the conversation, letting them know that the dog loved it. We hear an affirmative bark from the air ace, outside the sunroof.

As we approach the church, we see an amazing event taking place. Olive, fully dressed in her wedding gown complete with the long trailing train, is frantically running out of the church screaming. Vinnie, complete with coat, tails and top hat, is chasing after her. This track event is taking place in the parking lot and everyone from inside the church lines the lot, shouting out suggestions to each of them, as they run by.

I don't know why I'm surprised. Every time I get involved with Stuart or Vinnie, something outrageous usually takes place. This time I hope nobody lands in jail as a result of it all.

Myra and Suzi sit calmly watching. They both know the personalities involved. Olive jumps into her car and starts to drive away. Vinnie runs to the armored truck, jumps in and races after her. This scene reminds me of an old silent movie I once saw on PBS, starring a cockeyed group of police officers known as the "Keystone Cops."

I guess that there won't be a wedding today. That doesn't disappoint me, but I'm sure the dog was looking forward to some cold cuts. When we park and get out to meet all the other people there, most of whom we know, I learn what caused the problem. Being in a business that caters to funerals, Stuart and Vinnie had become quite friendly with a number of funeral directors and invited them to the wedding. What most people don't know is that quite often, undertakers live on the same premises as their business so they don't own their own private cars. If they have to go somewhere they usually drive a hearse or flower-car from the mortuary. This means that the parking lot looked like a funeral procession. Olive stepped outside the rear door of the church to take a swig from her flask and have a cigarette. At first she didn't realize what all those large dark Cadillacs were doing there, but when Victor pulled up in that mobile lab painted with his trademark logo of "1(800)AUTOPSY," poor Olive put it all together and started to come apart at the seams. I guess she flashed back to that day at the fast-food place when Harold jumped onto her lap. She freaked out, started to scream and ran.

Well, it wasn't a total loss. All the food was paid for, so a large group of us went to Pollo Meshuga and pigged out. It was a beautiful day and the buffet was laid out on the restaurant's patio. The dog ran around policing the floor. I don't think they needed any janitors that evening.

22

While we're all busy celebrating at the restaurant, Victor informs me that Harold died from a blood disease. He must have known about it for some time, because his body contained trace elements of the special medicine that's usually prescribed for people with that ailment.

When Victor tells me exactly what the medication was, I ask him if it's common. He tells me that the disease is rare and so is the medicine, which requires a prescription. There can't be too many pharmacies around that fill prescriptions for that stuff, so I get Jack B. to check it out. I want to know who his doctor was and if Harold knew how seriously ill he really was.

I don't have to wait too long for an answer because before Jack can start canvassing the local pharmacies, I get a phone call from the doctor who was treating Mister Blitzstien. He saw Harold's name mentioned in the newspaper after the trial and noted that I had been representing him. He wants to let me know that he was out of the country on vacation during the whole trial and didn't know anything about Harold's arrest, other than the fact that nobody contacted his office for prescription refills.

My only question for him is whether or not Harold knew how sick he was. The doctor realizes the patient-doctor privilege doesn't apply here now that his patient is dead, and he's obviously more worried about his own malpractice exposure for not having his office make some effort to get medicine to Harold. He tells me what I want to know. Harold knew that he only had six months to live.

That might answer another question. Why he didn't take more precautions to avoid getting caught for what he thought he did to Drago. He knew that he probably wouldn't live long enough to be convicted. All he cared about was making sure that Drago didn't survive, so that his family's share of the bank loot would be bigger. How nice. He was a family man, just wanting to do the best for his wife and kids. No wonder he made that remark to me about doing it for the money. And I'm the one who caused his estate to be diminished in value when the gang was arrested and the loot recovered.

He also had to suffer with the thought that he killed Drago for nothing. There would be no money for his family unless I got some reward money for him.

One last item from the doctor gave me a small hope that I could tie Harold into the robbery gang with something other than his confession. His prescriptions were delivered to a house – the one that the gang used as a staging area and where the 'dog lady' lived.

Okay, I'm part of the way there, but I still need more proof for Agent Snell. He'll be mad as hell when he finds out that there aren't any live gang members to arrest, so if I don't give him some concrete proof, I still might get screwed out of the reward money.

True to her word, the kid has some results on the face-recognition scans. We got lucky. Both Drago and Harold are seen inside all the banks before the robberies took place. I guess they all visited the scene of the crime in advance to block out their movements and time the escape and money retrieval.

The lobby cameras show that Harold was the maintenance man who walked through the lobby and picked the money and glasses out of the trashcans while the dog-lady did her act of diversion.

This raises an interesting question. If Drago was in the hospital, who took his place in the robbery of that bank where he fell? Sure enough, one of the lobby cameras picked up a different maintenance man, complete with phony beard and mustache. They got a substitute, but who was it? I check out all the newspapers for articles about the gang getting arrested and see names and pictures of the gang members caught that day. None of them were wearing a phony beard disguise... but the facial recognition software does make a match for the bearded maintenance man. When I gave Suzi the file, it contained everyone we had pictures of, including Drago's lawyer, Richard Handelmann.

Pictures of the people Snell arrested that day show one man in a business suit – obviously the inside man, who pulled the job without Drago's help, and the dog-lady. Nobody else. The loot was recovered, but no maintenance man. Handelmann must have driven his own car there that day. After the robbery, the dog lady drove around the block and got the moneybags from Handelmann first. She then picked up the inside man. By the time the feds caught up with the van, Handelmann was probably out of his janitor's jumpsuit and beard and was driving back to his office.

This is really hard to believe. They got their own lawyer to fill in for one of the gang. As hard as it is to believe, it's going to be even harder to prove. I checked the lobby security tapes of the job they pulled before the last one and sure enough, there was the bearded maintenance man again. He probably wanted to distance himself from the rest of the gang, so he didn't join their vanpool to work and back each of those times.

I call Agent Snell and let him know that there's an additional gang member that I'd like to add to the reward list. He tells me that he won't go more than ten thousand for the third identity. I tell him that it's a criminal defense attorney and I hear a sound over the phone that resembles the one I hear when the dog drools. There's nothing that cops like more than catching a dirty lawyer. This little tidbit allows me to get the reward up to a full twenty five thousand for the lawyer. Life is good.

The beauty of this last revelation is that no effort on my part will be required to prove Handelmann's involvement in the robberies. The Facial Recognition software program has the capability to see through phony disguises like Handelmann's. His goose is cooked and so is Drago's wrongful death claim.

Local news covering the progress of the gang's court case shows their lawyer making an announcement on the steps of the federal courthouse. Everyone wants to be like me. To my surprise, the gang's lawyer is none other than Handelmann. Why not? I should have figured it out before. How else could he have been retained to represent Drago's estate? I press the 'record' button on my VCR and tape him claiming that there were so many procedural errors made in this case that he's sure he can get it dismissed.

I have to agree with him about the errors part of his statement. If we did our job a little better, he'd be making this statement from his small room at the federal 'Grey-bar Hotel' now.

Stuart calls to let me know that Vinnie and Olive are back together again and says that Vinnie would like to ask my advice about whether or not he should bring Olive with him to his therapy session. This is definitely not my specialty. If I knew anything about how to keep a woman happy, I would still be married to Myra. Stuart asks if it would be okay for Vinnie to call.

When Vinnie calls, I ask him about his therapy sessions and who referred him. I don't know why but I'm not too surprised by his answer – the yellow pages. Maybe the telephone directory is okay for a plumber but I would think that a person might want to have a more personal type of referral to a therapist. But who am I to talk? My murder case was solved by a guy who I got from a fluke phone call made by Suzi when she dialed 1(800)AUTOPSY. The conversation continues. "Vinnie, do you know if your therapist is a psychologist or psychiatrist?"

"Not exactly, Mister Sharp."

"What do you mean not exactly? He's got to be one or the other."

"He's not a *he*, he's a *she*."

"Whatever. Okay, which one is she?"

"I don't think she's either one of those."

"Well what about her office... is it in a professional office building?"

"Actually, it's right down the street on Washington, between the dog grooming parlor and the boat broker."

"Vinnie, I'm familiar with that street and the only thing between those two places..." I stop short. It suddenly hits me. The storefront where he goes for his therapy certainly isn't the office of a psychiatrist or psychologist. In fact, if my memory serves me correctly, the sign on the window says 'Palm Reader.' Vinnie is going to a palm reader for therapy – and it's helping him.

"Mister Sharp, are you still there?"

"Oh yeah Vinnie, I'm still here... my cell phone must have cut out for a second."

What's the use? How can anyone expect to give advice to a guy who considers a palm reader his therapist? Ronald Reagan's wife consulted with an astrologer, and she advised the President, so maybe they know something I don't know. I politely end the conversation by telling Vinnie that if Olive wants to join him in a therapy session, then he should do whatever makes her happy. With Stuart's talent for filling out paperwork, I'm sure he'll get his insurance company to pay for Olive's therapy too. I wonder who'll pay for mine.

Later in the afternoon I go through some papers, trying to clean off my desk. I happen to see some further results from the facial recognition scan.

Included in the stack of videos given to the kid for scanning was the tape from the fast food place – and we got a hit off of it – the guy in the car planting a kiss on the boy. What a surprise. It's none other than Seymour, the acting District Attorney running against Myra in the election.

I like to work out, but my favorite exercise is definitely not jumping to conclusions. I figure that anyone running for an office these days must have a website, so I look for his and find it. On his personal history page, he claims to have gotten married just last year for the first time. Word on the street says it was to some socialite broad about five years older than him and that the main attraction between them was his desire for her money, to finance his campaign, and her desire to be the wife of some guy who will take her to black tie affairs.

Let's see. I can do the math on this one. Two adults who've never been married before, now together for only a year – that means the kid in the car with him was not his son.

This is tricky. I'm not into blackmail but this is definitely an item that can keep him from being elected. Being gay isn't the kicker here, it's the fact that his record of prosecution shows that he's especially hard on homosexuals, and a two-faced attitude like that can really come back to bite you in the ass, especially in an area with a large concentration of gay voters. Anyone who's been to West Hollywood can attest to the fact that after San Francisco, it's probably the second most densely populated area for gays... and they all pay their taxes and vote.

The problem now is how to use this information to Myra's advantage without letting either one of them know about it. Going to the press is out of the question. That would create a scandal that would ruin his career, his marriage, and also hurt the image of the district attorney's office. I'm not on a crusade and I certainly don't want to 'out' anyone. Whatever they do in their private lives is their own business – I just want to get Myra elected, like I promised.

I take another look at the video of the two of them in the car and call the lab to have them email me an enlargement of a particular frame that shows them facing forward as they pull up to the cashier's window.

When it comes in, I notice that both Seymour and his lunch date are wearing neckties. This elevates his companion out of the 'kid' category. He has a baby face, so I was misled into thinking he was much younger. It wouldn't surprise me to discover that they work in the same building together because the IDs that each one has pinned to his shirt look similar. It's not uncommon for people to get together for lunch, so they probably can easily keep their relationship secret. I e-mail just the young man's portion of the close-up to Jack Bibberman and tell him to stake out the district attorney's building employee parking lot. I want to know who this guy is.

23

The State of California has contracts with several large insurance companies from whom the state will accept policies that guarantee return appearances of criminal defendants in court. The policies issued are insurance documents called 'Bail Bonds,' and the insurance companies have agents located throughout the State who are authorized to issue these policies and procure the release of prisoners whose bail amount has been set by the court.

Bail bondsmen are sharp business people, and when they write one of their bonds they want to make sure that in the event the bonded person doesn't appear, the amount of the bond will be covered. This is done in several ways. On most misdemeanor bonds, a credit card can be used. For bail that exceeds a thousand dollars, a bondsman might demand someone execute a second mortgage on real estate. Bail for the dog lady and her accomplice has been set at a quarter of a million dollars each. The house they lived in was rented, so no second mortgage could be given and they're remaining in custody.

I have the kid send an email over to Handelmann's office letting him know of a wonderful new bail bond service.

To all California attorneys representing persons charged with crimes: this announcement is to inform you that the Bernard Bail Bond Company is offering a new service that will accept settlement drafts on civil cases as security for the issuance of bail bonds. If the settlement draft exceeds the combined amount of bail plus premium, the company will issue you a certified check for the difference. This service will be applicable to all State and Federal Court criminal cases.

Handelmann doesn't know it, but he is the only attorney that gets this message from me.

Two days later I convince Olive to make a phone call for me. Knowing that she's not the brightest bulb in the lamp, I rehearse her dialogue for several hours and then dial the phone for her. It rings and a female voice answers. "Handelmann law offices."

To play safe, I've had several three-by-five cards with dialogue filled out that cover different situations she might encounter. I now place the 'secretary answers' card in front of her. I nod to Olive and she goes on. "This is the Bernard Bail Bond Company, and we would like to tell Mister Handelmann about a new service we're offering." I'm listening on the extension phone, so I'll know if I should get the 'lawyer takes the call' card out for her.

"Handelmann here, what can I do for you?" Olive sees the next card and follows her script.

"Hello Mister Handelmann, this is the Bernard Bail Bond Company and we have a new service we'd like to tell you about..." He cuts her off mid-sentence.

"Is your boss there?" I tell her to hang up her phone and then I take over.

"Hello, this is the civil draft security division of Bernard Bail Bonds. Can I help you?"

239

"Yes, this is Richard M. Handelmann, attorney at law. I got your e-brochure and would like some information on how the service works."

"Okay, that's simple. First you fax us a copy of the draft, along with the name of the person you want to bail out and the booking number, along with his or her next appearance date and the amount of the bail. Once we verify the authenticity of the draft and the amount of the bail, we make arrangements to meet you in court at the next appearance date. At that time, you hand us the draft and we hand you the bail bond, all filled out and ready for presentation to the jailer, along with a certified check made out to you for any amount in excess of the bail and our premium."

"That's it? That's all there is to it?"

"Yes sir, that's how easy it is. If the settlement draft is made payable to you and your client, we would naturally need both of you present to endorse the draft, so that we can deposit it to our corporate account."

"No problem. The client is also one of the people being bailed out. There are two of them. Total bail for both is a half million, but that's no problem because the draft is for more than one million.

"Excellent. I'll give you back to our secretary and she'll give you our private fax number for you to use."

Olive takes the phone back and reads from the 'fax number' card. Mission accomplished. If this goes as planned I won't have to bother getting his account frozen or deal with the Probate court. Mister Handelmann will do the polite thing. He'll hand me the draft so I can return it to the insurance company, get even with Charles Indovine, and get my insurance defense job back.

Olive interrupts my reverie with a question. "Mister Sharp, where are we going to get the money to give him for his change?"

It never fails. There's always someone around to spoil a good plan. "Don't worry Olive, we won't need any money. He'll just give us the draft out of the kindness of his heart."

"Can I come and watch?"

"Sure, you can even bring your fiancée Vinnie with you."

"Are there going to be any dead bodies there?"

I assure her that on this assignment she'll only encounter the living. Now it's on to the second and third steps of the plan. I call Lieutenant Evans at the Van Nuys police station. I owe him a favor.

Olive told Vinnie about the new plan, so he calls and wants to know if I need any help. When I ask him what type of help he wants to offer, he informs me that Stuart sent both he and Olive to a special weapons training place, where they completed a course in firearm handling. With their certificates of completion and a letter of employment from Stuart's armored transport business, the state's Department of Consumer Affairs issued each of them an Exposed Firearm Permit, so that they can wear their holstered guns.

When I ask Vinnie why Olive would need one too, he tells me that Stuart's funeral escort business has grown so much that he's getting another armored truck and that Olive will drive it. I guess that carrying a loaded sidearm will make her feel safer around the dead body in a funeral procession.

I thank Vinnie for his offer and tell him that on this assignment there'll be quite a few 'regulars' around, in case anything goes wrong.

I feel good about the fact that there will be some reward money coming in for Harold's family, so I think it's time I actually speak to them. I'd like to introduce myself and express my condolences for their loss.

Whoever answers the phone at his family's house doesn't speak English. It's German, and I struggle to tell her that I don't speak the language and will call back at another time.

While attending undergraduate school I majored in Chemistry and planned to get a Bachelor of Science degree. The only thing holding me back was the requirement that B.S. candidates must complete one year of a foreign language.

I tried a couple of semesters of Spanish but failed miserably. French sounded too hard, so my last chance was to try German. I could never get the hang of how to conjugate verbs in a foreign language but my prior failing experiences gave me the idea that if I could memorize enough words and build a great vocabulary, I might be able to get through in some way. All summer before the fall term I memorized vocabulary. I knew so many words that I was almost able to understand what Colonel Klink was talking about when he scolded Schultz, the prison guard in *Hogan's Heroes* reruns.

I somehow managed to get through the first semester. Fortunately, the final exam was a written one and it required translation from German to English. My superb vocabulary came through for me and I easily passed with a well-earned C minus. This was encouraging, so I signed up for the second semester. If I could get through this one, I'd get my B.S. instead of a B.A.

The day of the final exam was a real shock for me. All of the hundreds of new words I learned weren't going to help much. The final was going to be oral, and our job was to translate from English to German. I knew this was going to be a problem, but I had to go through with it.

The teacher used the well-known story of William Tell and as she went from student to student, each one of us was required to translate a few sentences of the story from English into German. When she got to me, the sentence I was supposed to translate was the part where Tell used his bow and arrow to shoot the apple off of his son's head.

This was possible. I knew the German words for 'Arrow,' 'Apple,' 'Shoot' and 'Head.' However, vocabulary alone isn't good enough because there was a verb in there somewhere and my old problems with conjugation and pronunciation roared up. There are two words in German that are spelled almost the same, but are pronounced differently, and mean two different things. 'Geshiesen' is pronounced gesheesen. The vowel sound is an 'E' and it means *to shoot*. If you make the error of transposing two of the vowels in the middle of the word and it comes out 'Gesheisen,' the vowel sound is pronounced as an 'I' and the verb takes on quite a different meaning – one that was never covered in our class. The wrong spelling and pronunciation changes the verb from 'to shoot,' into 'to shit.'

The only person in the room who caught my error was the only person I wish hadn't caught it – the teacher. To say she was shocked would be a gross understatement, because my error changed the entire meaning of the story. As you can probably tell, instead of shooting the arrow off of his son's head, Mister Tell performed quite a different act to the top of that head. The teacher was not amused.

To make matters worse, not having the slightest idea that I had done something wrong, I had a completely straight face. The law school I enrolled in accepted my B.A.

Things are starting to come together. I have an appointment with Lieutenant Evans in a little while, so I'm casually driving through the Sepulveda Pass on the 405 Freeway planning my strategy. First, I give him all the details of the Drago case, complete with Immigration Service documents, photos, and fingerprint info. Next, I show him the case file in which Handelmann sued for wrongful death – and a copy of the settlement draft.

If I've got all the documentation together, I should be able to convince him that Handelmann has committed a crime by making a fraudulent claim to the insurance company, but he didn't stop there. By accepting the settlement draft, the crime steps up to grand theft, so if someone connects the dots properly, Handelmann is looking at some serious time as a guest of the State.

Because his law office is located on Ventura Boulevard in Encino, all of his criminal acts took place within the jurisdiction of Lieutenant Evans' Valley police division giving him authority to investigate the alleged crimes and make the arrest.

Some extra information from Jack B. also comes in handy. When he checked the hospital's outgoing phone logs he noted that Drago made only one telephone call from his room on the day he was admitted. That call was to Handelmann's office, no doubt to tell him where he was, because the rest of the gang in the bank that day were certainly not going to stick around and ask questions of the paramedics.

This means that we have a direct way to link Handelmann to the attempted murder of Drago. Handelmann was the only one who knew exactly what hospital and room that Drago was in. He can now be implicated in the murder conspiracy – and this is how I can get Myra involved in the case. She was appointed as a special prosecutor against Blitzstien when he was charged with murdering Drago. Blitzstien was found not guilty, so it certainly should be the continuing responsibility of the same prosecutor to bring the real killer to justice.

Seymour would probably explode if he knew that Myra was back on the case, so I think it best that we just let nature take its course. After I'm through with Evans today, I'll call Myra. If the cast of characters for next week's federal court appearance is to be complete, Myra will have to be there too.

Once at Evans' office it takes less than a half hour to lay out the whole case against Handelmann. After he's on the same page with me, he calls two of his detectives in and I go over it again for them. We talk about it for a while and the decision is made to go ahead and pick him up. Their only reluctance is about the deputy district attorneys who've recently been assigned to Van Nuys. They tell me that these deputies aren't experienced with criminal law, having been sent here from the district attorney's civil division as a reward for their loyalty to the present acting D.A. I tell them to hold that thought for a minute or two. A solution to their problem is in the offing.

At this point, I ask for a few minor conditions so that everything meshes with the other plans I've already put into motion.

First, I ask them not to get a warrant for Handelmann's arrest. If they do it the way I suggest, I'll personally be in the location where he's making a court appearance to point him out and make sure that they get the right guy. I show them his picture, so they don't worry about nabbing some other crooked lawyer by mistake.

Second, I don't want my name mentioned anywhere. On this case, the credit's all going to Evans and his boys, who will say that they received their information from someone other than me, who will also be in the courtroom at the time of the arrest. To answer their question as to the identity of that person, I inform them that it's none other than the next district attorney of this county - Myra, and she will owe them a big favor for this. As a newly elected official, she'll probably want to make some changes in the duty assignments. If they prepare a list of the deputy D.A.'s they've had good successes working with in the past, there's a good chance they may be coming back to the Van Nuys office.

This news brings out some smiles in the room. I also explain to them that the reason she'll be in court when they make the bust is to complete her job as prosecutor on the Drago murder.

I know that Handelmann will be making an appearance in court next Thursday to offer some discovery motions and try to have the robbery gang members' bail lowered, so I start to work on getting the rest of the entire cast of characters together. I've always dreamed of having my own 'showdown,' where like Nero Wolfe, I can see the culprit nailed. That's why I want to have everyone in that courtroom next Thursday, so I can wrap up all the loose ends.

My call gets put through to Myra's office. "What's up Petey?"

I really hate it when she calls me that. "Listen, I'll make it fast and only say it once. We know that Blitzstien didn't kill Drago, but someone told him to do it. That person is an attorney, who was also one of the robbery gang, so we've got him for conspiracy to commit murder. Never mind that it didn't work out the way he planned it, we both know that all you need to make the conspiracy case against him is the overt action – and we've got plenty of that.

"You were the prosecutor on the original case in that murder and since I haven't heard anything to the fact that you've been relieved of that responsibility, I think you have a further duty to see this case all the way through to arrest and conviction of the other member of that conspiracy.

"Your new defendant also filed a fraudulent claim against an insurance company I represent, so when he gets arrested, that charge will be added to the complaint.

"Don't worry about procedure here. I've already gone over this case with L.A.P.D. Lieutenant Evans and two of his detectives. Based on the information I gave them, they're prepared to make the arrest and turn their report over to you for the filing of charges.

"Your defendant will be making an appearance in court next Thursday afternoon. I will pick you up at your office at noon that day and we will ride to the courthouse together, where we will meet up with the police. The defendant hasn't the slightest idea of what's going on, so this should be a good show to watch.

"And if you're wondering, I have nothing to do with this whole thing. The press will be there because the case that Handelmann is appearing on is a high profile one – the bank robbery bust. I suggest that you get ready to make a statement outside on the courthouse steps.

"I'm sorry to throw you into the spotlight like this but I feel confident that you can handle it. I'll be faxing you the details of the case, so you'll be able to talk about it intelligently with the police and the press.

"All I want to hear from you is one word – yes, to the question of whether or not you will be in front of your office building next week when I get there to pick you up." The one word answer is given to me and another cast member is now in place.

Another job well done by Mister Jack Bibberman. He staked out the district attorney's employee parking lot and spotted Seymour's fast-food lunch date. After running his license plate we now know that he's part of a special law-student intern program that was started last year when Seymour took over as acting District Attorney. By using this program, second-year law students can work part-time in the D.A.'s offices and earn credit at school. When they graduate law school and pass the bar, they get placed on top of the prospect list to work at the prosecutor's office and have their previous part-time work period count for seniority and pension purposes.

By some devious questioning of other employees, Jack learns that our suspect has been working in that office since the first day Seymour started the program, about nine months ago.

Under the guise of working for a transcript service, Jack checks with all the local law schools but can't find any trace of our law student. If he's not going to one of the regular accredited schools, then he must be attending a storefront or correspondence law school that has a special requirement in California.

For screening purposes, the State Bar wisely requires students of non-accredited law schools to take a first-year law students' exam that covers the three main subjects they all take – Torts, Contracts, and Criminal Law. The students must pass this 'junior bar' exam before they're permitted to continue with their law studies and get credits for qualification to sit for the regular bar examination.

This system weeds out most of the crummy law schools and unfit students, so that the sad case of so many people wasting their time and money for four years doesn't result in a succession of bar exam failures.

If our law student falls into this group, it means that he must have taken the junior bar exam. Our computer expert searches the records and with a little 'hacking,' discovers that the student has just filled out his first application to take the junior bar exam. This means that he was not a law student at all when he joined Seymour's new program for second-year law students. In fact, he was working there all this time before finally enrolling in some correspondence mail-order law school.

If Seymour knew about this timeline, then we've just found another skeleton in his closet. Unfortunately, there's another career in danger and I don't want to destroy the student's chance of ever practicing law. This situation will have to be handled very delicately. It's not the type of thing I enjoy doing because neither of these guys has ever done anything nasty to me, and I'm just not the do-gooder whistle-blowing type.

I've been in touch with Handelmann's office for the past day or so, and after numerous faxes have been exchanged, he's under the impression that our bail bond company definitely will meet him in court and that the deal will be made.

When a legitimate attorney settles a client's case, he or she has the client sign off on the draft, endorses it, and then deposits it to a trust account. A draft is not a check because it is not instantly negotiable. You can't take a draft to any bank and cash it because it requires something to be done first – the claim for which it is being issued must be closed by the claimant's signing of a release form. Once the claim file is closed, the insurance company then authorizes its bank to honor the draft. This procedure can take as long as two weeks, during which time the draft sits in the attorney's trust account. If Handelmann were on the up-and-up, that's what he would do. When the draft clears his account, he could then have two certified checks issued in the sum of each of his client's bail, get them released and avoid the paying of a ten percent fee to a bail bondsman. But Handelmann is not a legitimate attorney... that's why he wants to use the services of our phony bail bond company. We don't need no stinkin' trust account. We don't exist.

If you're careful, you can usually recognize a con job when someone tries to pull one on you. There are two definite danger signs. First, there is an urgency involved. For some reason, whatever the con artist wants must be done now. If you delay, then the entire benefits you are promised will no longer be available.

Second, there is always some reason why other than normal procedures must be followed to expedite the urgency, and the reason given will usually have some grain of truth to it, to make it believable.

In Handelmann's case, he leads me to believe that he's willing to spend the fifty thousand for our fee because against his advice, the clients are ordering him to do so – they want to get out now, not two weeks from now. This sounds reasonable, but I know why. Two weeks from now, they will be many miles from here planning their next bank job. And they'll be a lot richer, having split what they think will be three quarters of a million dollars – the change received from their insurance draft.

I have to give Handelmann credit; he's a strong negotiator. He bargained my bail bond fee from fifty thousand down to thirty-five thousand.

Now that I'm pretty sure he'll be giving me that insurance draft, my next move is to get Indovine and his insurance company client into the courtroom next Thursday. If I can get them there too, then I can personally hand his client the draft and be the hero. I don't want to leave anything to chance, so I call the Uniman Insurance Company and ask to be put through to the boss.

Just like all other large organizations, there are many levels of people who try to screen people from getting to the boss – only letting those through who they think are important enough.

I've had enough of those Dilberts, so I cut right through them. The call is made. "Hello, this is Uniman Insurance, how can I direct your call?"

"I have a one-point-three million dollar draft from your company that I'd like to give back to you as a gift. Please connect me with Mister Uniman's office."

That should get her attention. Let's see how many schmucks I have to talk to before Uniman takes the call. I'm lucky today – only two other executives. The last one is especially snotty. He must be related to the boss. No employee who fears getting fired would ever talk to a stranger like that.

I finally convince him that I'm for real and after staying 'on hold' for about five minutes, the old man takes the call. "Uniman here, what's this about a draft of ours? We have legal counsel – you should talk to them. I'm giving you back to my secretary. She'll give you their telephone number."

I've got to make him understand exactly what's going on and I don't think he'll give me much time to do it, so I take my best shot. "Mister Uniman, this is attorney Peter Sharp. I believe you were in Mister Charles Indovine's office the last time I called there and he ignored my plea and advised you to settle that wrongful death case on Drago. Well, he was wrong and I was right. If you'll be in court next Thursday at one in the afternoon, I will be there to personally return that settlement draft back to you. The case will be closed and no further claim will be made."

A few seconds passes by while I hear him sputter. I go on to tell him a little more about how I brilliantly managed to save him the money. "The lawyer handling the case put in a fraudulent claim. I'll tell you all about it next Thursday when I see you in court. And oh, by the way, there are two things I want you to bring with you. Number one, I'd like Charles Indovine to be there with you. If he wouldn't have been so pompous and had given me the chance to present the evidence I had, you would never have had to settle this case in the first place and you would have saved all the legal fees you paid to Indovine's firm - and also a check for one-hundred- thirty thousand dollars made payable to me, as a ten percent fee for recovering your money. That's the second item.

"And while we're at it, if you're as great a businessman as they say you are, you'll also bring along one of your standard defense retainer agreements because notwithstanding the way I've been treated to date, I'd still like to work with you on a special assignment basis.

"Can I count on seeing you there next week – with Mister Indovine and my check and retainer?"

He gives me what's called a 'grumbling acceptance,' so it looks like we'll have a full cast in attendance. I'm sure that Special Agent Snell will be there too, because he's the main man in the Attorney General's case. I've let Myra and Lieutenant Evans know that when they grab Handelmann in court, to only tell him that he's being arrested for insurance fraud. Evans agrees with me that if Snell hears anything about a murder conspiracy, he might grab Handelmann as his own prisoner, for being a part of the robbery gang. That wouldn't be good for Evans and Myra, and it certainly wouldn't be good for me, because it would take all the wind out of my sails for getting that twenty-five grand for the third outstanding member of the gang. It would be tough to claim a reward for giving Snell someone who he already had in custody.

My next hurdle is the court. No judge likes surprises in the courtroom. Uniformed officers, detectives, a County prosecutor and a news crew all traipsing in for the arrest of an attorney during the middle of a Federal Court Motion Hearing definitely qualifies as a surprise. Having handled a few federal criminal matters, I know from personal experience how carefully they guard the constitutional rights of defendants, so I might as well use that premise as a way to get them on my page. I call the Federal Court and make an appointment to come in and speak to the judge of the courtroom where Handelmann will be making his appearance. I first have to convince the judge's clerk that in no way will I be discussing the merits of the case he'll be hearing. No judge will allow any person to come into chambers to discuss anything about a case unless all counsel involved are present. For this conference, I absolutely don't want the defendant's counsel there – and would rather not see Snell there either.

Fortunately, my explanation to the clerk about the fact that Handelmann will be arrested brings about a nice solution. Court normally starts its afternoon session promptly at one o'clock. On the day of Handelmann's appearance, the judge will refrain from taking the bench until fifteen minutes after one. This will give me a few minutes to get the insurance draft and allow Evans and Myra the opportunity to grab up Handelmann before court officially becomes 'in session.'

By doing things this way, the whole event is not placed on the official court reporter's transcript and when the judge does come out to take the bench at one-fifteen, he can handle it merely as a slight change of plans due to unavailability of defense counsel. A continuance will be granted so that new counsel can be retained and the case goes on as usual. I like this arrangement. It means that by one-thirty that day I can be having lunch with Myra and also be over a hundred grand richer. I won't mind picking up the tab.

Acting District Attorney Seymour calls. After his secretary lets me know that he wants to talk to me, I wait on hold for a few minutes for him to actually pick up the phone and start a conversation. Why can't these executive jerks just pick up the phone and call someone themselves? He finally comes on the line. "Hello, Mister Sharp, I wonder if you could please come to my office. There are a few details I'd like to discuss with you."

"Mister Seymour, I don't have any open cases with your office, so you'll have to give me an idea of what's on your mind."

"It's about your ex-wife and her candidacy for my office."

"Actually, it's not your office – you're just filling in temporarily, but if you really want to talk to me, I can be there next Thursday at about eleven in the morning. I have some business in Federal Court that afternoon, so I'll be downtown."

Pompous ass that he is, he grudgingly agrees to wait another couple of days for my appearance at his office. I have no idea what he wants to talk to me about, but I'm growing less and less fond of this guy every day. I think I should have some ammunition when I go to his office, so I prepare a file, hoping that it won't be necessary to use it.

There's one reporter who has steadily been following me on my cases. She's aggressive but can be cooperative when the situation requires it. The tough part is convincing her that the situation requires it. I make arrangements to meet her for lunch at the Jamaica Bay Inn Coffee Shop to make her an offer that I hope she can't refuse.

During lunch I explain to her that there will be an in-court arrest made of an attorney, who will be charged with a felony. She starts to salivate, immediately pressing me for more details. I lay out exactly what I want and how I'd like it to be handled. "Here's what you get. An exclusive on the in-court arrest of a prominent criminal attorney and an exclusive interview with the prosecutor."

"So, what's the catch? Seems straight forward to me"

"You're right, it is straight forward, except that there's a small transaction that's going to go down about thirty seconds before the arrest and I don't want it covered that day."

"Oh no, if it's news, I have to get it. The people have a right to know…"

I interrupt her standard reporter's line of constitutional bullshit. "Yeah, yeah, I know all about the people's right to know but the people also have a right to have the bad guys convicted without the case getting screwed up by a nosy reporter. During those thirty seconds, the lawyer will be handing me an envelope. What's in the envelope is the basis of his being arrested. If he sees reporters and a camera crew, he'll know something's going on, and I won't get the envelope. If I don't get the envelope, there'll be no arrest for you to put on the evening news – so here's the deal. You and your crew will be waiting down the hall in front of another courtroom door. Our court session is supposed to start promptly at one in the afternoon. I've made arrangements with the judge and the court staff to have the session delayed fifteen minutes, so that the arrest can be done off of the record. This means that since the court won't officially be in session, you guys can come in with your cameras, as long as you follow the cops and the perp out into the hall and clear the courtroom by a quarter after one because that's when the judge is coming out to take the bench.

"As soon as this lawyer hands me the envelope, a plain-clothes detective sitting in the back row of the spectator seats will open the hallway door signaling the uniforms to come in and make the bust. You already know in advance that it's okay to follow them in with the camera because I've arranged for the judge not to be on the bench. You get your footage, you get your story and as a bonus, you get an interview outside on the steps with a political candidate – and don't ask me who – you'll see when you get there. And in case you're curious, that interview will also inform you what transpired thirty seconds before you got into the courtroom and what was in the envelope.

"Do we have a deal?"

This is the fastest 'yes,' I've ever gotten from a female. She even lets me know that she's picking up the tab for our lunch. Knowing that the television station is buying, I order an extra tropical drink that contains Kahlùa and Bailey's Irish Cream. It tastes like a chocolate milk shake and I don't realize how powerful it is until we leave the table and someone points out to me that I'm walking on my knees.

There are only a few days before my grand performance in Federal Court. This is exciting. I'm finally going to reach my star potential and like a true martyr, I'll be stepping aside and letting Myra take all the credit. She won't be getting any part of my hundred and thirty grand, but I'm sure that the on-camera time means more to her. The publicity she'll get will be worth more than my reward check from Uniman and it'll also probably get her elected. Damn I'm good!

The only unknown remaining is what Acting Putz Seymour wants to see me about. It's tough to figure guys like that because I can't think like them. They're sociopathic sleazeballs and I refuse to try and get into their heads.

24

It's Thursday, the day of the big show. I feel like a Broadway producer on the opening night of his new play. Next time I bump into Neil Simon, I'll be sure to tell him that I understand what it feels like. I'm sure he'll be glad to know that I'm just like him.

I'm supposed to pick Myra up at noon, so I've about a half hour max to devote to my meeting with Seymour – and even less time than that if he makes me cool my heels in his outer office waiting for him.

I approach his secretary at about 2 minutes to eleven and make sure that she lets her boss know that I have to be out of there in about fifteen minutes, so if he's not available to see me, I might as well leave now and he can call me to reschedule the meeting.

This news probably doesn't sit too well with him, because he pops out into the waiting area in about a minute and motions for me to follow him into the inner office. No smile, no handshake, no pleasantries, no nothing. I guess this isn't a job interview. I follow him into the office, which looks like the interior of one of Saddam Hussein's palaces. He's obviously spent some of his own money bringing in fancy stuff because the last time I was in this room was to meet with his predecessor who was then Myra's boss – at that time, it looked like a typical government office.

I must admit that Seymour looks grand. When I first started practicing I was involved in a Federal criminal case where one of the defendants flew out here from New York for each appearance. He was sartorially splendid. The leather in his watchband matched the leather in his shoes. The silk in his necktie matched the silk in his breast pocket handkerchief. His suit looked like it was hand-sewed on him while he stood there. I'm sure he was in the upper levels of organized crime because his last name ended in a vowel and attorney Oscar Goodman (who was subsequently elected as the mayor of Las Vegas) represented him,.

Seymour's appearance is a few pegs below the crime boss' but it's still nice to look at, including the bright yellow suspenders he exhibits when removing his jacket to sit down behind that big expensive desk.

We aren't alone in the room. Sitting next to him is his trusted aide, the kissing law student. No introduction is made, but none is necessary. I know exactly who this guy is. He's in my photo scrapbook.

Seymour doesn't waste any time. As soon as I'm seated, he begins what is obviously a prepared speech. I can tell this isn't going to be a social event by his first word. It's my last name. That's big indication that his gloves are off and I'm probably in for a scolding from the big bad District Attorney.

"Sharp, I know who you are and that you were once married to my opponent in this race for District Attorney. I'm going to make this brief and to the point. I can be a good friend or a bad enemy… it's your choice. If you play along with me, report to me exactly what every one of her campaign plans are and don't try any bandstand tactics to get her elected, then you can have a good friend in this office – and that can mean a lot to a criminal attorney – access to the D.A.

"On the other hand, if you play your usual game and try to help her campaign, when I get elected, you're in for a rough time in my county. Every client you represent will be denied any kind of plea bargain. You'll have to either plead everyone straight up to all the charges or take the cases to trial, at which time I'll assign the best prosecutors we have and spare no expense in seeing your clients go to jail and your career as a criminal attorney destroyed. I intend to beat her in the race for this office, and I want to destroy her. And I'll destroy you along with her if I have to. I'm going to be the District Attorney of this county and I'll crush anyone who stands in my way.

"Do I make myself clear?"

I look down at my Timex to see how much time I have to surgically take this asshole apart. There's enough time.

"Gee, I'm sorry you feel that way about me, because I'm kinda fond of you. And I'd especially like to have a friend in this office, because one of my clients is considering bringing a misconduct action against a police officer that arrested him at a fast-food place recently. Of course, if this case goes to trial, we'll be introducing into evidence witness statements of the restaurant's employees – and one of them made the ridiculous claim that he saw you and your friend here kissing in the car. Now I know that it sounds a little out of the ordinary for a prosecutor who's been so tough on homosexuals to actually be one himself, but nevertheless, we have to take all statements seriously and present whatever testimony is available concerning the vehicles that were in line that day."

He stands up behind his desk and starts his best performance of the day. "Sharp, that's it. I was willing to give you a chance, against the advice of my closest advisors, but you've just put an end to any opportunity you might have ever had. Not only will your ex-wife lose the race against me, both you and she will probably be arrested and convicted of some crimes before the election. You know, it's not uncommon for people to be stopped for a minor traffic violation, only to have some restricted substance noticed in plain sight by the police. Many a career has been destroyed like that."

It wasn't only the things he said, it was the smug smirk on his face when he said it that really bothered me. I glance up at the clock on the wall and realize that I'm running out of time if I want to pick up Myra, so I open up my file folder and lay my cards on the table. I step forward and place on his desk in order, the ammunition I brought with me but didn't want to use.

"Okay mister District Attorney, here's how it is. I accept your apology. This is a picture of you and your friend here kissing on the lips. Let me know, I can get you some wallet-sized ones for a good price. And this is a copy of your friend's application to take the Baby Bar Exam. Note that he states under oath that he just started law school last term, so that when he took the job here in that program you instituted solely for the purpose of getting your lunch date a way to be close to you, not only was he not a second-year law student, he wasn't any kind of law student.

If all this stuff comes out at trial, not only will you be the one who's leaving town, but you'll be leaving without your wife and her money, and baby-face here will get thrown out of law school for lying on his application for a civil service position."

At this point they're both sucking wind like fishes out of water. As long as they're not interrupting me, I guess it's okay to go on.

"So, I'll tell you what I'm gonna do. I hate messy situations. Pretty boy, you will quit your job here and spend your time at home studying for your Baby Bar Exam. If you pass it and this stuff doesn't get revealed, maybe you'll have a chance at a law career and this will be a lesson to you that it never pays to act like your schmuck boyfriend here.

"And as for you, Mister Schmuck Boyfriend, I've just decided to convince my client that he shouldn't bring any action against the cops, so that none of this nasty stuff will be revealed. And that's a good thing because being forced to deal with vicious, evil people like you is a terrible experience.

"So here's what's going to happen. Copies of all this stuff, along with the audiotape I've been making of this meeting will be placed in a safe place, with the custodian instructed to give it to the press if anything nasty happens to either of us. She will win, make no mistake about that because as of this moment, you've just decided to instruct your campaign to immediately stop running those ridiculous negative campaign ads that are totally false and misleading. And without saying something bad about her, you're left with the alternative of saying something nice about yourself – and I don't think the best political advisors in the world can create something to fill that bill. Do I make myself clear?

"And by the way, I think you're wasting your time running for the office of District Attorney. That's only a County position. You're a bad enough person to qualify for a much higher position in our state's government. And with your wife's backing, the sky's the limit. I'd say that governor would be a nice stepping stone for you, on the way to Senator and then President."

The room is silent as I pick up my documents and exit with my file. I have a feeling that it's been a successful morning. There's a possibility that the outer office secretary may have been listening in on our meeting, because as I pass by her desk on the way out, she doesn't offer to validate my parking stub.

Punctual as usual, I pull up in front of Myra's office building and am surprised to see who's there waiting for me. Myra and Suzi. I'm informed that Suzi wants to see the Federal Court action, so Myra sent a taxi to bring her down here.

In a way, I'm glad. She was instrumental in getting most of the information together and she's entitled to watch a little bit of the action. The place will be full of cops and feds, so there's no danger for her. I wouldn't allow her to watch as we busted up the bank robbery gang, but the courtroom is a much more controlled place, so I feel okay about her being here.

5

The downtown Federal Building is quite an impressive place. It's nothing like the Municipal courts, with those halls full of drunk driving defendants and other forms of lowlifes meeting with their attorneys and arguing with their spouses.

Everything here is neat and in its place and there's a sense of order that pervades the building. No doubt about it - when you're in this building, you're in the major leagues of law.

When we walk down the corridor I see that my instructions are being followed. The reporter and her camera crew are stationed outside a different courtroom, so as to not give any sense of danger to Handelmann. There are always high profile cases going on in this building, so it doesn't look out of the ordinary to see a camera crew down the hall, outside of a courtroom.

Lieutenant Evans is down there with the reporter, along with one of his detectives and two uniforms. I'm sure that the other detective is already seated in our courtroom, ready to signal the rest of them that it's showtime.

A clock on the wall shows five minutes remaining until one. In Federal Court, it doesn't make any difference what time your wristwatch says because the judge will take the bench on Federal Courthouse time, as displayed on the wall clocks.

A tall, slender man walks past us and enters the courtroom. It's Handelmann. I look down the hall and see that Lieutenant Evans is nodding at me. He recognizes him too. Behind us, the elevator door opens and Charles Indovine steps out into the hall. We see each other. I nod to him. He ignores me. The executive-type with him must be the Uniman from Uniman Insurance. I hope he's brought my check with him.

Next out of the elevator is Special Agent Snell, followed by a small entourage of junior agents, a secretary, and a Federal Marshal. At least I get a nod of recognition from him as he passes by.

With Handelmann already in the courtroom, I nod a signal to Lieutenant Evans and the crew that it's okay now to come down the hall and gather outside this courtroom door, so they can all rush in when they get the signal.

Myra, Suzi, and I step inside the courtroom. Handelmann is already at the counsel table. I walk over to the clerk of the court. She tells me that the Deputy Attorney General has been informed of what's going to take place and he'll just step back out of the way and let everyone do their job. Suzi positions herself just behind the front railing, so she can get a good view of the event. She has to stand on her toes to see over the railing top.

I walk over to Handelmann. "Mister Handelmann? I'm from the Bail Bond Company. Do you have something for me? Just at that moment, the Federal Marshals bring in the two defendants. As the dog lady approaches Handelmann, they both exchange the same greeting. "Hello, Honey." Interesting. I now see another interesting aspect of this strange group of people. Handelmann turns to me "Yeah, just a minute, I've got to get this draft signed by my client." He takes it out of his briefcase and puts it down on the counsel table so that the dog-lady can sign off on it, just under where Handelmann has already affixed his signature.

I glance toward the spectator seats and see Mister Uniman's eyes bulge out as he sees the draft on the counsel table being signed. That old cocker's vision must be pretty good for him to be able to recognize one of his company's drafts at over twenty feet away. I look in his direction with an expression of confidence on my face. Charles Indovine is sitting next to him, not at all amused.

Once the draft is signed, Handelmann picks it up off of the table and hands it to me. "Okay Mister Bail Bonds, do you have something for me?"

Of course I have something for him. I motion to Myra that it's her turn to step forward. At the same time, Evans' detective, who is sitting in the back row, gets up and opens the hallway door. The reporter rushes in with the camera crew behind her. There's also a guy with a long pole and a fuzzy attachment that's probably a microphone. There's a bright light on top of the camera and the whole crew is rapidly approaching the counsel tables, including Lieutenant Evans, the reporters, two detectives, and two uniformed L.A.P.D. officers.

Handelmann turns around and sees the crowd approaching. He looks like a deer caught in the headlights. I glance toward the spectator seats and see a portion of the kid's head peeking over the rail... she's staying low, taking no chances.

Myra steps up to Handelmann and makes me proud. Turning her head so that she's partly facing the cameras and also facing Handelmann, she makes a brief announcement. "Richard Handelmann, my name is Myra Scot, special prosecutor for the County of Los Angeles District Attorney's office. I'm placing you under arrest for the felony of insurance fraud." With that, she looks at the Lieutenant. "Book him, Lieutenant Evans." She then turns partly back towards Handelmann. "This is Lieutenant Sidney Evans of the Los Angeles Police Department. He will be taking you to the Van Nuys Division and you will be booked there." She then turns to the Federal Marshal. "You can leave these defendants here…the judge will be out in a minute."

Wow, she really can perform. Not only does she announce to Handelmann what's going on, she even goes so far as to give instructions to the police and the Marshal of the courtroom.

The five policemen cuff Handelmann and slowly escort him out of the courtroom, so that the reporter and camera crew are able to easily keep up with them. I look back towards the rail and see an entire little head sticking up over it. I guess the action is all over so she thinks it's safe to stand up.

Myra walks out, following the parade. She doesn't want to be too far from the press, because once Handelmann is in the squad car, they'll be focusing on her – and she wants to make it easy for them.

Settlement draft in hand, I walk back to the spectator section and approach Indovine and Uniman. Indovine seems to be having some difficulty looking me in the face. Uniman stands up and speaks to me. "Mister Sharp… can I call you Peter?" I nod yes.

"Peter, I understand you have something for me." He holds his hand out.

"Yes, Mister Uniman... can I call you Murray?" I decide to anyway, even though he never nods his acceptance of my assumed familiarity with him. "I certainly do have something for you. Am I correct in assuming that you also have something for me?"

I'm correct. There's a trace of a smile on his face as he looks at Indovine. "Go ahead Charles, give it to him." At this point, I hope it's my check he's talking about because I'm sure that Indovine probably feels like really 'giving it to me' with at least thirty-eight calibers.

Per Mister Uniman's instructions, Indovine stands up and hands me an envelope. I peek inside to make sure it's the correct amount. It is, and I hand the draft to him. "Here, Charles, this is for your client. If I'm still working for you, you're the one who hired me to bring this case to its conclusion, so you should take the credit for getting his money back."

Indovine is taken aback by my act of graciousness. "Listen here, Sharp... er, uh, Peter, I'm sorry about any misunderstanding we may have had in the past. I hope that you'll continue to let us avail ourselves of your services."

That's very nice of him. Uniman probably forced him into it. "No problem Charles, I can understand your actions. Your firm isn't experienced in the seamy side of insurance fraud, so your advice to Mister Uniman to settle the case was probably the most prudent thing to do at the time."

Mister Uniman looks pleased. We all exchange nods and they leave the courtroom. Special

Agent Snell passes by me on his way out. "Sharp, I don't know how you do it, but as long as you don't get in my way, I guess it's okay. I'll probably be hearing from you soon with that information, right?"

I let him know that he's right. I look down and see that the kid is standing right next to me, trying to get her share of the credit. I want to make sure that the Asian boys continue to deliver those Chinese gourmet meals to the boat, so I toss away a little credit. "Oh by the way, Agent Snell, this is my office manager, Suzi Braunstein. She's the one who coordinates all my information."

Suzi looks up at Snell and decides to finish my sentence for me, as she gently grabs Uniman's check out of my hand.

"And makes the bank deposits."

Snell looks down at her. "Nice work Miss Braunstein, when you're tall enough to see over the rail, come and see me… the F.B.I. is always looking for a few good people." I look down at her. She's actually blushing. Any other kid her age would probably be walking on cloud nine after getting a compliment like that from a senior special agent but we both know that she could never work for the FBI, or anyone else, for that matter. She'd never want to take the cut in pay.

I take her by the hand and we start to leave the courtroom to find Myra, who has probably already made her statement to the press. We'll catch it later tonight on the news.

At exactly fifteen minutes after one, the Federal Marshal calls the court to order and the judge takes the bench. I feel a tug at my hand. The kid wants to stick around to see what the judge does, so we sit down in the back row. The case is called and the clerk hands a note up to him. He looks down at the defendants.

"This court has been informed that your attorney will no longer be available to represent either one of you. Therefore, this case is being continued for ten days, at which time I would like to have a status report on your efforts to retain other counsel. In the meantime, I will instruct the Federal Defender's Office to contact both of you, to assist you in your efforts to obtain counsel."

That having been said, he bangs his gavel, gets up and heads for the golf course. Suzi is impressed. We go outside to locate Myra the media star.

Flush with our insurance reward money, I think it's time to go shopping. Last year I told the broker at Purcell Yachts to keep his eye out for us. We're looking for a Grand Banks 50 that's in good shape. Suzi could easily write a check for the fiberglass model, but with me being forced to carry my end, we still can't afford one of the newer ones, but there are quite a few beautiful old 'woodies' out there that have been meticulously maintained.

Now that Purcell thinks I can actually afford to buy a boat, his search has miraculously found a few for me to look at. Combining the reward money with everything I've got in my bank account and his giving us a decent amount for the forty-two footer we're now living on, I think we should just about be able to swing what a wooden Grand Banks will cost.

The Californian we're now on is a nice boat but there's nothing like a 50-foot Grand Banks, complete with parquet floors, raised pilothouse, extra staterooms and lots and lots of room. We stayed on one for a while last year that was inherited by Stuart, but thanks to his letting the I.R.S. think he was the invisible man for about ten years, they decided it would be nicer in their Marina than ours.

Purcell wants me to come and look at one nearby, so I'm on the way. I see that the lights are on in George Clooney's boat. I leave word with the kid that if George stops by while I'm gone, to tell him that I'll be back in less than an hour. I surely want to be on the boat in time for the six o'clock news, so I can see how Myra's appearance came off. Suzi is sitting there waiting. She wants to watch too.

Myra looks great on camera. It loves her almost as much as she loves it. There she is. The camera is shaky as it's being hand-held and quickly carried through the double doors leading into the courtroom, following Myra and the reporter – and then there's Myra making her announcement to Handelmann and bossing everyone in the courtroom around. She really knows how to take control... especially when I arrange to give it to her. I see that the reporter kept up her part of the bargain. I'm nowhere to be seen. It's all Myra's show.

Next we see the camera follow her out of the building. Handelmann is rushed into a waiting squad car and whisked away. The reporter knew in advance what station Handelmann would be taken to, so I'm sure she arranged to have another crew standing by to see him brought out of the squad car and into the Van Nuys jail. The 'perp walk.'

Myra did a great job with her outdoor press conference. She explained how during the trial, her investigation led her to believe that there was more to the case than just Harold Blitzstien, but that Seymour didn't want to hear any of it. Great! She took a little shot at him. It couldn't happen to a nicer guy.

Finally, and at my express instruction, the reporter asks her about her campaign plans. Myra really sticks it to Seymour by explaining that the office of the District Attorney should be more open to the policy of not getting too locked in on any one suspect – even after charges have been filed. That's not fair to the people accused of crimes or to the public at large. She then does a beautiful job of explaining what's wrong with the way the District Attorney's office is being run now and how she intends to reform it after she takes office. Also as agreed, she praises the cooperation of Lieutenant Evans and his men, in her ongoing investigation and the arrest. Now I'm even with him. It's nice to be able to pay off debts.

Myra gets a million dollars worth of publicity and another bad guy gets brought to justice. At this point, even if Snell is watching her statement, there's no way he can figure Handelmann as the third gang member, because at this time he doesn't even know that Blitzstien and Drago were in the gang. I love it when a good plan comes together.

I'm a little short of the full price for the Grand Banks I just made an offer on, so it's probably a good time to get my finances in order. The time sheets on the Blitzstien case have been amended to include investigation hours spent in clearing him and finding the real killer. The court shouldn't mind those extra hours, especially when it resulted in bringing in a real bad guy. That should cover my trip to Hawaii with Myra and still leave enough left over to almost cover the boat.

The FBI's twenty-five grand for fingering Handelmann will finish the new boat's purchase price. I'll send the Blitzstien portion to his family. The Drago share of the reward will be distributed between Suzi and Jack B. They put all the information together and they deserve it.

Now that I can give Snell an address that I'm sure Handelmann will be at for a while, his documentation package is complete. Jack B. will hand-carry it to the FBI office for me.

I've got some time to pack for Hawaii. We'll be leaving in a couple of days and I want to get ready for this romantic vacation with Myra. The room reservation has already been made there at the Pioneer Inn. I bought the plane tickets the same afternoon that Blitzstien's not guilty verdict came in. Myra's ticket was given to her while we were on the way to the Federal Courthouse.

I take some time to go through the travel brochures, lining up a bunch of things for us to do during the day while we're in Maui. This time, I want to make sure we get to take one of those evening dinner cruises. We'll also be renting a jeep for the curvy drive over the mountain to reach Hana, a secluded place on the farthest east end of the island,

and also stopping to walk through the park that has the IAO Needle, a twenty-five hundred foot tall volcanic spire. While I'm at it, I might as well reserve some scuba gear. A fellow member of the Lahaina Yacht Club has the video concession on a large tourist dive boat, so we'll probably spend a day out there with him. I don't think I'm the only one on the boat who's interested in Hawaii, because this morning I see that the travel brochures on the dinette table are not in the same order that I left them in last night.

Myra likes to play golf. Not being from a family with money and plenty of time to waste, I never got around to learning it. If I'm going to use a stick to make a small ball move around, it won't be on a golf course with a bunch of fat old white guys, it'll be in a pool hall, where the real men go. There's no quiche served in poolrooms.

When I was a kid back in Chicago I used to work at a bowling alley that hadn't yet converted to that new automatic pin-spotting equipment, so they employed boys like us to set the pins several nights a week when the leagues were bowling. If you were a pin-spotter, you were allowed to play pool for free during the afternoon. After a while I got pretty good at it – good enough to work my way through high school by doing a little hustling in between jobs playing piano at weddings.

After a couple of years in smoke filled rooms, you get pretty good at spotting hustlers and con artists of every kind, and that knowledge has served me quite well over the years. I had no problem spotting Handelmann and Seymour as people to avoid doing business with. Vinnie still gives me a slight problem, but Olive and Stuart have rehabilitated him nicely, so I think he'll be okay as long as he stays away from trees.

Special Agent Snell calls. He is not a happy camper. "Sharp, are you crazy? We checked out the addresses you gave us on those remaining three gang members. One of them is the County Morgue and the other is the Van Nuys Division of the Los Angeles Police Station. Is this a joke?"

"No joke Agent Snell. That's where they are. Handelmann is the guy you saw getting arrested in court the other day. If you hurry, you can still catch him in Van Nuys. After tomorrow, he'll be transferred to the County Jail downtown, to await trial. The County Morgue is where Vlad Drago and Harold Blitzstien are and if you hurry, you can still catch the bodies. After another day or so, you can have the ashes."

"And you expect us to give you fifty thousand dollars for turning in two dead bodies and a city jail prisoner?"

"No, I expect you to give me fifty thousand dollars for providing you with their identities, proof of their involvement in the bank robberies and their present addresses."

"This sucks."

"Sorry Snell, but if you work things right, you can still get some good press coverage out of it. After all, if not for my work on getting Handelmann busted for insurance fraud, he would have used the one point three million dollar fraudulently obtained settlement to bail out the other gang members. You know what would happen then... they'd skip bail and turn up in some other location where banks are located on the first floor of large office buildings.

"Your work on this case has put an end to that. You should be getting a medal of some kind and when I talk to a certain reporter I know, your name will be prominently mentioned. I'm sure she'll be contacting you for an interview, so make sure you're Bar Mitzvah suit is pressed. Blue looks really good on camera."

"Okay Sharp, you've got a point there. By the way, is she the one who you brought into court for the Handelmann bust?"

"Yep, she's the one and she owes me big time, so when I tell her about you, an interview is a certainty."

"When do you think you might be speaking to this reporter friend of yours?"

"I'll be telling her all about you at the dinner I promised to take her to. She picked a really expensive restaurant, but I can't afford it without that reward money you'll be sending me. The sooner you authorize that payment, the sooner I can tell her about you."

Snell doesn't sound too happy about our conversation, but I have a feeling that the reward check will be coming in shortly.

I think that the best place to entertain the reporter will be on our boat, so I'm working on a new pasta recipe.

Myra calls to tell me that she had to change her flight plans. She has an important interview the morning of our flight to Maui, so she's booked a later flight and will meet me on the Island, either late that night or early the next morning – and I'm not to worry about transportation because she's arranged for a car service to bring her the twenty-seven miles from the Maui airport to Lahaina.

That's a disappointment, because it means we'll be spending one less night together in my hotel room. Oh well, I guess you can never really have everything you want.

I spend my remaining time here on the mainland laying out my island wardrobe and packing. As usual, I'll be using a car service to take me to the airport. They send a Lincoln Town Car to pick me up and the driver usually gets here at least fifteen minutes early and calls me on his cell phone to ask if I need any assistance in bringing my luggage up to the car. This car service thing is really a class act. When you get into their vehicle, a brand new bottle of some expensive foreign water is waiting for you, and it's personal, door-to-door service.

A dock neighbor who's really into computers has shown me the proper way to access my email, so I'm also packing my laptop. I'm sure the kid will want me to check in with her a couple of times each day. Stuart has offered to stay on the boat to keep an eye on her. She would probably rather stay alone, but Stuart insisted, because she's helping him brief his cases for the law classes he's taking. He already told me that some day soon he intends to be my law partner. I can't wait. That's just what I need – another person to take part of my hard earned fees.

The phone rings and my caller ID display shows a familiar number – the Van Nuys Police

Station. Thinking it's Lieutenant Evans, I pick up the phone with a happy greeting. It's not Evans – it's Handelmann.

"Hello Sharp, how's the bail bond business?"

"I don't owe you any explanation or apology. You broke the rules and I nailed you. What do you want?"

"I need a favor."

"And you think I'll do it for you?"

"Yeah, because I've got something to trade."

"I'm listening."

"I can't go into details, but I've made a deal with the Feds. They're going to take me out of here soon."

That figures. He's been flipped and will now rat out his other clients, so the feds will put him into some witness protection program. I know he's a con man, but I'm still curious to know what he's going to offer me for whatever favor he wants. I tell him I'm still listening.

"I know that you're getting a nice reward for turning me in and the favor I'd like is for you to deposit some money into my wife's inmate account. She may have to serve a year or two before I can get her out."

"And why would I want to do this for you?"

"Because I know that your ex-wife, the ball-busting broad who's prosecuting me, is running for D.A. and my conviction on her record will look really good to the voters."

This guy may be a criminal, but he's one smart cookie. If I get his drift, he's offering to plead guilty to the charges Myra's bringing against him because he knows he won't have to serve the time.

"Okay Handelmann, let's say just for conversation's sake that I go along with your program. What exactly do you have in mind?"

"First, I call her up and tell her I want to make a plea. Then she comes and visits me and we both sign the plea agreement. I plead guilty to whatever she wants. After the deal is signed, you deposit the maximum one thousand to each of our three accounts. That's it. Your squeeze gets a fast conviction and gets elected as District Attorney and we have plenty of money to spend on candy and cigarettes until I can spring us."

"Okay, go ahead and make the call, Handelmann. When your conviction is entered on the court's record, I'll deposit the two thousand to their accounts and when you're transferred over to the Feds, I'll make the last deposit to your account. And you'd better make it quick, because if Snell takes you out of there before the plea bargain is signed, our deal is off."

The deal is done. Now I wait to see Myra on the evening news, announcing that she got the confession and guilty plea. I call the reporter and give her an anonymous' tip about the upcoming plea. I'm sure that in her report she'll refer to me as a 'high-ranking associate of the district attorney.' Seymour will be pleased to hear that.

Myra makes her announcement on the evening news. The timing is perfect because the next day Lieutenant Evans calls to tell me that the Feds came and took Handelmann away. He wasn't disappointed. This means there'll be one less prisoner to spend money on clothing, housing, feeding, and taking through the judicial system. Evans got his press coverage out of it, so he's happy.

Myra calls. She tells me that one of her spies at the District Attorney's office tells her that Seymour is planning on making an announcement after work today. He's called a news conference. She wants to know if I have any idea what's going on, because she also has found out that I met with Seymour that morning before we went to Federal Court to bust Handelmann.

I tell her that Seymour threatened to destroy me if I helped her campaign and that he wanted me to spy on her for him. At first, she's a little put out that I didn't tell her about it sooner, but when she remembers all the things I did to help her election campaign, she realizes that I have no intentions of doing anything that would hurt her.

My suggestion is that we meet at Pollo Meshuga for an early dinner and to watch Seymour's announcement on one of their six hanging television sets. If there's no Hispanic team playing soccer somewhere in the world, they'll probably let us tune one set in to the news.

She took my suggestion, and I'm now sitting at our favorite table waiting for her to come in. After our salsa and guacamole appetizer is brought to the table, we see our friendly reporter on the steps of the Criminal Courts Building, prepping the audience for Acting District Attorney Seymour's announce-ment.

When he saunters down the steps to where the cameras are, I notice that his lunch date is nowhere to be seen. As usual, Seymour looks wonderful... he's definitely dressed too good to be a district attorney. He starts out with the usual crap about how glad he is to see the press and about how his office finally got a conviction on the Drago murder. Our friendly reporter interrupts him with a question. "Excuse me Mister Seymour, but wasn't that conviction obtained by your opponent, Myra Scot?"

Seymour brushes off the question, but you can tell that it got to him. "Any conviction that's obtained by any person working for me is a victory for the People." Smooth. He turns Myra into one of his flunkies, just doing her job. We're still waiting for the other shoe to drop. You can't just call a press conference. You've got to have something to say or you lose credibility and the next time you try it, no press will show up. He doesn't disappoint them.

"The reason I've brought you here is because I've had a long discussion with my family, and the consensus is that I shouldn't be in this race for District Attorney." Audible gasps are heard in the crowd. Myra squeezes my arm.

"Did you have anything to do with this?"

I don't answer her question with anything but a 'who me?' look. Seymour goes on.

"This was a difficult decision to make, because I love the job of District Attorney and am sure that I would win the election, but I feel that I can do much more for the People if I'm in a higher office. Therefore, effective immediately, I am withdrawing my name from the list of candidates for the office of District Attorney of Los Angeles County and notifying the Board of Elections that I intend to be entering the race for Governor of the State of California."

One of the other reporters shouts out a question to him. "Mister Seymour, does this mean that you'll be telling your people to support Myra Scot?"

"Well to tell you the truth, if I was just a private citizen, I'd be glad to answer that question, but now that I'm a declared candidate for Governor, I don't think it's my place to comment on a local county election."

That was a nice way of avoiding the question. There's no way he'd publicly support Myra, but it doesn't make any difference now. She's got a lock on this election and I feel that I fulfilled the promise I made to get her elected.

Hearing this, Myra tells me something that makes me very happy.

"Petey, I don't know how, but I do know that you've had plenty to do with me getting in position to win this election, so I've got a special gift for you."

I wish she'd stop calling me that but I know that if I asked her to, that would provide her with just one more button she could press to annoy me. "I'm all ears." Myra's got tons of money she inherited from her grandfather. Maybe she's finally going to spend a little on me.

"When you get to Maui, I want you to make sure that you don't waste the whole night getting drunk at the club on Margaritas. I want you to get to your hotel room at exactly eleven that evening, because there's going to be a surprise on your bed waiting for you. I'm not going to tell you what it is, because I don't want to ruin the surprise, but I can tell you that it will be warm, wet, and breathing hard.

That's it. My life is now complete. I've finished my last few years' work and gotten Myra's respect back. In another day or so, I'll be in Myra on Maui.

It feels like the time until my plane leaves tomorrow is taking about five years to pass by. I'm so preoccupied with my second honeymoon with Myra that I can't even concentrate on a Sherlock Holmes or Nero Wolfe story. Instead, I spend the day on the other thing I lust for, the fifty-foot Grand Banks. Purcell Yachts has arranged with the owner for permission to board the boat and I'm now sitting in the main salon, dreaming of how great it's going to be living here. I've already got some new furniture in mind. The thing I really like about it is that it has separate levels. My master stateroom isn't just through a door leading to the rear of the boat, like on the Californian we're now on. The Grand Banks has a teak spiral staircase leading below to the walk-in engine rooms, guest staterooms and aft master stateroom, complete with walk-around king-sized bed, and plenty of bookcases for my mini legal library. I think I'll also spring for one of those big flat-panel plasma television screens.

The kid will appreciate the much larger forward stateroom area, usually reserved for the crew. It has its own private head with shower. The Saint Bernard will appreciate the engine rooms, where he can go to be alone.

285

If Snell's reward money comes in as promised, the deal should close while I'm in Hawaii and Suzi can supervise the move, with the Asian boys doing most of the work.

Title to boats pass quite quickly, not like houses requiring up to ninety days of escrow. Boat ownership changes are just like automobile sales. Purcell will arrange for picking up the old Californian and bringing the Grand Banks over to our regular slip for us.

26

The day has finally arrived. It's early morning and I'm waiting for the car service to pick me up and take me to LAX for my flight to OGG, which is the official designation for Kahului Airport on Maui.

The car comes early, but there's no need for the driver to call me. I'm already up by the gate waiting for him. Stuart will be by later this morning to start his tutoring program, so I'm not worried about the kid. I sit back, drink from my bottle of expensive water and enjoy the nine-mile ride to the airport.

My luggage fits neatly into one carry-on bag. All you need in Maui is shorts, tee shirts and underwear, so it's really easy to travel there. I've been paying all my bills with a credit card that gives air miles, so I've accumulated enough of them to upgrade to first class. And why not? This is the way that a Grand Banks 50 owner should travel.

Once we're at thirty thousand feet, I notice that my carry-on bag has a swelling in it. I remove the two puffed-up separately packaged Hostess Cupcakes. The difference in air pressure between on the ground and up here has caused the packages to inflate like balloons. I brought them along because I wasn't sure that they'd have room on the plane to upgrade me. Now that I'm in first class, I feel a little silly having brought a snack along. Some of the other first class passengers give me one of those 'my goodness, they'll let anyone fly first class nowadays' looks.

287

The food and service are both pretty good up here and you have a lot more legroom, but it's still a multi-ton metal plane up in the air. When I'm on the Grand Banks, I feel comfortable knowing that wood naturally floats. Metal doesn't naturally fly.

Fortunately, it's a beautiful flight and I get the usual lei around my neck when we land. A rented Chrysler PT Cruiser is waiting for me at the airport. I could have arranged for a Hummer, but there are too many small parking lots to negotiate in Lahaina and the PT will do just fine for me to take Myra around to the restaurants and other places of interest.

After a pleasant forty-minute drive from the airport, I reach the Pioneer Inn. Once at the registration desk, I make sure to let the guy know that if an attractive woman wants to get into my room while I'm not there, he should absolutely allow it. He hesitates and tells me that it's against the rules to let anyone but the registered person into a room. Ten seconds and ten dollars later, he agrees that it's okay. I tell him that her name is Myra and that she's my wife. He couldn't care less. He says that he'll be working late tonight, so when I return at eleven this evening, he'll give me a 'thumbs up' sign if she arrived and he let her into the room. That was a nice touch the way she tried to make me believe she wouldn't be coming for another day or so.

Now that everything's taken care of at the hotel, it's time to trot across the street to the Lahaina Yacht Club. I've been carrying my plastic membership card in my pocket for the last week getting ready for this moment. I flash it at the door and sign in, handing my credit card to the bartender and tell him to start running a tab for me – but to collect for tomorrow night's dinner from my guest. That's part of our deal from the Blitzstien trial.

I now have the rest of the day to relax, throw away a couple of hundred dollars getting monogrammed Lahaina Yacht Club items from the gift shop and schmooze with other yacht club members as we all sit there, watch the sunset and get wasted on the club's balcony that overhangs the Pacific Ocean.

Several of the members ask me if I've got an appointment somewhere because I'm looking at my watch so often. It finally dawns on me that I forgot to reset the time. Hawaii is two hours behind Los Angeles, so it's now an extra two more hours until I get to be alone with Myra.

The food is great, the drinks are great, and the company is great, so the time passes by quickly. Boaters from all over the world belong to the club, so there's always someone like me visiting the Island, and plenty of interesting cruising stories about other countries.

The sunset is beautiful, and after dinner I decide to voluntarily cut myself off from any more booze. I want to be able to remember this evening. I'm glad it's after ten in the evening because I've looked at my watch so many times, I think I've developed carpal tunnel syndrome.

It's now ten minutes to eleven and I can't wait any longer. I'm walking back to the Pioneer Inn and if the guy at the desk doesn't give me a 'thumbs up' sign, I'm going back to the club and drinking myself to death.

I slowly walk into the lobby. The guy behind the registration desk sees me, winks, and gives me the long-awaited thumbs up. Great! I walk a little quicker now, and almost break off the key as I open the room's door. It's dark in the room, but the moonlight brings in just enough light for me to make out a form on the bed. Just what I've been waiting for – something warm, wet, and breathing hard.

I don't waste any time, quickly dropping my shorts and almost ripping my shirt as I pull it up over my head. I jump into the bed and grab what's waiting for me - the Saint Bernard.

27

I must have had too much to drink at the club. This can't be happening. Maybe the plane crashed and I'm actually dead right now. This must be the afterlife, because there's no way that this can be a real dog. I turn on the light. I am not dead. Maybe I wish I was, but I'm not. This is Bernie, Suzi's dog, and he's got a message in his collar.

More than two thousand miles away and the kid still manages to send me dog-mail. It's a note from Myra.

Peter Darling:
    Suzi saw your travel brochures, and when I learned how much she'd like to see the island, I

arranged for her and Bernie to fly over with me. They wouldn't let Bernie stay with us here at the Kapalua Ritz-Carlton, so we thought that you wouldn't mind him staying with you. We've hired a limo for the next few days, so we'll pick you up tomorrow morning for breakfast.

It happened again. Just as I'm about to achieve my dream moment, I wake up.

Just North of Lahaina is the very nice resort area Kaanapali, where most of the Island's beachfront condos are. If you go another few miles to the Northern tip of the Island, you reach the super-rich Kapalua area where the golf courses, million dollar estates and expensive hotels are. I'm sure that Myra's spending about four hundred a night for the room she and Suzi are staying in, and that doesn't count the greens fees she'll have to lay out to play on the hotel's fifty-four champion-ship hole golf course.

Maybe that's the way it should be. The millionairesses are staying at the Ritz Carlton and I'm staying here with the dog.

EPILOGUE

Our vacation in Maui was a lot more fun than I thought that any period of celibacy could be. I rented an electric cart for Suzi that's identical to the one she has at the Marina. She took the huge dog, put on her 'Bubba Gump Shrimp' tee shirt and drove that thing all over the Island, becoming an instant icon. Every tourist and shop-owner wanted to meet her, and after the second day, she was forced to drive with only one hand so that the other was free to wave at her fans. She probably had enough conversations to last her until we return here next year, so she won't have to have any with me until then. Her annual quota of Peter talk has already been used up. She liked Maui so much that I think she's considering buying some property there. I hope she'll let me stay with her once in a while.

Of course as expected, Myra won the election in a landslide. Her only remaining opponent didn't have the courtesy to concede and congratulate her, so Myra probably won't return any courtesy by giving that candidate's drug-legalization demands much thought. When I stopped by the office to say hello one day, I noticed that Seymour's old lunch-date law student wasn't there any more. He'll probably be on the Governor's staff in another year or so.

Myra offered to bring me in as a consultant on an occasional insurance fraud case, but I told her we'd probably be better off not associating. There are too many people out there waiting to take pot shots at her and giving a consulting contract to her ex-husband would be just too damn convenient for them.

The new love of my life is now sitting in our slip. A fifty-foot Grand Banks Trawler Yacht. Stuart, Vinnie and Olive all helped the Asian boys move our stuff. When we returned from the Island, we boarded our new home and had a grand first night dinner. Suzi hired Sally the sign painter to put the name on the back of the boat. Like the last one, this is the 'Suzi

B,' which is probably much better than our second choice of 'the Peter S.'

Now that we've got this beautiful new yacht, I decide to show it off a little. I owe that female reporter Hedy a dinner, so using my brand new pasta recipe I entertained her on the boat. She enjoyed the service so much that she stayed for breakfast too. I think I've given new meaning to the phrase 'manipulating the press.' She'll be a good contact to have every time I decide to give one of my 'outside the courthouse' performances. Nothing helps a bad case more than good press - there's a famous dream team that will attest to that adage.

Charles Indovine and I are on the 'do not invite to the same party list,' but he still assigns a case to me every once in a while, just to keep Uniman Insurance happy.

The only interesting new thing going on in my life now is a client that came in the other day. He was referred by Stuart and told me the most amazing things about a situation he's involved in. If I decide to take his case, it will no doubt be the most interesting adventure I've ever been involved with... but that's another story. I see that a message is coming in by dog-mail, so it must be time for me to go back to work.

Yesterday the kid told me that a man walked by and said hello to her, on his way to that big boat on the end tie. I asked her if it was George Clooney, but she didn't know. When I inquired about his appearance, her answer was "he was old... like you."

...By Reason of Sanity

The Peter Sharp Legal Mystery Series

#1: Single Jeopardy

Attorney Peter Sharp has been wrongfully suspended from the practice of law and thrown out of the house by his soon-to-be ex-wife, a newly appointed deputy district attorney. As a result of the eviction, he's forced to live in their back yard on an old, poorly wired, 40-foot Chris Craft cabin cruiser he's restoring, that is in danger of burning up at any time.

To make matters worse, as the result of trying to help someone fill out some claim forms, he gets arrested for conspiracy to defraud an insurance company. His alleged co-conspirator, a man charged with murdering his own wife to be with a beautiful flight attendant, is about to discover that Peter is also sleeping with her while the man is out of town.

As Peter fights to get his law license reinstated, he discovers the secrets behind two murders, a fatal plane crash, and who framed him with the State Bar - all with the help of his legal ward Suzi, an adorable, quiet (at least to Peter) twelve-year-old Chinese girl and her huge Saint Bernard.

Peter also gets involved in matters concerning sexual harassment, vexatious litigation, double jeopardy, and a groundbreaking case of *Negligent Nymphomania.*

#2: *...By Reason of Sanity*

In his second Adventure, Attorney Peter Sharp gets retained to defend a man accused of capital murder. The only things making this case a little harder to defend than most others are that the client's acts were captured on videotape, he confessed to the police, and he wants to plead guilty. To make matters worse, the District Attorney's office has brought in a special prosecutor for the trial: Peter's ex-wife Myra.

While he's preparing for trial on the murder case, Peter is also hired to represent an insurance company, to defend it against a man who slipped and fell while inside a bank that was coincidentally robbed later that same day. Peter thinks the case would have died when the claimant was murdered, but at usual, he's wrong.

In this adventure, while Peter is involved representing Vinnie, the prolific, peeing pornographer, he also helps solve several bank robberies by catching the entire gang, and makes the acquaintance of a new friend who runs an autopsy store - all with the help of his legal ward, the adorable twelve-year-old Suzi and her huge Saint Bernard.

3: *A Class Action*

In his third Adventure, Attorney Peter Sharp is retained to represent a man accused of murder, by the planting of bombs in vehicles. The client is also suspected of being part of a conspiracy to assassinate the President of the United States in an upcoming Fourth of July parade.

With the assistance of his legal ward Suzi, Peter cracks the case, identifies the real murderer, and at the same time solves the mystery of a dead body found in his friend Stuart's automobile trunk... all while falling for a lesbian lawyer, winning a Will contest, breaking up a stolen car ring 4,000 miles away, and battling with his ex-wife, who has been elected to the office of District Attorney.

In the adventure's finale, Suzi miraculously manages to get 'Bernie,' her huge Saint Bernard into a courtroom, where she makes her first official court appearance, holds her first press conference, and becomes a local television hero.

#4: *"Conspiracy of Innocence"*

Suzi once again saves Peter's case by finding the connection between two crimes that allegedly took place in different parts of the State, one of which Peter was arrested for. And once again, Peter falls for a woman who he thinks could really 'be the one' this time.

Peter's ex-wife Myra must make the decision as to whether or not she should resign from prosecution of a case in which she may have a conflict of interest – Peter's murder charge.

Everyone including Peter is sitting on the edge of their chairs as this double murder mystery comes to a shocking conclusion that involves a mafia hit man, revengeful drug dealers, a local police chief, and the ever-popular FBI.

#5: ...*Until Proven Innocent*

Tony Edwards, A dock neighbor of Peter's, is charged with murder. Unfortunately, he is a suspended police officer with a known dislike for people who are the color of his alleged victim. He's also the subject of many citizen complaints for using excessive force in the minority community.

At Suzi's request, Tony has taught her how to help him re-load his target practice ammunition, also giving the little girl a basic course in ballistics.

When a local black movie producer who Tony was working for gets killed, Suzi and talks Peter into handling Tony's defense... which doesn't look too good because he was arrested at the scene of the murder with his gun still smoking.

Along the way, Peter once again gets involved with who he thinks might be 'Miss Right,' represents a 500-pound woman who is being discriminated against, uncovers a white supremist militant organization, and also stumbles onto a group of people who are pirating DVD copies of recently released major motion pictures.

Peter's ex-wife, District Attorney Myra Scot, makes a mistake when she subpoenas little Suzi to come and testify as a prosecution witness against the defendant, Suzi's friend Tony.

After what Suzi does to solve the mystery and destroy Myra's case in court, everyone knows that the District Attorney's office will never subpoena Suzi again.

#6: **The Common Law**

Peter Sharp encounters a client with amnesia, who not only can't tell Peter what his own name is, but who also has absolutely no recollection of the crime he is charged with committing. In lieu of his memory, Peter's obtains video surveillance footage that establishes his client's guilt beyond a reasonable doubt.

The usual crew also gets involved, including Peter's close friend Stuart, Jack Bibberman the investigator, Laverne the 'amorous houseboat lady', and Stuart's employees Vinnie and Olive – who are having some disagreement as to whether or not they're legally married; and last but not least, little Suzi B. and her big Saint Bernard.

The law firm is still operating from their 50-foot Grand Banks trawler yacht in Marina del Rey, California… the vessel that Peter still doesn't know how to drive. As in past adventures, all involved continue to visit the local haunts.

One way or another each of Peter's cases winds up being a conflict with his ex-wife Myra, who is the county's chief prosecutor. He also may be more closely involved with FBI Special Agent in Charge Bob Snell than before, as they share a dangerous high-speed situation on a winding road.

Suzi's new friend Lotus and her mother also play an interesting part in this adventure as Peter finds that he is fighting a ring of credit-card fraud experts.

7: The Magician's Legacy

Little Suzi has decided that she wants to study magic in this eighth legal adventure she participates in. Unfortunately, her teacher is the main suspect in what appears to be an 'impossible' crime... the shooting of a man in his completely locked 'safe room.'

In order for Suzi to clear her magic teacher of liability for this crime, she must convince Peter to handle the case, which he does under one condition: Suzi must help him by solving the mystery of this locked-room murder.

Her task is made difficult because all events took place in a secure 'panic room,' with steel doors in place, and no windows. Somehow, the alleged murderer is believed to have committed the crime and successfully escaped from a room that could only later be opened by a crew using blowtorches.

Suzi is especially motivated to solve this enigma when she learns that an attorney who she dislikes may be involved.

The Magician's Legacy may be the most baffling locked-room murder mystery of this century.

#8: *The Reluctant Jurist*

There's a mini flu epidemic going around in Los Angeles and it has especially taken its toll among Superior Court Judges in Santa Monica, who all seem to have been infected at the same conference they attended.

Peter has been 'drafted' to fill in as a temporary judge for some civil matters, but winds up getting stuck hearing a big criminal trial involving a devious attorney as the defendant... the same attorney who Peter crossed swords with in a previous situation.

Suspense enters the picture when Peter's legal ward Suzi fails to appear as guest of honor at her own birthday party, and every local state and Federal peace officer in California wants to locate her.

This is the second adventure that Peter and Suzi B. have been involved where Suzi's Saint Bernard may be partly responsible for a successful conclusion.

#9: *The Final Case*

Suzi dislikes a certain devious attorney who Peter keeps coming up against. She feels that he has no business being licensed to practice law in the State of California.

When Peter's new romantic interest invites him to a cocktail party, Suzi and the other guests are shocked by a loud noise down the hall, coming from their host's study.

Other guests at the party include the chief of police, mayor, and district attorney, who unanimously conclude that the dead body they discover is the result of a suicide.

Even Suzi is inclined to go along with their conclusion... until she learns that the devious attorney she dislikes may be involved in handling some legal matters for the deceased.

Suzi won't let go of this one. Against everyone's advice, she keeps working to prove her suspicions about that devious attorney and his connections to what Suzi believes must have been murder.

The conclusion to this mystery is a complete surprise to everyone.

#10: *An Element of Peril*

In this tenth Peter Sharp Legal Mystery, Peter faces a double task: defending a person who is charged with murder, and also trying to locate the missing victim, who was allegedly killed in a completely locked room.

Somewhere behind the tangled mess of a down-ward-spiraling celebrity starlet, a battling married couple, a missing currency trader and a disappearing corpse, attorney Peter Sharp and his legal ward Suzi must find where the truth lies.

As in the past, while Peter's client's trial nears, Suzi has failed to come up with any workable solution that can save Peter from certain defeat and humiliation in court.

You'll be sitting on the edge of your chair as you see the courtroom drama that takes place during the last few minutes of the trial.

#11: *a Good Alibi*

In Latin, the word "alibi" literally means "somewhere else," and to any person charged with a crime, it is an extremely valuable asset to have because it can mean the difference between an acquittal and a conviction.

However, just having an alibi isn't enough: it has to stand up to scrutiny, because any good prosecutor knows that breaking an alibi and proving it was fraudulently concocted can lead a sure-thing conviction.

In this eleventh adventure of the Peter Sharp Legal Mysteries, Peter is drawn into a role he never thought he'd be playing – that of a prosecutor, being brought in as for the singular purpose of trying to break a defendant's apparently 'airtight' alibi.

#12: *Legally Dead*

Nobody likes a killer, but sometimes you have to put your personal feelings on hold when you're a trained professional called upon to do a job.

When attorney Peter Sharp's former wife Myra calls to ask a favor, he finds it difficult to refuse her, because any occasion to work with her is always a pleasure for him.

The favor that District Attorney Myra asks is for Peter to represent a client in court who wants to plead guilty to a crime. A plea bargain the defendant agreed to is already in place.

Peter agrees to the contemplated one-hour of work as a court-appointed defense attorney and makes the court appearance. But when the case is called, the surprises start, and don't stop until the unexpected end of this twelfth of the Legal Mystery series, during which time Peter gets his first opportunity to defend a dead person charged with murder.

All thirteen of the Peter Sharp Legal Mysteries are now available at bookstores and can easily be ordered online from Amazon.com.

To order at your local bookseller or online, simply provide the title's ISBN (International Standard Book Number), or insert it into Amazon's search block.

Single Jeopardy _____	ISBN	1-882629-19-1
...By Reason of Sanity _____	ISBN	1-882629-13-2
A Class Action _____	ISBN	1-882629-66-3
Conspiracy of Innocence ___	ISBN	1-882629-09-4
...Until Proven Innocent ___	ISBN	1-882629-51-5
The Common Law _____	ISBN	1-882629-39-6
The Magician's Legacy ____	ISBN	1-882629-15-9
The Reluctant Jurist _____	ISBN	1-882629-72-8
The Final Case _____	ISBN	1-882629-81-7
An Element of Peril _____	ISBN	1-882629-76-0
A Good Alibi _____	ISBN	1-882629-84-1
Legally Dead	ISBN	1-882629-75-2
How to Rob a Bank _____	ISBN	1-882629-05-1

See www.LegalMystery.com for details

Editor's note:
  If you notice any blatant typographical errors in the text of this book, we suggest you bring them to the attention of the author, who was the last person to sign off on the manuscript. We feel quite comfortable shifting the blame onto him for any errors he may have missed.

He can be reached at: editor@MagicLampPress.com

About the Author

Gene Grossman worked his way through high school, college, and law school as a shoe salesman, welder, process server, bail bondsman, tire changer, saloon piano player and 'extra,' appearing in seven motion pictures. He then spent 20 years as a trial lawyer, during which time he served as Dean of a small local law school, where he also taught several classes.

His film & video company produced over fifty special interest DVD titles on everything from boating, to bankruptcy. Now retired from the practice of law, Gene writes aboard his yacht in Marina del Rey.

You can see pictures of Peter Sharp's boats, yellow Hummer, Suzi's e-cart, and Laverne's houseboat at

www.PeterSharpBooks.com